LT Cleage
Cleage, Pearl
Till you hear from me /

# TILL YOU HEAR FROM ME

This Large Print Book carries the
Seal of Approval of N.A.V.H.

# TILL YOU HEAR FROM ME

# PEARL CLEAGE

**THORNDIKE PRESS**

*A part of Gale, Cengage Learning*

GALE
CENGAGE Learning

Detroit • New York • San Francisco • New Haven, Conn • Waterville, Maine • London

## GALE
### CENGAGE Learning

LIBRARY OF CONGRESS CATALOGING-IN-PUBLICATION DATA

Cleage, Pearl.
    Till you hear from me / by Pearl Cleage.
        p. cm. — (Thorndike Press large print African-American)
    ISBN-13: 978-1-4104-2809-7
    ISBN-10: 1-4104-2809-5
    1. African American women—Fiction. 2. African
Americans—Politics and government—Fiction. 3. Fathers and
daughters—Fiction. 4. Large type books. I. Title.
PS3553.L389T56 2010b
813'.54—dc22                                      2010016263

Published in 2010 by arrangement with The Ballantine Publishing Group, a division of Random House, Inc.

Printed in the United States of America
1 2 3 4 5 6 7 14 13 12 11 10

*For my father, Rev. Albert B. Cleage Jr.,*
*and for Kay*

"Do nothin' till you hear from me.
Pay no attention to what's said . . ."
*Do Nothin' Till You Hear From Me*
DUKE ELLINGTON AND BOB RUSSELL

# PROLOGUE

*West End News, November 5, 2008*

"Well, the first thing they gonna have to do," Mr. Charles said the morning after the election, "is rethink that whole Black History Month idea."

Mr. Eddie frowned. "How you figure that?"

"We got a black president now, brother! What do we need with one month? Every month can be Black History Month!"

"Man, you crazy! You not even gonna give the white folks one month like they gave us?"

"They didn't give us a damn thing," Mr. Charles said. "We took that month, just like we took the White House!"

"Now you gettin' carried away." Mr. Eddie shook his head. "We not the only people who voted for him. A lot of everybody saw the same thing we did. An honest man who could handle the job."

"Okay, so while he's handlin' the job, he can just issue a decree saying from henceforth, *every* month will be Black History Month, except for *one* which the white folks can have to focus on their history."

"How are they supposed to fit all their history into one month? These white folks been around a long time."

"Now you showin' your ignorance. We been around a lot longer than they have. We had libraries and museums when they were still swingin' through the trees and we had to tell it all during one little month, and the shortest month at that!"

"So why can't we do better than they did and just let history be history?"

Mr. Charles looked disappointed, but his voice was patient. "You not gettin' into the spirit of things, man. What's the point of having a black president if you can't pull rank now and then?"

"You talkin' about pullin' rank and the man is trying to figure out how to save the country!"

"He ain't gonna figure out how to save nothin' if he don't pull rank every now and then."

"He figured out how to get elected, didn't he?"

# ONE:
## TACOS AND SANGRIA

When the phone rang at 5:25 A.M., I was already up, pretending to meditate. Miss Iona didn't even wait for me to say hello.

"You have to come home."

"I am home," I said.

"That is where you live. This is home and you know it. I called you last night. Where were you?"

"Probably somewhere minding my own business," I said. "And good morning to you, too."

Miss Iona Williams had been my parents' friend for as long as I could remember. On a lot of the nights when my father would be out late at meetings and my mother was defiantly finishing up her graduate studies, it was Miss Iona who came to sit with me and fix me dinner and hear my prayers and tuck me in. When my mom left the Rev and moved to the West Coast, he got custody of Miss Iona. She's one of the few people he cannot intimidate, although he never stops trying.

Five years ago, at sixty plus, she got married for the first time to Charles Larson, but refused to take his name.

"I'm not trying to make a statement," she had explained to my mother who tried to offer feminist congratulations at the wedding. "I just don't see the point."

Miss Iona wasn't maternal in the traditional sense of being motherly. She was more like a really great friend who never took any shit from you, but never gave you any either. When my mom was being too ideological and my father was being too omnipotent, I always knew I could trust Miss Iona to give it to me straight.

"Good morning, good morning, good morning! Did I wake you?" she said without waiting for an answer. "I've been up for hours, but I was trying to wait for a more civilized hour before I called you."

She was just trying to be polite. Miss Iona always called very early or very late. Other people's schedules were of little or no concern to her. She had that in common with the Rev.

"I'm up," I said. "What's wrong?"

"Just what I said. You have to come home right away. Your father needs you."

12

This was not a crisis. This was a delusion.

"The Rev doesn't need me," I said, calling him by the name everybody called him, except my grandmother who died when I was five, and who always called him *Dunbar.* Even my mother still called him Rev, although she had disavowed the practice in an essay on the patriarchy that won an award in a big-time feminist journal. It was a good piece, too, but after a lifetime of calling him *Rev,* what was she going to substitute? *Sweetie Pie?* "He hasn't even spoken to me in five months."

"Well, he needs to speak to you now because he has completely lost his mind."

"There is a difference," I said, "between insanity and intractability. He's not crazy. He's just stubborn."

"Have you seen yesterday's paper?"

I haven't lived in Atlanta in more than a decade, but I knew Miss Iona meant *The Atlanta Constitution.*

"No, I . . ."

"That's why you're not on a plane down here right now," she interrupted me. "If you had seen it, that's where you would be. On your way to talk some sense into him before he undoes the work of his whole lifetime."

Miss Iona was known for her unflappability, but she was really getting wound up.

The Rev must really have put his foot in his mouth.

"What did he say?"

"What did he say? How about when they asked him about those signs Reverend Patterson put up at the church . . ."

"What signs?"

"Bilingual signs. You know, first in English, then in Spanish right under it. We've got a lot of Mexican families coming on Sundays now, nicest people you ever want to meet, but a lot of them don't speak much English yet and Reverend Patterson thought the signs would make them feel welcome."

Reverend Patterson had become the senior pastor at the Rock of Faith Community Church last year after my father retired and the Rev had always been supportive.

"So what's wrong with that?"

"Nothing!" Miss Iona said. "That's the whole point, but not according to your father."

I could hear the paper rustling while she found the part of the article she wanted to quote exactly.

"The Rev said, and I quote, 'you can go overboard with this multicultural thing. Next thing you know, we'll be offering tacos and sangria for communion Sunday.' "

"What?!" My father was a champion of

14

diversity. This had to be a misquote.

"It gets worse. 'Before they start worrying about teaching these kids to speak Spanish, somebody needs to teach them how to speak English. That's why they can't get decent jobs. Our president is content to bask in his own rhetorical flourishes without acknowledging that most of our kids can't even speak their own mother tongue, much less read it. And that doesn't have anything to do with white folks. That has to do with being sorry. Why doesn't Barack Obama talk about that?' "

I closed my eyes and felt a familiar throb behind my right eyeball. My father's relationship or lack of relationship with President Obama was the reason I was up at five o'clock in the morning trying to calm my ass down in the first place. My father once had been a big supporter of then-candidate Obama and had spearheaded an independent voter registration drive that put 100,000 new names on Georgia's books. From my position inside the campaign, I let people know that my father had offered access to this list of enthusiastic new voters in a state where Republicans were expected to make a clean sweep everywhere but the city of Atlanta, where, of course, Obama was expected to cream all comers.

The Rev's voters, already organized and easily targeted, had been gathered from one hundred churches spread throughout the state who had participated in a program called One Hundred Percenters. Each church pledged to register 100 percent of the eligible voters in the congregation and make sure those voters got to the polls. Nobody thought they could do it, but they did. Access to that list would have given our campaign a huge leg up on the competition. His timely offer would also improve both my father's access to the candidate and my own currency as a bright, energetic, but undeniably mid-level staffer. *Enter the Rev. Jeremiah Wright.*

Reverend Wright and my dad shared a belief in the Black Liberation Theology that had always been a strong strain in the African American religious tradition, but had remained largely unknown to most white Americans who first encountered its passionate, prophetic cadences when a thirty-second video of Reverend Wright surfaced on the Internet. His fiery declaration that rather than saying "God bless America," his parishioners ought to "God-damn America," for her long history of racial crimes, set off a storm of outrage that led to the candidate's decision to craft and

16

deliver as eloquent and unapologetic a treatise on race as has ever been heard anywhere. Rejecting the sound bite, but refusing to jettison Wright, Obama's support for his pastor went too far for some, but not nearly far enough for some radical clergymen who leaped to Wright's defense, charging the media with racism and ignorance and candidate Obama with abandoning a man who had been his pastor for more than twenty years. My father planted himself firmly in the latter camp and stayed there throughout those long, strange weeks when the full weirdness of American race relations was on display for all the world to see.

Jeremiah Wright scared the hell out of those of us who were spending every waking hour working to send Barack Obama to the White House. Trying to explain Liberation Theology to people whose only other exposure to black preaching is Martin Luther King Jr.'s "I Have a Dream" speech is like trying to explain classical ballet to a group of wiggly eight-year-olds in tutus; a thankless task. By the time the smoke cleared, my father had reneged on his promise to share 100,000 new voter names and the campaign had decided I wasn't the rising star they thought I was.

I'm not saying it's the Rev's fault that my

17

dream job hasn't materialized yet, but I don't think his unwavering support of Rev. Wright, even after the man's disastrous visit to the Washington Press Club, did me a whole lot of good either. Our last conversation before we mutually cut off communication with each other was a terrible exchange of defiance (him) and desperation (me), where we both said things we shouldn't have. But you know what they say: *shoulda, coulda, woulda.*

"He's not plugged in anywhere," Miss Iona was saying urgently, trying to make me understand. "Nobody's asking his opinion on anything and you know that man needs to give his opinion!"

At least we could agree on that. "Go on."

"You should have seen him on election night," she said. "Me and Charlie had some folks over, but the Rev was just in a funk all night. He wanted to be somewhere with a little more light shinin' on it, but nobody invited him but us."

I sighed. This is exactly what I had warned him about. "Do the Obama people really have that much to say about what happens in Atlanta?"

"It appears they do. Precious Hargrove had a big party at the Regency and your father's name was nowhere on the guest list."

State Senator Precious Hargrove was a strong contender in the upcoming Georgia governor's race. She had been a member of Rock of Faith as long as I had known her and the Rev had been the one who first encouraged her to go into politics when she was a young mother, newly arrived in West End, struggling to raise her son alone and make her way in the world.

"Now he's going all over the state, bad-mouthing her."

"Bad-mouthing her about what?"

"About supporting the president is what I'm trying to tell you! He called her a . . . wait a minute. Let me get it right. He called her 'a card carrying member of the Ladies for Obama fan club who can be counted on to follow their handsome hero wherever he may lead them.' "

This was awful. I had never heard the Rev talk like that to anybody, much less a reporter from *The Atlanta Constitution.* His comments to the guy were bigoted and sexist, bitter and petty.

"Do you think he's having some kind of breakdown?"

"I don't know what he's having," she said. "He called a press conference last week and

19

nobody came, so he read *The Constitution*'s editor the riot act until they promised to do a big feature story on him. He spent the day talking to the reporter and this, *this,* is the article that came out of it."

"What's the headline?" I said.

"Angry Icon Blasts Obama."

I took a deep, meditative breath. *Calm down,* I said to myself. *This doesn't have anything to do with you.*

"I don't know what you think I can do."

"Talk to him!" she said. "Tell him he's making a complete fool of himself."

That was not going to happen. The very idea of judging my father and then offering him my opinion was not within the realm of possibility.

"I'd like to live to see my thirty-fifth birthday, if it's all the same to you," I said. "What about Mr. Eddie?"

Miss Iona snorted. "You know Ed Harper is not gonna tell the Rev nothin' he don't want to hear. That's why they been friends so long."

"Why don't *you* tell him?"

"I *have* told him! He's not paying me a bit of attention. He doesn't think I know anything about politics."

"This isn't about politics. This is about bad judgment."

"Exactly what I said. So will you come home and talk to him?"

I walked over to the window and looked outside. It was still dark and quiet, but a few miles away the D.C. rush hour was already shaping up. I couldn't see it from this tree-lined Georgetown street where I was renting a tiny garage apartment from the parents of a well-connected friend, but I could *feel* it. If you're addicted to politics, and I stand accused, this is the town that manufactures your drug of choice. The fact that the Rev's craziness was splashing over into my life here was infuriating. I took another deep breath.

"Will you come?"

"For what? He's not even speaking to me. You know that."

"Are you speaking to him?"

Miss Iona knew all the gory details of our feud so she was not really asking for information. She was building a case. I had to choose my words carefully.

"We have not spoken to each other since before the election."

*Good job,* I said to myself. *Stick to the facts.*

"So if he was ready to speak to you, you would be ready to speak to him?"

"He's the one who started it!" It never helps your argument to sound like a whiny

21

six-year-old. Miss Iona heard her advantage and took it.

"Listen to yourself, Ida B," she said.

In a rare confluence of his black nationalism and her incipient feminism, my parents named me after Ida B. Wells Barnett, pioneering journalist and tireless anti-lynching activist. Although I'm just *Ida* in the outside world, everybody in West End, *which is a world of its own,* still calls me Ida B.

"I'm sorry," I said, "but I can't just come down there, walk into the house, and say, 'I know we've been out of touch recently, but what's going on with you? That article in the paper made you sound like an angry, bitter old man. Say it ain't so, Rev. Say it ain't so!' "

"You're being sarcastic, but why not? That would be perfect!"

"No, that would be crazy. Listen, Miss Iona, the Rev did a terrible thing. He let his ego make him refuse to help in the most important election of our lifetime."

"He was being loyal to a friend."

"There's a limit to loyalty."

She let that lie there for a minute, too. An unfortunate choice of words. Unconditional support is the essence of loyalty. *Limits ain't in it.*

"Let me ask you something," she said

finally. "Have I tried to insert myself into this difference of opinion between you and your father?"

"It's a little more serious than a difference of opinion," I said, going for highly offended and sounding peevish instead.

"Granted. But have I ever?"

"No," I said. "You have stayed remarkably neutral."

"Have I ever asked you to come home?"

She had me there. In all the years and through a dizzying variety of crises, she had never called and demanded that I get my ass on a plane and get down there *posthaste*. "No, you never have."

"No," she said, repeating my words for emphasis. "No, I never have, so I would think the unique nature of this conversation would at least make you consider my request before dismissing it out of hand."

She was right, of course, but I didn't want to go to Atlanta. My feelings were still hurt, and besides, I had other things to do, like finding a job. D.C. was the place where I needed to put my focus. I had to look out for myself first. The Rev would have to wait.

"Even if I wanted to come," I said, "it's just not a good time. I've got so much to do here . . ."

"Look, I know you're going to work at the

White House and everything," she said. "I know you're busy, but you haven't started yet, have you?"

A guilty flush crept over my cheeks and I was glad she couldn't see my face. I had shared my working with Obama *fantasy* as working with Obama *fact,* and now my story was coming back to bite me on the butt.

"No, they're still doing the vetting," I said, hoping it might be true.

"All the more reason for you to be on top of this," she said. "Think about it, Ida B. What are you gonna say when they call and ask you was that your father all over the Internet talking about tacos and sangria?"

The throbbing behind my right eye moved over to include my left one. This was my worst nightmare. I was hoping enough time had passed so that I could be evaluated by Team Obama on my own merits, but Miss Iona was right. If this interview is as bad as she says it is, who knows how far its effect might ripple? On a slow news day, anything was possible. Look at Joe the Plumber.

"Just do this for me, will you?" Miss Iona said gently, correctly judging from my silence that her arrow had landed. "Look at the video of the whole interview on YouTube and then if you don't think we need to worry, I won't call you about this again."

That wasn't too much to ask. I felt guilty about not clearing up that White House thing, but as much as I hated to admit it, I guess there was a part of me that was still hoping I'd get that call: *Will you please hold for the president?* No way I was going to let the Rev mess that up for me if I could help it.

"All right," I said. "You've got a deal."

"Great," she said. "Call me back as soon as you see it."

"You want me to look at it right now?"

I don't know how you can hear somebody raise their eyebrows through the phone, but when I said that, I heard Miss Iona raise hers. "You got something better to do?"

"I was trying to meditate."

"Girl, *please*," she said. "You got the rest of your life to meditate. This is your future we're talking about!"

# Two:
# Every Trick in the
# Book

Wes walked into the small room where he kept his treadmill and his weights, flipped on CNN for background noise, and laced up his new cross-trainers. They felt good. He was glad he could afford an apartment big enough to accommodate his workout. Wes Harper hated his body. Not the perfectly conditioned, well-muscled one you could see. The one he carried around inside his head. The fat one. The one his mother had so lovingly overfed that at thirteen, he had soft, fat thighs that rubbed together when he walked. He was the one with the cheeks too chubby not to pinch. The one who never made the team, never got the girl, and was the butt of every fat joke known to man, no pun intended. When he got to prep school, football changed all that, but it was the memory of his adolescent body that kept Wes motivated. He liked to sweat.

Even when his head was elsewhere, like it was today, he got on that treadmill for forty-five minutes, six times a week. He also played tennis and golf when called upon and was good at both. He liked doing business on the golf course and few things compared to the pleasure of trouncing those shit-talking white boys from the first tee to the eighteenth green.

But this meeting wasn't about kicking their ass. It was more about them kissing his. Wes Harper Communications had officially arrived. Some of his so-called friends had actually laughed out loud when he said he was going to open his own full-service public relations firm in New York City, and now, ten years later, he had an impressive client list that included corporate giants and rap star moguls, politicians eager to move up, and businessmen eager to break into the always lucrative African American urban market. Wes had the ideas, the energy, and the contacts. No one could beat him for *getting it done,* and everybody knew it. Even the guys who had been waiting for his country ass to fail up here in the big city, playing with grown folks. *Who's laughing now?* he thought. *Who's laughing now?*

Wes could feel the sweat running down his back as he reviewed the conversation he'd had late this afternoon with a Republican contact who had become almost a friend during the long months of the last presidential race, although using the word "friend" with these guys was stretching it. Oscar said there were some people interested in talking with him about a few things, but they were very concerned about not drawing attention to their activities. Could a meeting be arranged for Sunday morning at Wes's offices, not theirs?

Of course Wes had agreed and then asked if he should prepare anything specific or just come ready to listen and react. His contact had said no preparation would be necessary. They wanted to talk about recent high-volume voter registration efforts in Georgia, the man said, and since he was from Atlanta, and still had family there, they thought Wes might be able to offer some insight.

Of course he could offer some insight, Wes thought, turning up the speed on the treadmill to a lazy trot. Insight, access, and the one thing you can hope, but never plan for: personal history. Rev. Horace A. Dunbar, the mastermind behind all those shiny new voters, had not only christened Wes as the infant son of his closest friend, Eddie, but had performed the ceremony at Wes's first wedding, which Wes didn't hold against him even though it ended badly, just like his second one.

Horace Dunbar had been pastor, mentor, friend of the family all his life. The man was practically his surrogate father. When he left Atlanta for boarding school, the Rev had given him five books — the King James version of the bible; a copy of *Muhammad: His Life Based on the Earliest Sources* by Martin Lings; *Old Path White Clouds*, a biography of the Buddha written by Thich Nhat Hanh, an activist monk who Martin Luther King nominated for the Nobel Peace Prize; *The Autobiography of Malcolm X*, with Alex Haley; and *The Big Sea*, the first volume of poet Langston Hughes's autobiography. He included a note that said, "Great men are defined by great ideas. Here are a few to get you started." If they wanted information about Rev. Dunbar's operation, they had hit the mother lode without even knowing it. All they knew was that Wes was from Atlanta. They had no idea how close his connection was to exactly what they needed. He couldn't have asked for a better break.

All he was waiting for now was the best available research on what the Reverend had been up to since he sided with Jeremiah Wright and effectively removed himself from access to all things Obama. He caught

Toni Cassidy, his newest associate who was as fine as she was smart, on her way out the door and told her he needed everything she could get him on Rev. Horace Dunbar by seven o'clock. With only one day before the meeting, he wanted to make sure he was current. The question about whether or not he needed to prepare was rhetorical. Wes *always* prepared. She promised to bring whatever she could find by his apartment later and he dashed out to meet another client for drinks.

He glanced up at the clock. He would have just enough time to take a quick shower before Toni arrived with the research and some Chinese takeout from his favorite spot around the corner. That's one of the things Wes liked about living in New York. The Chinese food in Atlanta was a joke and the offerings in New Hampshire, Chinese and otherwise, were not much better.

When Wes arrived at prep school, carrying sixty extra pounds and a hearty appetite, he was shocked at the blandness of the New Hampshire cuisine. With no decent collard greens for miles and only a blank stare in response to his request for cheese grits in the Phillips Exeter cafeteria, Wes found it easy to stick to his new self-imposed diet. He started lifting weights and as fat turned to muscle, he drew the attention of the football coach, who encouraged him to try out for the team and afterward awarded him a spot on the squad.

The rigorous training program imposed the physical discipline he was looking for and the plays seemed second nature to him after just one practice session. The coach was delighted. Wes was fast and strong and smart, willing to take a hit and deliver one, but he had a truly special gift for plucking impossible passes out of the air with a grace that was almost balletic. Exeter had gone co-ed thirteen years before Wes got there in 1983 and his new body, plus his football hero status, guaranteed him the female attention he'd never had before and he loved it. As one of only a handful of black Exonians, Wes reveled in his uniqueness and so did many of the white girls he met, whose previous experiences with African American men were largely limited to the service capacities and a *super nigga* or two they might have met under rigorously supervised circumstances.

At thirty-eight, he had racked up enough real world accomplishments not to miss the glory of catching that Hail Mary pass to deliver the big game for the home team, but he knew women appreciated a man who

31

kept in shape and Wes liked women. He didn't consider them his equals, although like most of the middle-class men of his generation, he was fluent in the feminist rhetoric required of men who had worked *with* and *for* women most of their professional lives. When Wes thought about women, it was as sexual partners or employees. Necessary, certainly, but highly interchangeable. The large pool of smart, attractive, ambitious black women without romantic partners gave Wes an endless supply of lovers and entry-level associates who expected nothing more than whatever he was prepared to give.

Toni was a perfect example. She was smart, sexy, and as ruthless as he was, maybe more. At twenty-seven, she was engaged to a guy finishing up his medical residency in Boston. His schedule was brutal and they were lucky if they saw each other once every couple of months. In between visits, she indulged herself with Wes, which made their working relationship more interesting for both of them and didn't compromise her commitment to her fiancé, who understood that she was not the kind of girl who liked to be alone. In exchange for his tolerance, he extracted a promise that she would always be super safe and postponed any expectation of monogamy until after the wedding, which would not be for another two years. In the meantime . . .

*What the hell was he doing, thinking about Toni?* This was no time to get distracted. Daydreaming about pussy was not on the agenda. These next twenty-four hours were all about *focus.* If he could get his firm on retainer with the Republicans while they rebuilt what was left of their increasingly marginalized party, his business would close out its first decade in the black, in more ways than one. He had made his bones with these guys during the long, bizarre march of the McCain-Palin team toward the crushing defeat that was election day, 2008. By the end, they were prepared to try any and every trick in the book. That was Wes's specialty.

After a few recommendations from some fellow Exonians on the inside of the doomed campaign, he became attached to a shadowy squad of saboteurs who traveled around the country nonstop, disrupting Democratic events, distributing false or misleading information about Democratic candidates, and fueling the fringe element who still thought Barack Obama was the scariest thing they'd seen in ages. Although they were ultimately unsuccessful, his creative efforts to try to hold back the tide of history on their behalf did not escape the notice of those scrambling to salvage what they could of the GOP. He knew this meeting was the next step in formalizing a long-term relationship that would make him and his small firm an integral part of that ongoing process.

He also knew some of his Obama-obsessed friends would think he was making a deal with the devil, but he didn't intend to broadcast the relationship any more than he had told anyone about his work during the campaign. They wouldn't have understood, even though some of the stuff turned out so perfectly, he wanted to tell somebody who could celebrate his genius with him. Just his work on the Joe the Plumber narrative was worth its weight in gold. But he wasn't in this business for bragging rights. He was in it for money and power. The meeting on Sunday was going to place him a lot closer to both. All he had to do now was focus and stay loose.

He turned up the machine another notch and loved the burn in his legs as he started to run. These Obama motherfuckas were used to being the smartest niggas in every room, he thought, but all that shit was about to change.

# THREE:
# THE ENEMY OF MY
# ENEMY

As bad as I thought the Rev's YouTube debut might be, it was so much worse. Within the space of fifteen endless minutes, my father managed to offend or insult Latinos, gays, feminists, black parents, the president of the United States, and the pastor who had succeeded him in the Rock of Faith pulpit, not necessarily in that order. The reporter's first innocuous question — "Do you think that the election of Barack Obama signals the dawn of a new America?" — set the Rev off like a firecracker on the fourth of July.

"A new America?" he roared in the grainy video. "Looks like the same old place to me!"

And he was off. Ranting and raving, charging and countercharging, in a swirl of angry words/words/words that sounded like they ought to make sense, but didn't. I had never seen him like this and it was all I could do not to turn away, but there was something that wouldn't let me. Something almost as disturbing as what he was saying and that was the way he was saying it. For as long as I've known him, the Rev has moved through the world chin up, chest out, eyes focused unblinking on whatever lay ahead. But now, sitting on the dark green leather sofa in the new pastor's study, spitting out the most cynical, simplistic views about the most complex, sensitive issues of the day, he didn't look strong and focused and certain. He looked sad and saggy and *old.* Even his magnificent voice sounded hollow and lacking in conviction.

"All I'm saying is this," the Rev practically spat out the words. "Being black is different from being a member of these other groups you're talking about. They have their issues. We have ours. The problem is these other groups — the gays, Latinos, women — all of them learned how to organize and confront for change from the African American freedom struggle. They all acknowledge it if you ask them when there's no cameras on them, but once the media boys get there, they act like they never even heard of Dr. King."

I closed my eyes, but I could still hear him, angry and strident. "The gays fighting back at Stonewall? The women marching around and burning their bras?"

*Burning their bras?* Had the Rev slipped through some kind of time warp? Half the women in America these days have probably never even owned a bra!

"Those Latino kids staging a walkout over immigration issues? They learned all that from us, but do we ever get a thank-you? Not likely."

"But didn't they learn their lessons well?" the reporter asked off camera. "Didn't those lessons help to put the first African American president in the White House?"

The Rev leaned toward the unseen reporter and pointed a long, slender finger in his direction. "And so what if they did? Brother Malcolm used to say when white America gets a cold, Black America gets pneumonia. It's the same today. New paradigm, old paradigm, race is, was, and always will be the dominant force in American life and the sooner Barack *Hussein* Obama realizes it, the better off he'll be."

Then he turned directly to the camera, which up until that point he had ignored so completely, I didn't think he was even aware of it.

"You owe Reverend Jeremiah Wright and the whole black community a public apology, Mister President, and until he gets it, I remind you of that old saying, *the enemy of my enemy is my friend.*"

He paused for what I guess was supposed to be dramatic effect. "Jeremiah Wright is my friend."

*What the hell did that mean?*

Was he using the Internet to declare himself an enemy of the president? The same president I was still hoping might offer me a job? There weren't enough Excedrin Migraine tablets in the world to stop the throb that was now beating in my brain nonstop.

I closed my eyes and pinched the bridge of my nose tightly, which didn't do anything but make me want to sneeze. I picked up the phone and punched in Miss Iona's number.

# FOUR:
## OLD-SCHOOL

"Tell me again why you needed all this stuff so fast on a Friday night?" Toni said as soon as Wes opened the door. She was standing in front of him close enough for Wes to smell her perfume. "Because I'm beginning to suspect this was just an excuse to get me up here so you can try to have your way with me."

Wes had already showered and shaved, set two plates and a couple of forks out at the counter, and put a bottle of Pinot Grigio in the freezer for a fast chill when Toni rang the bell and he buzzed her in. He felt good, energized, and on top of the situation. He smiled to himself. The situation wasn't the only thing he hoped to be on top of before the evening was over. He had just wrapped up a busy week with no time for anything but business and Toni's exhausted fiancé had flown in the weekend before with roses so she wouldn't think the poor man was too distracted to remember her twenty-seventh birthday. Wes hadn't been in the mood to call in a backup, so the truth was, he was horny as hell. Toni probably was, too. Her fiancé had a bright future, but based on what she'd told Wes, he didn't seem to be very creative between the sheets.

Wes took the bag of Chinese food out of her arms and pulled her gently inside. She slipped off her coat and tossed it casually on the closest chair. She was wearing a slim black skirt, a white silk blouse, and black pumps with four-inch heels.

"Exactly what *stuff* are we talking about, Miss Cassidy?" He grinned. "My research? My dinner?"

Toni ran her fingers through her hair in a lovely gesture that Wes had only ever seen in the movies and tossed her head, her smile revealing small, white, slightly pointed teeth. He spread his grin a little wider.

"My pussy?"

She raised her perfectly arched eyebrows. "Getting a bit presumptuous, aren't we?"

"Don't worry," Wes said, putting the food down and leaning over to give her soft, fragrant cheek a quick kiss. "Your secret is safe with me."

She laughed and handed him a bright red

40

file folder. "I have no secrets. You know that."

"It is your greatest charm," he said, opening the slender folder. "Is this all you got?"

"There's a lot more online," she said, opening the white takeout containers and sniffing the contents of each. "I put the links in the email for you. These are just to give you a sense of what the guy's been up to."

Wes took a cursory look through the things she had printed out. A piece about the kickoff of the registration campaign. A piece about the Rev's group BAC-UP! — Black Activist Clergy United for Progress — and how they had managed to get all these churches to work together. Some pictures of the Rev standing on somebody's front porch with voter registration forms.

*Talk about old-school,* Wes thought, glad all over again that he had had the good sense to head north as fast as he could figure out a way to get there.

"Why are you so interested in this guy all of a sudden?"

"My boy called me from the Republican National Committee. His people are worried about Georgia in the midterms, and the presence of one hundred thousand new, energized Democratic voters does not make them happy."

Toni was spooning out the meal on both plates while Wes's eyes scanned the pages quickly. He would check the videos tomorrow. The food aromas demanded his attention and he heard his stomach growling loudly. He closed the folder and put it aside.

"Go on," she said, as he removed the wine from the freezer and reached for two wineglasses.

"They want to know three things," Wes said, opening the wine efficiently and pouring them each a glass. "How he did it. How they can stop him from doing it again, and how they can get hold of those names."

"Your contact told you all that on the phone?"

Wes shook his head. "Paranoid as these guys are, they'll barely tell you when they want to meet, much less why they're calling. All he said was they wanted to talk about the recent high-volume voter registration efforts in Georgia and since I was from there, they thought I might be able to assist them."

"And can you assist them, Mr. Harper?" she said, raising her glass.

"I can do better than that," he said, clinking his glass against hers lightly. "I can introduce them to my pastor."

She took a sip of her wine. "Are they also

in need of spiritual counseling?"

"My pastor happens to be Reverend Doctor Horace A. Dunbar, the man of the hour."

Her eyes widened. "He's your pastor?"

Wes nodded and took a bite of his Mongolian Beef. "I grew up in his church."

Toni put down her glass and shook her head.

"What?"

"Why can't I picture you as a little kid sitting in Sunday school?"

"Because you have a woefully limited imagination," he said. "I was a member of the junior choir and treasurer of the Youth Fellowship for three years running."

She laughed again. "What happened the fourth year?"

He grinned at her again. "I discovered the pursuit of pussy and my church attendance fell off a little, but you didn't let me finish."

She took another small sip of her wine. Toni wasn't a big eater. "By all means, finish."

"The Rev. Dunbar is also my dad's best friend."

"You're kidding."

Wes shook his head. "I kid you not. They have coffee together three or four mornings a week. All I have to do is ask my dad if I can stay with him for a couple of days and all the information I need will come walking up the front steps."

"Well, that wraps it up with a bow," she said. "You can sell out the race and betray your father's trust all in one fell swoop."

"It's a gift."

That was another thing he liked about Toni. She shared his ability to dismiss any claims of racial solidarity that conflicted with the interests of their clients. He thought of the two of them as part of the vanguard of post-racial African American professionals who were free at last to pimp the race without pretending they were trying to save it.

"Did you tell the RNC guy all this?"

"Hell, no," Wes said, refilling their glasses. "Too much information all at one time isn't good for white folks. Anything of particular interest in the video clips?"

"Not much," Toni said, nibbling a piece of broccoli delicately. "There is one with the good reverend and some of his contemporaries really roasting Obama and then one from two days ago where he suggests in an interview with *The Atlanta Constitution* that unchecked diversity may result in black churches being forced to serve tacos and sangria on Communion Sunday."

Wes choked on a spring roll. "He said *what?*"

"Tacos and sangria," Toni said when Wes stopped coughing. "The whole thing is kind of bizarre actually. He's apparently still really mad at the president."

"All those old guys are still mad."

"Because of Jeremiah Wright?"

"That's part of it," Wes said, helping himself to the last spring roll. "But I think it's just hard for them to admit that whether they were ready or not, the torch has been passed."

"But that's what they were all working for, wasn't it? A chance for black folks to rise and be first-class American citizens?" she said. "Well, they did it. They won. They should be celebrating their victory."

"They don't know how to celebrate," Wes said. "They're warriors. What they know how to do is fight, struggle, organize. Stepping aside to make room for new blood isn't part of their makeup."

She looked at him and grinned. "So I guess Etta James spoke for them all when she offered to whip Beyoncé's young ass for singing her song at the inauguration."

"Exactly," he said. "That wasn't about the song. That was about being *iconed* to death when all she really wanted to do was sing."

45

"What does the Reverend Dunbar want?"

"I won't know that until I get down there and have a chance to talk to him. These guys are ripe to flip their party affiliations, and that would be a real coup. It's just a matter of using that anger to our advantage."

"I think you are the most perfectly amoral person I've ever met."

"Coming from you," he said, "I'll take that as a compliment."

"I meant it as one."

"They're being so damn secretive about the meeting, they want to get together on Sunday morning at seven A.M. They told me to come alone, but I said I had to have one staffer there. *You.*"

"Why thank you, sir. You know I always like to be the only girl."

"You just be on your best behavior."

"Don't worry. I'll wear my corporate drag. Dark pants suit. String of pearls."

"But not too conservative," he said. "These guys always like to see a little leg."

"Oh, yeah? Any of 'em ass men? Or are they just assholes?"

He laughed and stood up. "I love it when you talk dirty."

He picked up the plates and stacked them in the kitchen. That was enough business for one night. He sat down on the couch and took the wine with him. Toni came to sit beside him, kicking off her shoes and tucking her feet up between them.

"You figure you'll have to go down there awhile if all this works out?"

"Probably," he said, gently massaging the foot closest to him. "Why?"

She leaned her head back and closed her eyes. "Maybe I can come and visit you. We could make out on the couch in your dad's rec room."

He squeezed each well-pedicured toe gently. "My dad doesn't have a rec room."

"Well, where did you make out when you were a kid?"

"I was in boarding school. Most of my making out was between me and my strong right hand."

She laughed and opened her eyes. "Why does that turn me on?"

"I don't know," he said. "But forget about it. If you have to come down, which I do not anticipate, you'll stay at the Four Seasons."

"Why is that?" she said, touching him softly without unzipping his pants. "Are you ashamed to introduce me to your father?"

He looked at Toni's perfect face, perfect hair, perfect skin, perfect teeth, perfect, *perfect* breasts, and smiled at the very idea of anyone being ashamed of anything associated with this girl.

"Shame has nothing to do with it," he said, squeezing her left breast lightly. "My father is an old man with a weak heart, and you, beautiful girl, are a screamer."

She threw back her head and laughed, then ran her hands through her hair again in that movie star gesture he loved. "Whose fault is that, Big Daddy?"

"Yours," he said, not caring if she was just buttering him up. Lying was his favorite kind of foreplay. "Which is why you've got to be punished."

She stood up, slid her skirt down over her hips, stepped gracefully out of her silky pink barely there thong, but slipped back into her black stilettos. That was one of the sexiest things about Toni, he thought. She always wore heels that lifted up that fine ass like she was putting it on a platter.

"If there is any punishing to be done," she said, unbuttoning her blouse and dropping it to the floor, "I will be the one doing it."

"Oh, yeah?" he said, but as he pulled her close, she suddenly grabbed his balls and squeezed them hard enough that he actually yelped in protest. *"Hey!"*

"Now who's the screamer?" she cooed, releasing him with a grin.

He pulled her down onto his lap and buried his face between her breasts. He was going to miss this girl when her man finally finished med school and made an honest woman of her. But for tonight, her heart belonged to Daddy.

# FIVE:
## GREETING THE GHOSTS

When I pulled up in front of my father's house, in my little white rental car, I was glad he wouldn't be there. Not because I didn't want to see him. In spite of everything, I love the Rev like I love my life, but coming home has a certain rhythm to it if it's going to be done right. A certain sacredness, and a big dose of self-preservation. That's why I always try to arrive when the Rev is occupied elsewhere, so that I can close that big front door behind me and spend a few minutes alone, greeting the ghosts and reviewing the protocols.

This is, after all, the house of Rev. Horace A. Dunbar, gifted orator, fearless Civil Rights warrior, Founding Pastor, now Pastor Emeritus at Rock of Faith Community Church, advisor to mayors, congressmen, and even a president or two. Loving father, misunderstood husband, lifelong servant of the people. Attention must be paid. My father was one of the lions of the Atlanta Civil Rights Movement and although his name is not as well known as some of his contemporaries, his courage is legendary, his contributions undeniable. I grew up in a house where a bona fide hero sat at the head of our table, and we all knew it.

If you doubted it for a minute, the photographs are everywhere to remind you. There he is hanging on the wall in the hallway, leading a picket line in front of Rich's Department Store downtown because black folks could buy clothes there, they just weren't allowed to try them on first. There he is on the desk in his study, shaking hands with Martin Luther King Jr., two days before The March on Washington, or on the living room mantel talking head-to-head with Brother Malcolm, or on the wall of the breakfast nook, receiving a proclamation for Rev. Horace A. Dunbar Day from Mayor Maynard Jackson, or even in a candid shot, laughing in the backyard with Mr. Eddie. It doesn't matter what he's doing, it's always there. In his eyes. In the way he smiles. There's that *certainty.* That absolute conviction that there is a right and wrong of things; that the arc of the universe is long, but it does bend toward justice.

I took my suitcase upstairs to my old

bedroom, still decorated with the pale pink wallpaper my mother let me pick out for my tenth birthday. The one picture of her the Rev allows in the house sits on my dresser in a little silver frame. It's a picture of the three of us on Tybee Island, near Savannah, when I was still a toddler. I don't know who took it, probably Mr. Eddie, but my mother is young and beautiful and happy to be standing in the crook of my father's arm. She's holding me by the hand, but she's looking up at the Rev, who is looking right back, and it is such an intimate, sensual glance between them that whenever I see it, I feel almost like I'm intruding on their privacy, even all these years later.

That photograph used to be downstairs on the mantel, but after Mom left, he moved it up here. I guess he couldn't stand to put it away, but he couldn't take seeing it every day either. I don't remember my parents being in love like that. By the time I was old enough to notice, things had already cooled considerably. Sometimes I think she was just waiting for me to graduate and go off to college before she made her move. I always appreciated that. They've been separated now almost as long as they lived together, but neither one of them has ever gotten around to filing for divorce. They talk to each other more than either one ever admits to me, but unless they drag me into those discussions, I steer clear. My parents did not raise a fool.

This house is full of ghosts. Not the chain clanking, *boo* in the night kind. More like spirits. Energy left behind when the courageous souls who used to fill this house with endless talk of revolution and resistance, the possibility of transformation and the necessity of love, finally passed on, or moved on, or in my case, moved *out*. And not a moment too soon, I might add. That self-preservation thing again. It was hard to find room to breathe in this house when I was growing up, much less get a word in edge-wise. My father needed all the air and he sure had a lock on all the words.

His voice seemed to have an infinite capacity to convey every human emotion, but no ability to modulate itself to everyday exchanges. The Rev's voice didn't just resonate. It *boomed,* commanding the attention of everyone within the sound of it. Whether he was calling for a march on City Hall or complimenting Miss Iona on her Easter Sunday hat, when he spoke, you had to listen. Or if you had any sense you did, because that was the other thing about my father. He was always right. I was twenty-five before I ever heard him admit to a mistake, and it was, of course, a minor infraction. That's what makes him such a great leader. He's always absolutely certain that what he's suggesting is the right thing to do.

I need somebody like that in my life again. Somebody who can look me in the eye and say, *This is what is happening and this is what you need to do about it.* My father used to fill that role, but since he stopped speaking to me five months ago, or, let me be fair, since we stopped speaking to each other, I'm kind of out here on my own. My mother is entirely too ideological to be much good in the personal advice area. Tell my mother that some dude just broke your heart and she will tell you why the patriarchy is the root of all evil, which may or may not be true, but which is not very useful to a recently deflowered sixteen-year-old who just realized her first lover wasn't going to be her only one.

I know as a thirty-four-year-old woman, I'm supposed to be able to do that for myself, but lately I've been kind of falling down on the job and I don't really trust myself to do the right thing anymore. Take my *Sitting at the Right Hand of Obama* fantasy. Where did that come from? I've been trying to figure it out for weeks and I still don't know how I could have been so wrong. Maybe it was just the unavoidable spillover of an extended idealistic perfect moment, or maybe it was a grievously overinflated sense of my own importance to the campaign, but whatever it was, I was so sure I was going to get a White House job offered to me that I didn't even have a backup plan. *I still don't!*

When my old boss called me while I was working on the campaign in New Mexico to tell me that there were going to be cutbacks in my area, I wasn't worried. I just knew I would have other options. After all, I had carried out my first few assignments without a hitch and moved up in the campaign hierarchy quickly. I'm not going to lie and say I was flying around with Valerie Jarrett and David Axelrod, but I met the candidate enough times for him to remember my name once and for the first lady to compliment my haircut at an event in Santa Fe.

The campaign was an exciting, all-consuming, alternate universe. There was so much work to do, and I was good at most of it. I was surrounded by a steady stream of interesting people who were as passionate about the possibilities as I was and we worked nonstop at whatever tasks were at hand. In the early days, there were more computer geeks around than community organizers. Most of the young people who were volunteering had all the technical expertise in the world, but when it came time to motivate a bunch of hopeful voters huddled together in a community center some place where people still get most of their mail deposited out front by a guy who knows their names, these kids were clueless.

But being the Rev's daughter, I was right at home. That kind of house-by-house organizing is in my blood. My father is still the best I ever saw at taking a scared group of nervous neighbors and helping them shape themselves into a cohesive political unit, capable of great courage in the face of even the most implacable foe. The lessons I'd learned riding all over Georgia with the Rev and Mr. Eddie came back strong and those basics became part of one of the most successful grassroots campaigns the country has ever seen. The president gets big respect for using the Internet in revolutionary ways, but he deserves equal praise for his ability to adapt old-school techniques to new-school possibilities. I'm as proud of the role I played in all of it as I've ever been of anything I've ever done. The Rev would be, too, if he could ever stop fussing long enough to enjoy it.

For the first time, I felt like I was part of something that was going to change America forever. I wondered if this was what the best of the sixties felt like to my father's generation. When I asked him, he laughed and said I was what they used to call *freedom high,* drunk with the possibility of living free. Whatever you call it, I was caught up in a moment unlike any other I had experienced and I was prepared to go where it took me. The campaign became my whole world and whatever pitiful personal life I'd had fell by the wayside without a whimper.

To tell the truth, it wasn't much of a loss. A halfhearted boyfriend who didn't like oral sex. (The giving of; he was fine with the receiving.) A circle of girlfriends who were getting increasingly antsy as the years went by and nobody in our group was even close to a serious, committed relationship, regardless of gender, much less marriage. Professionally, I had been working my ass off for the last eight years as a fund-raising consultant for struggling nonprofits, but the economy had forced many of our clients to close their doors and the others were too broke to hire us to tell them what to do about it. *Like we knew.* When I asked for an unpaid leave to work full-time for the Obama campaign, I think my boss was glad to see me go. It meant she didn't have to tell me face-to-face that I wouldn't be coming back.

When I called her last week, she was struggling to keep on her two remaining staffers, so even if she had wanted to rehire me, there was no money to make it happen. I wasn't in panic mode yet. I've always been careful not to pile up a lot of debt and I'd had a couple of interviews that seemed promising, but everybody was scrambling to meet existing payroll and they couldn't commit right now. All I could do was wait and hope to pick up a little freelancing here and there to see me through.

The other problem was, neither job was even remotely connected to the world I'd been moving around in for the last eighteen months or so and I wasn't ready to give it all up and go back to trying to change the world by inches. I didn't believe my political life was over because I had helped elect one amazing president. I knew there was more work I wanted to do and more work he needed me to do, even if I wasn't going to be able to do it sitting at his right hand. Sure, my feelings were hurt. My ego was a little bruised, but I'm a big girl. I'll get over it.

This might not be a bad time to get out of town for a minute, all things considered. In D.C., the first question anybody asked, no matter where they saw you — restaurant, grocery store, health club — was *Where are you working now?* I tried to stick with a mysterious smile and that old line about being "between engagements," but everybody knew I had worked my ass off in the campaign and it was no secret that I was hoping to get tapped for the White House. Realistically, I know that the inauguration was only two weeks ago and there are still spaces to be filled, but try explaining that to the person who's just asked what you've been up to lately and it comes out sounding more desperate than devil-may-care. Any whiff of panic as the great jobs were picked off one by one was sure to be reported back to the community at large and would not improve my increasingly shaky place on the A-list. Making myself scarce for a few weeks might be the best move I could make.

The Cinderella clock on the nightstand said it was only twelve o'clock. Services on first Sunday are always longer because of Communion, and this was the first Sunday in Black History Month, so it was safe to assume that the Rev probably wouldn't be home until after one thirty, which left just enough time for a sweet little catnap. I kicked off my shoes and jumped in the bed like I used to when the Rev would listen to my prayers every night before he tucked me in, and even though he wasn't there to hear me, old habits are hard to break. So I snuggled down under that pink chenille bedspread, closed my eyes, and spoke a few words I know as well as I know my own name:

Now I lay me down to sleep,
I pray the Lord my soul to keep,
If I should die before I wake,
I pray the Lord my soul to take.

# Six:
## The Race Card

The first thing Wes clocked when Toni tapped on the door and ushered two men into his office was that they were both white. That gave Wes the answer to the one question he needed to ask, but couldn't: How many African Americans did they have moving around at this level? If they already had a brother, Wes knew, he'd be here. Right-wing Republican white folks love to bring one of their own in-house brothers to meetings like this. Takes away any opportunity for the other black person to play *the race card.* That didn't matter to Wes. He was holding all the cards he needed.

Besides, to Wes's mind, any additional African American presence just increased the risk of this unholy alliance becoming known to the black folks whose job it is to holler about such things, as well as to the Obama people who had eyes in the backs of their heads and a 110 percent approval rat-ing in Black America. Wes had no interest in being identified by a guilt-ridden coconspirator, suddenly stricken with a bout of racial solidarity and desperate to be invited back to the big party in progress at 1600 Pennsylvania Avenue. Being the only dark face in this particular room suited him just fine, *thank you.*

Wes came around his desk quickly, hand outstretched, his smile of welcome untainted by even the slightest hint of obsequiousness. He exuded the same calm confidence that the new president seemed to exemplify so effortlessly, and just that quickly, Stan Bridges, who was meeting Wes for the first time, felt himself relax. Maybe everything Oscar had said about this guy was true, he thought. Stan sure hoped so.

Oscar Thames (*just like the river,* he said whenever he introduced himself), had recruited Wes during the campaign and he greeted him now as a friend.

"Good to see you, buddy!"

"Welcome," Wes said, as the two shook hands. "How was your flight?" He knew they had flown in from Houston on a private jet a few hours ago.

"Not bad," Oscar said. "Let me introduce you to Stan Bridges. Stan, Wes."

"Welcome," Wes said again, shaking Stan's

hand firmly.

That's one point in this guy's favor, Stan thought. He didn't do that macho hand-crushing shit some of the black guys tried to pull. It always made him mad. If you're such a big dick badass, he'd think, why don't you run the world instead of standing here squeezing my hand like it means something.

"Good to be here."

Stan and Oscar took seats on opposite ends of the couch, positioned to give visitors the best view of Wes's little piece of the New York skyline. Wes took a chair that allowed him the best view of his visitors. Oscar looked about the same; tall, thin, unassuming. With his pasty skin, washed-out brown hair, perpetually wrinkled suit, and thick glasses, he could have been an absentminded professor. But looks can be deceiving. Oscar was anything but absent-minded. At forty-two years old, he was well respected for finding creative ways to throw the opposition off its game. He was the one who concocted the story line about the big, black Obama supporter who mugged an innocent McCain/Palin voter at an ATM and carved the candidate's initials in her cheek. Of course, it had been exposed as a cruel exploitation of an already troubled girl, but for at least one whole news cycle, the words "young white woman," "black mugger," and "Barack Obama" were being uttered in the same sentence, and that was always a plus.

Stan was about fifty, blond, and permanently ruddy from hours spent at the helm of his beloved sailboat, with watery blue eyes and a mouth that seemed disinclined to arrange itself in more than the most perfunctory smile. His clothes were expensive and tasteful, but he wore them without any hint of personal style. From his oxblood wing tips, to his three-striped tie and starched white shirt, he was the very model of an old-money, East Coast WASP. Oscar had told him Stan had a son with an undistinguished academic record applying to Exeter and implied that he might welcome a reference from a well-respected alum, which Wes most certainly was. Wes wondered if Stan, wrapped tightly in the last shreds of white privilege, would be able to humble himself enough to ask for it.

"We appreciate your making time to see us on this Sunday morning," Stan said, making an effort to smile.

"Oscar and I are used to working irregular hours," Wes said, watching approvingly as Toni took a seat behind him in a smaller chair. She was wearing a dark suit, a white silk blouse, and her pumps from the other night. *Perfect.* Oscar had specified no computers, so she would be making any notes on a yellow legal pad. Their eyes met briefly, but neither one tried to telegraph anything personal. *Pussy was pussy.* This was *business.*

"Coffee?" Wes said, knowing Toni would already have asked.

"I'm good," Oscar said. "Stan?"

"Nothing for me, thanks," Stan said. "I'd prefer to get right to the business at hand, if that's all right with everybody."

It was clearly a rhetorical question. Wes was there to listen and Oscar was there to facilitate. The ball was in Stan's court. He was just being polite and they all knew it. Toni held her pen poised.

"By all means," Wes said, neither impressed nor intimidated. He had met a lot of white men like Stan. Rich, powerful, steadily projecting class and doing dirt. They were scrambling to figure out a place for themselves and their kind in an increasingly diverse America, and like all cornered animals, they were dangerous. Wes sat back, crossed his legs, and waited.

Stan leaned forward and frowned slightly. "It's no secret that our last showing was a disaster. There's no need to go over the whys and wherefores. That is yesterday's news as far as I'm concerned, Wes. My focus is on the future, not the past."

"I couldn't agree more, Stan," Wes said. "How can I help you?"

It was important at times like these to remind the Stans of the world who had asked who for assistance. Otherwise, they would start acting like they were doing you a favor when it was you who was saving their asses.

Stan smiled his tight-lipped grimace. "I like a man who can get to the point."

Wes's smile was wider, but no less insincere.

"You come highly recommended," Stan said, inclining his head slightly toward Oscar, who pushed his glasses up on his nose and nodded. "Your work with the Palin camp around positioning Sarah with a black female constituency based on the fact that she had that pregnant, unmarried daughter was brilliant. The fact that they couldn't figure out how to use it more effectively is not your fault. None of us could have anticipated that level of sheer . . ."

Stan stopped himself and Wes squashed the impulse to supply the word. *Incompetence?*

"The point is you were thinking creatively

66

and specifically and that's what we're going to need in Atlanta."

He turned toward Oscar. "Why don't you give Wes the broad picture and then I'll fill in the specifics."

Oscar ran a hand over his hair, which did nothing to tame it. "We identified four African American leaders who seem unaffected by the country's current infatuation with all things Obama. Jesse Jackson, Jeremiah Wright, Tavis Smiley, and Horace Dunbar." Oscar ticked them off on his fingers like a hostess counting her dinner guests. "Jesse was not considered a good potential partner in our upcoming efforts because he can't be counted on not to have a change of heart and switch sides at the last minute. Jeremiah Wright has so much light on him already, any attempt to involve him in something where discretion is required is immediately doomed, and Tavis Smiley is impossible to predict and therefore to control, which brings us to Reverend Dunbar. Well known, well respected, mad as hell and he's not going to take it anymore. He's ripe for a change in party affiliation and I don't have to tell you what a PR bonanza that would be for us. Not to mention access to the list of those hundred thousand new voters he put on the rolls in time for November fourth."

"Needless to say, those votes are over-whelmingly Democratic," Stan said, like the word itself left a bad taste in his mouth. "And if I may speak frankly, neutralizing his efforts is going to be the cornerstone of our first Georgia initiative."

Now we're getting to it, Wes thought. "Define 'neutralize.' "

Stan passed the question off to Oscar with a glance. "We want to purge the Georgia voter rolls of as many of those new Democratic voters as we can," Oscar said carefully. "Since these churches all did their registration drives at the same time, we can easily isolate and remove them if we can get a crack at that list."

"Go on."

"We've got somebody on the inside of the elections office, but we need the membership lists from those churches. There are at least ten of them in the network, as best we can tell, but there doesn't seem to be a master list anywhere."

*Old-school,* Wes thought. "How can I help?"

Stan was pleased at Wes's directness. This was going to work out just fine. He'd deliver the money they had picked up in Texas and be on a plane back to Boston by noon. *Piece of cake.*

"First thing we need is a solid assessment of what we're dealing with," Stan said. "It could be a hundred thousand names, but it could be twenty-five thousand. Who really knows?"

Oscar nodded. "As soon as we get the lists, we'll compile a master list and shoot the whole thing over to our guy in elections. The ones we can purge on technicalities, we will. The ones we can't, we'll target with misinformation. You know, bogus changes in polling places, threats to put folks in jail for back child support — the usual."

He smiled at Wes. They both knew how to do this kind of work and they both knew the other one was good at it.

"At the same time, we'll begin setting up speaking engagements for Reverend Dunbar in front of audiences who will respond positively to criticism of the White House agenda. With this guy's movement credentials, press coverage is a given."

Wes got up and walked over to the window. It was always good to appear to consider the full ramifications of the proposed trickery. He folded his arms and gazed down at the people in the street below; the very picture of a man in the midst of careful internal deliberations.

"Can you help us out, Wes?" Oscar prompted him gently.

Before he could answer, Stan spoke up quickly. "There is one more thing."

Wes turned back to the two men and smiled as if pleased to be released from his reverie.

"There's always one more thing," he said.

"We've got a bit of time pressure. Our guy down there in elections is retiring at the end of April. That gives us just three months to work with. Is it doable?"

"Is there support for it at the appropriate level?"

"Top priority down the line," Stan said. "Whatever resources you need are already in place."

Wes walked back to his chair and sat down, aware that Stan's watery eyes were following his every move closely. "I'll need to go down and make an initial assessment before I can suggest an approach that makes sense," he said.

Stan nodded. "Of course."

"But I can practically guarantee that we can work within your timetable."

Stan's face almost managed a real smile. "That's good to hear, but what makes you so optimistic?"

*Wait for it,* Wes thought. *Make him wait for it.*

"Because, gentlemen," he said, leaning back in his lovely leather chair. "Reverend Dunbar is my father's best friend. I grew up in his church."

Oscar's mouth dropped open with surprise and Stan's face flushed ever redder with surprise or delight, Wes couldn't tell. It didn't matter. At that moment, Wes was golden.

"Well, then," Stan said, reaching in his pocket for a thick white envelope and placing it on Wes's desk without comment. "I don't mean to rush things, but we've got a plane going to Atlanta at midnight, don't we, Oscar?"

Oscar nodded. "Twelve fifteen."

"Can you be on it?"

Wes leaned over, picked up the envelope without comment, and slid it into the breast pocket of his dark blue suit. "Have your car pick me up here at ten thirty."

"Done."

Stan stood up then. "Oscar will continue to be our point man on this. If we need to talk, Oscar can set it up within twenty-four hours."

"He's always got my numbers," Wes said, turning to Toni. "Will you show our guests

71

out, Miss Cassidy?"

Toni stood up gracefully. "Of course. Gentlemen?"

Oscar chuckled. "Bless you, young lady. I admire your boss's security provisions, but we would never have found our way back to the parking deck alone."

Toni offered him her dimpled smile and followed him out the door. Stan and Wes were a few steps behind.

"Two thousand and eight was tough," Stan said. "I don't intend to let anything like that happen again. I'm a man who likes to win."

"That makes us even," Wes said. "I'm a man who hates to lose."

Stan slowed, stopped, looked at Wes, and blinked those watery eyes almost like he was on the verge of tears. *Here we go,* Wes thought.

"Oscar tells me you're an Exeter man."

"I'm an Exonian to my soul. Class of 1990."

"Did you have a positive experience there?"

"Some of the best years of my life," Wes said. "I hear your son is interested."

Stan shot another quick glance at Wes, trying to read his tone. If he knew Junior was interested, did he also know the kid's chances of being admitted on his own merit were slim and none?

"Yes," he said carefully, hating the position in which his overindulged son had placed him. "We've done all the paperwork and sent in references from some of his favorite teachers . . ."

*Of whom I'm sure there are many,* Wes thought.

"I thought we were done with all that, then the admissions office told my wife it might *strengthen* his application if he had a reference from a distinguished alum."

This was Wes's cue to offer to write the letter, make the call, put his reputation on the line for a kid he'd never met who was probably a spoiled little fuckup, but Wes couldn't resist making Stan squirm just a little bit longer.

"I've heard they do take those things into consideration."

Stan looked pained. "So it seems."

Wes knew he could prolong Stan's uncomfortable moment simply by asking the next logical question: *How are Junior's grades?* But what was the point? It was a done deal. He was going to write a glowing recommendation and then whether the kid got in or not, Stan would owe him a favor for putting in a good word on behalf of his idiot son. Both men knew the only thing more valuable than a favor well done was a secret well kept. This had the potential to be both.

"I'd be happy to write a letter for your son if you think it would help," Wes said, touching Stan's shoulder lightly.

A look of relief and something else crossed Stan's face. Probably *shame*, Wes thought. Stan's definition of being a "winner" did not include having to ask a black man for a favor.

"I would appreciate that, Wes," Stan said, knowing there was still one more embarrassing question he had to ask.

"No problem," Wes said. "Is Truman Jarrett still running the shop over there in admissions?"

Stan nodded. "I'll have my girl send the address over."

Wes smiled. "No need to. I think I still remember it."

At the door he saw Oscar glance in their direction. It was time to go, but he had to ask.

"Do I need to . . ."

Wes looked as if he had no idea what was coming next, although of course he did.

Stan bit the bullet. "Do I need to send over his transcripts?"

And here was the wonderful moment

when a favor becomes a secret shared, Wes thought. In his world, that was as good as money in the bank. Or in a plain white envelope.

"That won't be necessary," he said and lowered his voice conspiratorially even though Toni had engaged Oscar's attention in the hallway and there was no danger of being overheard. "I know what to say."

Stan's gratitude was almost palpable. "Then you're my man," he said, extending his hand one more time, smiling his first real smile of the day, and heading for the door. "I'll be in touch."

*Well, Mr. Mystery Money, that's one more thing you're wrong about,* Wes thought, watching Stan and Oscar follow Toni out into the hallway and back through the unnecessarily confusing exit path he'd created for their benefit. *I'm nobody's man but my own.*

# SEVEN:
# FAST-TALKING
# CHICAGO NEGROES

*Catnap, my ass.* I was sound asleep when the front doorbell woke me up with a start. I use the word "bell" loosely. What the Rev has is a door *siren* that makes an amazingly unpleasant, impossibly loud sound, that can best be described as a cross between an old-fashioned alarm clock and a fire engine. We have all begged him to replace it with some chimes, or even a less insistent buzzer, but so far, he hasn't gotten around to it.

All that was, of course, beside the point. The question was why was he ringing his own doorbell at one thirty on a Sunday afternoon? The answer is, he wasn't. When I went down and opened the front door, Miss Iona was standing there, all alone, beaming and wearing a beautiful dark green coat, a matching hat that clung to her salt-and-pepper bob at an impossibly sassy and undeniably stylish angle, and a pair of beautiful suede heels, also dark green, that clicked softly on the hardwood floor when she stepped in and threw her arms around me. Miss Iona was a power hugger. She grabbed you fast, squeezed you hard, and then stepped back to extend the appropriate greeting.

"Welcome home, darlin'," she said. "Tell me I didn't wake you up at this hour of the day!"

"No, I was just . . ." Of course she didn't wait for an answer. She took off her coat and dropped it on the coatrack, revealing a dress of the same dark green wool. This was clearly one of Miss Iona's famous churchgoing ensembles. She liked everything to match and on this day, she had achieved her goal and topped it all off with the gravity-defying hat.

"The Rev's on his way to Madison," she said and rolled her eyes. "Black History Month waits for no man! Eddie's driving him, of course, so I'm charged with being the official greeter and with getting you over to my house in time for supper. That way you can see everybody at one time and the Rev will have to be on his best behavior because we'll all be there watching him."

I wondered briefly what the Rev would look like on his best behavior, but when I opened my mouth to respond, a big yawn came out instead.

Miss Iona raised her eyebrows. "I *did* wake you up, didn't I?"

"I was up late," I said. "Sorry!"

Her eyes twinkled at me and she lowered her voice. "Anything you can talk about?"

"Nothing like that," I said quickly, wishing I had never uttered the words "White House" to Miss Iona or anybody else. "Just some freelance work to hold body and soul together."

She looked disappointed, but regrouped fast. "Well, go on upstairs and throw some cold water on your face or something and I'll make a pot of coffee. Can't have you yawning at my guests."

"How many people are coming?" I said, heading for the stairs and wondering if a public reunion was the best way to go to bring out the best in what was probably going to be a fairly awkward moment, no matter how well Miss Iona had been able to smooth the way.

"Just the usual suspects," she said. "My Charlie, of course."

She always referred to her husband as *my Charlie* in a tone that was equal parts affection and ownership. He loved it.

"Flora and Hank Lumumba, if he's in town. He's traveling all the time now. Do-

78

ing something mysterious. Politics or something. I hope they'll bring their daughter, Lu. She's going to Georgetown in the fall, so you should know her anyway. Abbie and Peachy were here from Tybee for the weekend, so they're coming by before they head back to the island. Probably Blue and Regina Hamilton, you remember them, right?"

Blue Hamilton was a former R&B singer who had been West End's unofficial godfather for the past ten years or so. He was the reason West End was always a peaceful oasis, no matter what went on beyond its twenty or so square block borders. I was already away at school when the neighborhood got hit bad with the crack epidemic and a sudden rise in unemployment and homelessness. Women were being robbed and raped like it was a sport. When a member of Blue's band had a sister assaulted and murdered on her way home from the grocery store, Blue decided something had to be done. He organized the men in the neighborhood, guaranteed the safety of the women, and required the children to have respect for their elders and a sense of responsibility for their futures.

I had met him and his wife, Regina, a couple of times and been struck by their obvious affection for each other. They are one of those couples who always seem to prefer each other's company no matter how many other people are around. The rumor is that they knew each other in a past life, but how can you prove something like that? Of course, West End is full of visionaries, clairvoyants, and prophets of all kinds, so there's no reason to doubt it either.

"I remember them," I said.

"And of course your father and Eddie when they get back from Madison." She shook her head with a rare show of impatience. The smooth brown feather on her green felt hat trembled delicately. "Isn't that just like a man? The gathering is in his honor in the first place and he's going to be the main one walking in late."

"In the Rev's honor?"

"No, Mr. Eddie, but you know he won't let anybody else drive your dad, so what are you gonna do?"

This was a classic case of Iona overload. I hadn't even had a chance to ask her how the Rev reacted when she told him I was coming and we had already moved on to one of the Sunday gatherings for which she was rightfully famous. Sometimes she and Mr. Charles cooked everything themselves. Sometimes it was potluck, but even then, Mr. Charles always cooked a ham or a big

80

turkey and Miss Iona always made a big pan of mac and cheese to start things off.

"What *I'm* going to do," I said, "is take your suggestion, go splash some water on my face and then come back down here for a cup of that coffee you promised me before you thrust me right back into the never-ending West End social whirl without some caffeine to fortify me."

She laughed. "You talk more like your father every day!"

Hoping that wasn't true, I hurried back upstairs to wash my face, brush my teeth, and run a comb through my hair. I have always been a low-maintenance girl and being on the road for almost two years straight required that I learn to go from jumping in the shower to walking out the front door in fifteen minutes flat, and I got good at it.

The Rev hates that I wear my hair so short. He's definitely of the *women's hair as crowning glory* school, but I think it's really because I look more like my mom this way. One of the worst arguments I ever heard between my parents was when she cut her shoulder-length pageboy into a curly cap of natural ringlets. He accused her of doing it to spite him. She accused him of being a male chauvinist pig and it went downhill from there.

As I straightened the neckline of my dress, I realized I hadn't even taken off my pearls when I lay down. They were part of my protective campaign coloration and now they're just a habit, I guess. I met lots of new people every day when I was on the road and it was my job to make them comfortable with our candidate. Some of them had heard really scary things about Barack, but nobody's afraid of a smiling woman with a strand of pearls around her neck. Ask the first lady.

Before heading back downstairs, I examined my reflection for obvious signs of stress and saw looking back at me what appeared to be an attractive, confident woman. The contrast between how I looked and how I felt was so stark, it actually made me smile. *Who is that serene-looking bitch?* I thought, remembering Richard Pryor's famous line during his divorce proceedings when his wife showed up looking like a sixteen-year-old virgin instead of his willing partner in crimes too numerous to detail here.

The funny part is the woman in the mirror looking back at me seemed to be totally on top of things; cool, calm, and collected. Maybe I'm more in control than I think and just maybe Miss Iona's right about surrounding the Rev with a crowd to bring out the best in him. He's good at crowds. It's the one-on-one that makes him crazy. *Me, too.*

Thankfully, the smell of freshly brewed coffee floated up the stairs before I could head down that road, so I slipped on my shoes and joined Miss Iona in the kitchen.

"Can I help you?"

It was a purely rhetorical question. Miss Iona was bustling around efficiently, her amazing little hat still in place on top of her salt-and-pepper hair, her suede high heels clicking daintily on the tile floor. To paraphrase Gloria Steinem, she needed my help like a fish needs a bicycle.

"I've got it under control," she said. "Sit down, sit down. How's your mother doing? Still stirring up trouble on the West Coast?"

"Every chance she gets," I said, taking a seat at the table where I had eaten countless bowls of Cheerios, innumerable platters of fried chicken. "She just led a demonstration against her new department chair and they've been friends for fifteen years."

Miss Iona laughed. "I knew they shouldn't have given her that tenure. I told you she was going to run amok out there!"

Miss Iona was only a few years older than my mom, but she had remained untouched by the rush of the Women's Movement that swept my mother along in a torrent of revolutionary fervor, redefining her life and her tribe and finally giving her the strength to override the Rev's shocked disapproval and leave him so she could focus her considerable energies on becoming a fully liberated woman, which she did, although last time I checked, neither one of them had filed for divorce.

On the other hand, Miss Iona seemed never to have imagined herself anything other than completely free. She was the first woman I knew who always had her own money, who never had children, who didn't marry for the first time until most of her friends were already widows, bought a house at thirty, paid it off at forty, and never asked any man any of us had ever seen for permission to do anything. My mother's defiance was amusing to Miss Iona.

"Defiance means you got somebody with power over you," she said once after listening to my mother speaking at a pro-choice rally. Miss Iona wasn't much on demonstrations, but she'd come along to look out for me while my mom was doing her thing. "If that's the case, you don't need to be defiant, you need to be gone."

"What about the women who can't go?" my mother would say, but Miss Iona couldn't even wrap her mind around that whole idea.

"Can't go?" she'd say. "Who's holding them?"

"It's complicated," my mom would say.

"Seems pretty simple to me," Miss Iona would say gently but firmly, like she didn't want my mother to be insulted, but was unwilling to feign agreement just to keep the conversation moving along in whatever was my mom's current direction. "Either you're free or you're not."

And my mom would give me that *She's wrong, I'm right, I'll explain later* look and smile at Miss Iona, who smiled back, just like she was doing now.

"Your mother always took everything so seriously," Miss Iona said.

"She still does," I said, wondering why she was taking so long to get to the heart of the matter: what the Rev said when she told him I was coming.

"Old folks don't change," she said, "except to get more like they already are."

"Amen to that," I said, as she poured us two steaming cups of coffee and then went to the refrigerator for cream, to the small cabinet over the sink for the sugar bowl, and then back to the silverware drawer for two spoons.

"So," I said when she finally stopped bustling around and sat down across from me, still without removing her beautiful hat. "What did the Rev say when you told him I was coming?"

Miss Iona raised her cup to her lips and blew delicately. That's when I knew. I groaned loudly and involuntarily.

"Oh, Lord, please tell me he knows I'm coming!"

"Don't blaspheme," she said. "I think he *suspects*. You know how hard it is to slip anything past the Rev."

"He *suspects?*" I set down my cup harder than I meant to and stood up. My first inclination was to dash upstairs, grab my stuff, and run for my life. "You didn't tell him?"

"Now calm down, Ida B, before you break up your mother's wedding china and the Rev demands both our heads on a platter. I tried to tell him, but I couldn't find the right moment. Everything has been so hectic with the beginning to Black History Month. He's speaking all over the state, not to mention half the pulpits in Atlanta. They all booked him before he lost his mind, of course, but I don't think they even care. As far as these Negroes are concerned, the Rev can do no wrong."

The Rev's waning popularity among the people who were running things didn't translate into smaller crowds among the people upon whom he had always counted. He could still draw a crowd in every town in Georgia just by showing up.

"This was not our deal," I said, refusing to be distracted by the Rev's busy schedule. "You promised me."

"I know I did," she said, reaching up now to remove the little hat and place it carefully on the table beside her. "And I meant to do it, you know I did . . ."

Her voice trailed off and then she looked up at me suddenly with a bright smile. "But you're here now, aren't you? And you know once he sees you, all will be forgiven."

"I haven't done anything to be forgiven for," I said. "He's the one who needs to say he's sorry."

She looked disappointed. "He's still your father, Ida B. Don't you think he deserves that respect?"

How had we gone from her not keeping up her end of our bargain to my alleged lack of respect for the Rev? My head was throbbing again.

"That's not fair," I said, "and you know it. He can't keep going back and forth between being my father and being a hot-shot Civil Rights leader."

"He has no choice," she said, shrugging her shoulders gracefully. "He's always both. Always has been. Always will be."

This conversation was going nowhere. I sat back down across from her, suddenly feeling exhausted and grumpy. I needed a hot shower and a hot meal.

"So now what?" I said, wondering what were the chances I'd get either one anytime soon.

"Calm down," she said again. "Don't I always have a plan?"

"Okay, let's hear it," I said, picking up my coffee and suddenly wishing she'd put some brandy in it.

"Like I told you, I'm having a little something tonight at my house in Eddie's honor," Miss Iona said. "His garden over at Washington High just won a big award. You should see what he's done with those kids. Tomatoes you wouldn't believe!"

"Go on," I said, stopping her before she got too far off the track.

She frowned as if she didn't understand what I was still concerned about. "That's it. Soon as they get back from Madison, Eddie will bring the Rev right over."

"And then what?" I could hear the stress rising in my voice. What happened to that serene girl in the mirror? Probably gone back to bed like she had some sense.

"Then I'll say . . ." She put on a big happy smile. " 'Surprise, Rev! Look who's here!' And then you step up and say, 'I love you, Daddy! I have missed you so much and no crowd of fast-talking Chicago Negroes should ever come between us again!' Then hug his neck and I swear to you he'll be the happiest man in West End."

The scene was straight out of a Tyler Perry movie, but real life is always a little more complicated.

"What makes you so sure?"

"Girl, please," she said. "He's already so proud of you he's about to bust. It's that ego that wouldn't let him call you."

Just when I thought things couldn't get any worse, I knew they were about to. "Proud of me for what?"

"Your new position at the right hand of *you know who,*" she said, and actually winked. "He may have issues with Obama, but he's been bragging on you all over town."

I wondered if it was too late to get on a flight out of here this afternoon. "You told him I was going to work at the White House?"

"Guilty as charged," she said cheerfully.

"I'm sorry, sweetie, but it was just too good to hold. We're all so proud of you."

My heart sank ever lower, if that was possible. "All? Who else knows?"

"Well," she said, "I had to tell my Charlie. You know that. And Eddie was there when I told your dad and I don't know who all he's told."

I stood up again and walked over to the window. I couldn't look her in the eye.

"What's wrong, sweetie?"

I took a deep breath. "I didn't get the job."

"At the White House?"

"Anywhere."

Now it was Miss Iona's turn to be confused. "But I thought you said you were going to work for the president."

"I was wrong," I said, and that was the whole truth of it. I had dreamed up a fantasy job and then discovered that was exactly what it was: a fantasy. It felt good to tell her the truth, but I sure do wish she hadn't spread the word quite so fast.

"Oh, darlin', I'm so sorry. What happened?"

She sounded so sympathetic, I almost teared up. "I don't know. I guess I wasn't quite as indispensable as I thought I was."

She was quiet for a minute and then she said my fear out loud. "Do you think the

Rev . . . *being the Rev* . . . had anything to do with it?"

I sat back down and took a sip of my coffee. "I don't think it helped."

She pursed her lips and sighed. "You know I wouldn't have breathed a word if I'd thought it wasn't a done deal."

"I know." There was no point in blaming Miss Iona. She had only repeated what I'd told her. The fault was mine.

"Is there any chance it's just taking them a while to find the right place to put you?" she said, grabbing at the same straws I'd been clutching for weeks. "You know, someplace where they could use all your talents to the best effect."

"There's always a chance," I said. "Probably not at the White House, but, you know, somewhere else in government."

"Well, if they don't make you an offer," she said, covering my hand with her own and giving it a protective squeeze, "they're not as smart as they think they are."

I appreciated her loyalty, although the thing that's so impressive about the new administration is that they are *exactly* as smart as they think they are. But right now, I had to focus on damage control. This fantasy had the potential to blow up in my face, *repeatedly,* on the very night I wanted to keep everything, and *everyone,* on an even keel.

"So does everybody who's going to be at your house know?"

She nodded. "Pretty much."

"Then I can't go," I said.

"Why not?" She looked surprised.

"What am I going to say to all those people who think I'm headed for the West Wing?"

She thought for a minute, than brightened again. "Tell 'em you're in delicate final negotiations and everything is still hush-hush until things are finalized."

I was impressed. As excuses go, that one wasn't half bad. "You think they'll buy it?"

"Of course I do," she said. "Nobody knows how anybody gets those jobs. The more mysterious you make it sound, the better. Then after you and the Rev have a chance to talk, you can straighten it out with the others, no problem."

She said "no problem" the way people say "no worries," as if to imply that your insistence on obsessing about the matter at hand is simply a choice of perspective, which could easily be corrected by a little positive thinking. I wish I could say her confidence was infectious, but all I felt was a growing conviction that this whole evening was going to hell in a handbasket, Miss Iona's good intentions notwithstanding.

She was looking at me sympathetically again. "You want me to put some brandy in that coffee?"

"That's the best offer I've had all day," I said. She got the bottle from the pantry and poured a dollop in my cup and another in hers.

"Don't let me forget to put it back," she said. "Don't want the Rev to know we got into his private stash."

We clinked our cups in a wordless toast, each took a nice long swallow, and sat looking at each other.

"This will never work," I said.

"Of course it will." She patted my hand again. "Trust me."

# Eight:
## Business
### Opportunities

While Toni shepherded Stan and Oscar out of the building by a circuitous path that satisfied their strange need for cloak-and-dagger security measures and included a ride down a freight elevator, Wes took the moment alone to call his father and see if Mr. Eddie, as everyone but Wes called him, could put him up for a few days. He'd probably be too surprised to say no, even if he wanted to, Wes thought, punching in Mr. Eddie's number.

How long had it been? Wes tried to call his father every couple of weeks, just to check in, but things had been so busy lately, he couldn't actually remember when they'd last spoken, much less laid eyes on each other. After four rings, his father's ancient answering machine clicked on and the familiar voice greeted him, sounding vaguely uncomfortable like old people always do as if they never really trust the technology to take a message.

"Good afternoon. You have reached the house of Edward Harper. Please leave a message and I'll call you back quick as I can."

"Hey, Pop," Wes said after the beep. "It's me. Listen, I've got a couple of business opportunities I need to check out down there and I was wondering if I could stay with you at the house for a couple of days. I know we haven't been able to spend much time together lately and I thought we could . . ."

*Could what? Catch up?* His mother had been the conduit through which father and son had always communicated. When she died a decade ago, Wes and Mr. Eddie rode in deep silence from the church to the cemetery and back to the house. In the ten years since, neither one had found a way to break it, other than with an occasional, nonbinding "How you doin'?" Or a strangely formal "Merry Christmas."

Not that his father ever gave him any grief about not calling, any more than he chided him for not showing up for the birthdays and retirement parties and other stuff he missed or arrived at so late he might as well have missed them. His father was always happy to see him, but he never seemed to mind very much when he didn't.

"We could have dinner or something." He sounded like he was talking to a stranger. "Anyway, I'm not sure what time my flight gets in, I'm coming in on a private jet this time, so I'll call you. Okay, Pop. Looking forward to it."

He clicked off, wondering if he should have said "I love you."

# NINE:
# THE KNOWNS AND
# THE UNKNOWNS

When we got to Miss Iona's house, we could hear somebody growling a much nastier version of the Rolling Stones classic "Let's Spend the Night Together" before she even opened the front door.

"That man's gonna get us all sent straight to hell playing that Muddy Waters mess that loud on Sunday afternoon," Miss Iona said as she stepped inside, shedding her coat and heading down the hall toward the kitchen.

"Turn that down, will you?" she said, over her shoulder. "I can't hear myself think!"

I took off my coat, too, and turned down the volume on their ancient but active stereo system where Mr. Charles was actually playing the *album,* not the CD. He had tossed the cover on the coffee table and Muddy Waters's face was looking up at me from under the carefully constructed waves of that amazing process. For some reason, he was also wearing a long robe, which may have given Mr. Charles the idea that God wouldn't mind adding Muddy's voice to the heavenly choir.

I hung up our coats in the hall closet beside the front door. Down the hall from the kitchen, I could hear Miss Iona and Mr. Charles and another couple of women's voices I didn't recognize. At least I didn't hear the Rev's *boom* yet. I needed a few minutes to gather myself together. I took a deep breath and looked around. Miss Iona and Mr. Charles lived in the cozy West End bungalow she had occupied solo for thirty years. The décor definitely reflected her taste for antiques and several small tables were crowded with souvenirs and bric-a-brac from the ports of call she'd visited on one of her beloved cruises. She had graciously accommodated Mr. Charles's fondness for television by giving over what had been her sewing room to a large flat-screen television and his favorite burgundy *pleather* Barcalounger. She added a love seat and a cashmere throw for when they wanted to cuddle up and watch something together and ordered a cable service with all the sports and movie channels, but no Playboy.

"I don't need the competition," she'd said when the cable company salesman made the offer to Mr. Charles as part of a package.

Although appropriately muted, I could see the large screen was alive with one of the nature shows Mr. Charles loved. A herd of graceful gazelle were in panicked flight from a tawny pair of lionesses who probably had cubs to feed and no time to waste.

But Mr. Charles wasn't watching TV today. He was cooking, and from the aromas wafting around the house, cooking up a storm. Of course, I was still nervous about the Rev's reaction to seeing me, and mine to seeing him. I still had no idea how I was going to break the news to him about my fantasy job going up in smoke, or how I was going to lie my way through an evening with people who shared his pride in my nonaccomplishment, but something about the coziness of this house where I had spent so many happy hours and learned so many valuable lessons really calmed me down a lot. Maybe it was the music, or maybe it was because the whole place smelled like the soul food supper of your dreams. Roast chicken, baked ham, collard greens, and Miss Iona's famous mac and cheese were sending out such amazing messages from the kitchen that for just a second or two, I forgot all about the knowns and the unknowns and just enjoyed being home.

Before I could fully indulge my sudden

wave of nostalgia, I heard Mr. Charles headed my way down the hallway. He was wearing a snow white chef's hat and a big black apron that said "Don't make me poison your food!" across his chest in huge white letters. He was followed by a smiling woman with her hair pulled back into two thick French braids and a girl in a bright pink sweater who looked to be about sixteen or seventeen.

"Ida B. Dunbar, you are a sight for sore eyes!" he said, wrapping his long arms around me in one of many welcome home hugs I anticipated before the evening was over. I had known Mr. Charles as long as I had known Mr. Eddie, which is to say my whole life. "Welcome home, baby girl!"

"Thank you," I said, kissing his cheek and pointing to the writing on his apron. "Should I be concerned?"

"Not for one second, darlin'," he said. "Louie Baptiste gave us all one of these for Christmas."

Louie Baptiste was a wonderful chef who had been permanently displaced by Hurricane Katrina and was now the chef at Sweet Abbie's, a new Tybee Island restaurant owned by Peachy Nolan and named after Miss Abbie, Regina Hamilton's aunt and West End's self-proclaimed *visionary advisor.*

"You know those New Orleans folks are serious about their food." Mr. Charles laughed and waved one long arm to include his two other guests in our moment. "Miss Ida B, meet two of the finest women in West End, Miss Flora Lumumba, gardener extraordinaire, and her daughter, the lovely and talented Fannie Lu Lumumba."

"You better stop all that before your wife hears you." Flora laughed and reached out a warm hand. "Good to meet you."

"You, too," I said.

"Everybody calls me Lu," her daughter said, also offering a handshake and a smile.

"I'm just Ida," I said, smiling back.

Miss Iona appeared in the doorway wearing a frilly white apron that tied at her trim waistline with a bow and carrying a tray of ice tea with a wedge of lemon delicately balanced on the lip of each tall glass. Summer or winter, sweet tea was a Sunday staple.

"So did everybody meet everybody?"

Mr. Charles hurried across the room to take the tray and set it down on the coffee table.

"You know I took care of my duties as official host," he said. "Tell her, Lu."

"He said we were two of the finest women

in West End." Lu grinned at Mr. Charles, who grinned back.

"I said it and I'll say it again," he said, handing a glass of tea to me and one to Flora.

"They heard you the first time," Miss Iona said. "Come on back and taste these collard greens for me. You know I never get them hot enough for you."

"I've been tasting all day," he said. "We need a clear palate. Come on, Lu."

She shook her head. Her hair was pulled into two big Afro puffs, one over each ear. "I can't. It's got pork."

Lu had Flora's face, but not her cocoa brown skin. Her sandy hair framed a light tan face with a delicate dusting of freckles across the bridge of her nose.

Mr. Charles groaned. "Oh, Lord, are you still on that *no meat* kick?"

"It's not a kick." She looked at me. "We go through this every Sunday. Don't pay us any mind."

"You come do it then, Flora. You're not swearing off pork, too, are you?"

"Not me," Flora said. "All things in moderation."

"Find some more music, Lu," said Miss Iona as the two cooks and their official taster headed back down the hall. "And get the doorbell if it rings, will you?"

"Yes, ma'am," Lu said, smiling at me and heading for Mr. Charles's well-organized album collection that was heavy on blues and a little pre-bebop jazz, and Miss Iona's CDs, which included mostly female vocalists from the fifties as well as a healthy dose of Motown, the complete Anita Baker collection, every album Aretha Franklin ever made, and a recording of Leontyne Price singing *Aida*. As I recall, there's also a pretty good selection of Mahalia Jackson. I wondered what Lu would pick.

She squatted down in front of Mr. Charles's two shelves of albums and began to flip through them. I sat down on the couch, took a sip of my perfectly sweet tea, and relaxed a little more. Lu pulled out John Coltrane's *My Favorite Things* and flipped over to the liner notes. I wondered if she had ever heard it. The Rev was a big jazz fan so I had learned a lot just by osmosis.

Lu grinned up at me, returning the Coltrane to its proper place and continuing her search. "Are you named after Ida B. Wells Barnett?"

"Yep." I grinned back. "Fannie Lou Hamer and Patrice Lumumba, right?"

She nodded, pleased I had recognized the name of the martyred Congolese leader.

"You're good! Some people get the Fannie Lou part, but nobody knows anything about Patrice Lumumba. He was my dad's favorite revolutionary so when he decided Jones was a slave name, Lumumba was a natural."

"We're a walking history lesson," I said as she pulled out Anita Baker's *Rapture*. Every woman I know who's my mom and Miss Iona's age has this album in their collection, but Mr. Charles had his own copy. Men who like women learn to like women's music. Mr. Charles loved women, especially the lady of the house, so I wasn't surprised.

"You're Reverend Dunbar's daughter?"

"Do you know my dad?"

She lifted the needle on Muddy Waters, replaced him with Anita's masterpiece, and adjusted the volume to accommodate our conversation. "I interviewed him once for a history project," she said. "He told me all these stories about the Movement and about working with Dr. King. He made it seem so real."

*I wish they had put her interview on YouTube instead of the one they're running,* I thought.

"It is real," I said, but I knew what she meant. Their courage and commitment were bigger than ordinary life. That's why they were able to change the world.

"My dad told me your father is one of his

104

heroes."

"Mine, too," I said, and it was true. Which didn't mean I wasn't getting more nervous the closer it got to the time for him to lay eyes on me. I had missed him a lot, and more than anything, I wanted him to be glad to see me here among his friends and neighbors.

"What was it like to —" Before Lu could finish her question, the doorbell rang. My heart started pounding immediately, wondering if this was the Rev; hoping it was, hoping it wasn't.

" 'Scuse me," Lu said. "Gotta play hostess."

To my great relief, she opened the door to a smiling young woman and a little girl of about five or six who was dressed in what looked like a Halloween costume under her coat, complete with a small tiara.

"Hey, now!" said the woman, kissing Lu's cheek. "Sorry we're late. I couldn't find Princess Joyce Ann's crown."

"I'm Cinderella, Mommy," said the little girl. "There isn't any princess named Joyce Ann."

"Well, there should be," her mother said, spotting me as Lu helped the girl with her coat. "Hi! I'm Aretha."

"Ida Dunbar," I said.

"And this," Lu straightened the girl's tiara and turned her toward me, "this is Princess Joyce Ann Hargrove."

"*Cinderella,* Lulu!"

"Princess Cinderella," Lu said.

I remembered a brief attempt on the Rev's part to call me his *little princess,* and my mom's outraged reaction that turned a sweet nothing into a slave name. I guessed the woman to be about thirty with close-cropped hair and three small gold hoops in each ear. She was wearing a long black dress with a high collar that accentuated her graceful neck, and a pair of Doc Martens on her feet that gave her outfit a funky, boho look that seemed just right. I can never pull that off, but I always admire a sister who can. Under her left arm, she was carrying a large black portfolio. I wondered if she was an artist. She looked like one.

"Good afternoon," I said to the princess. "I love your dress."

"Thank you," she said, with the confidence that royalty must confer. "My daddy got it at Target."

Lu smiled and took the child's hand. "Let's go show Miss Iona."

"And Mr. Charles?"

"He's out there, too," Lu said, guiding the princess past her mother. "How'd the pictures come out?"

"Amazing, if I do say so myself." Aretha grinned, looking around for a place to put down the portfolio.

"Great," Lu said, disappearing down the hallway. "I can't wait to see."

"Put it here," I said, moving the ice tea tray to a smaller table in the corner that was full of small sweetgrass baskets that I slid over to one side.

"Thanks," she said, laying the portfolio down gently and taking the seat Lu had just vacated. "You're the Rev's daughter, right?"

West End was a small town in the middle of a big city. Everybody knew the Rev and even the people who had arrived after I went away to school and then to work knew he had a daughter.

"That's me," I said. "Are you a photographer?"

She nodded. "I'm a painter mostly, but I do a lot of photography, too. Some video."

"Is that some of your work?"

Her hand fluttered over it protectively, although I don't think she was even conscious of the gesture. "Yeah, I've been documenting the garden project at Washington ever since Mr. Eddie started it two years ago. They're giving him an award for Black History Month, so I made a set of prints for them to hang in the main hallway right beside the basketball trophies."

This neighborhood has always been big on backyard gardens. A couple of years ago, after Blue Hamilton became the godfather around here, he started encouraging people to plant community gardens on any vacant lot he owned and now the West End Grower's Association had plots all over the place, growing everything from juicy jumbo tomatoes to giant sunflowers. The Rev never liked to work in the dirt and my mother never had time, so Mr. Eddie taught me everything I know about making things grow. He had a real flair for it and the patience to show a young person how to do it right.

"I think it's great Mr. Eddie is getting an award."

"Yes," she said, "but you know how he hates anybody to make a fuss over him. He's threatening to boycott the ceremony."

That sounded about right. Mr. Eddie was notoriously shy. If the Rev craved the spotlight, Mr. Eddie was content to bask in reflected glory.

"Can I see them?"

"Sure," she said, carefully untying the black grosgrain ribbon that held the thing together. I moved my glass out of the way to avoid even the possibility of a spill as she opened it.

Aretha was a wonderful photographer. The very first image caught your eye and your heart and held you right where she wanted you. There was Mr. Eddie with a serious look on his face, standing in the center of a group of high school kids who were clustered around him wearing overalls and the sheepish, hopeful grins of people about to embark on a journey together. Some of them were holding shovels, and off to the right, you could see a pile of bagged manure from Lowe's Garden Shop. Two girls were holding a sign that said "Booker T. Washington High School Garden Project," and behind them, you could see the statue for which the school is famous, Dr. Washington himself pulling back the veil of ignorance from the face of a newly liberated bondsman.

"That was the first day," Aretha said. "There's Lu right there next to Mr. Eddie."

Lu had linked her arm through his affectionately and I could see a great big Obama button pinned to the bib of her overalls.

"She's the one who got him to do it in the first place. They had a perfect plot of land to work with, but nobody had ever done a garden there, so when Lu asked about getting some other kids together to grow stuff, they told her she needed an adult volunteer to make sure they did it right, and a budget they could raise themselves since the school didn't have any funds to support them."

There was loud laughter from the kitchen.

"But you know Lu, right? She didn't let that stop her for a minute. With the parents she's got, she came out of the womb organizing people."

We could hear the group from down the hall coming our way. Princess Joyce Ann came first, still holding Lu by the hand, followed by Flora and Mr. Charles, who was still wearing his apron, and Miss Iona, who was not.

"Are those the photographs?" Flora said, sitting down on the arm of the couch and looking over Aretha's shoulder.

Aretha nodded. "I just started showing Ida."

"You started without me?" Lu said. "Go back to the beginning, then!"

Aretha laughed and carefully turned back to the first photo. "You're getting as bossy as the princess."

Mr. Charles leaned over to take a closer look at the group shot and nodded approvingly at his friend's photo. Mr. Eddie was the only person I had ever seen who could make garden overalls look elegant. Picture a sepia-toned Fred Astaire weeding a patch of perfect collard greens and you get the picture.

"You made the old boy look good. Pretty soon, ol' Ed's gonna have to start signing autographs."

"Everybody told him those kids wouldn't want to get their hands dirty, but you know Eddie," Miss Iona said proudly. "He just went over there and started digging."

He probably made it look so cool, they couldn't resist, I thought.

"Now the school board wants to use it as a citywide model," Flora said.

Aretha turned to the next photo and we all leaned forward to see.

"I'm in there, too," said the princess, pointing a chubby finger at herself, sans regal apparel, standing in the garden beside Lu, holding a tiny rake and smiling for the camera.

"Wait until we get these up online," Lu said. "Every high school in the city is going to want a garden!"

"And who's going to coordinate all that?" Flora groaned, as Aretha turned to another photograph that showed two boys talking earnestly to Mr. Eddie about something on

the back of what looked like a seed cata-
logue. "We're having a hard enough time
finding somebody to take this job already
without piling on more for them to do."

"You're the one with the grand vision."
Aretha grinned and turned another page.
"You have no one to blame but yourself."

"Look at Dad," Lu said, pointing at a shot
of a tall, sandy-haired man with a big
Angela Davis–style Afro, spreading mulch
between the rows of new plants.

Flora smiled at her husband's image.
"What a faker! The man can't keep a tomato
plant alive and there he is looking like
Johnny Appleseed."

"Where is Hank anyway?" Aretha glanced
around like she might have missed him, an
impossibility in the cozy room.

"He's in D.C. until Friday," Lu said.
"He's been gone for two weeks."

Aretha shook her head in Flora's direction. "If I didn't know that man was madly
in love with you, I'd swear he had a mis-
tress."

"There are children present!" Lu said,
covering her own ears, but Flora just
laughed.

"It's only until June," she said, draping
her arm around her daughter's shoulders
affectionately. "Soon as Lu graduates, we'll

get on up the road."

"Daddy only took that job because I'm gonna be at Georgetown," Lu said, rolling her eyes. "They can't live without me."

"But we keep on tryin'!"

"Well, don't try too hard." Lu grinned at her mother. "I'll tell you when."

"That's the only problem with raising princesses," Flora said, and kissed her daughter's cheek. "Always with the orders!"

# TEN:
## A PERFECT MORNING

Toni rapped on the door lightly.

"Come on in," Wes said, pleased that she had been in the meeting to witness his performance. What's that corny line from *Mahogany,* "Success is nothing unless you got somebody to share it with"?

"Congratulations," she said, holding up a bottle of champagne and two glasses.

"Where'd you get that?" he said, noting that it was Dom Perignon and unable to stop himself from also noting that he hadn't authorized any such expenditure.

She set the glasses on the table and opened the champagne without asking for assistance. "You are my new hero."

She filled both glasses, handed him one, and raised hers in a toast. "And don't worry. This didn't come out of petty cash. I paid for it myself."

He laughed, touched his glass lightly against hers, and took a sip. She did, too.

"You know me too well."

"Probably," she said, sitting down on the chocolate-colored suede love seat and crossing her lovely legs, "but the point is, you kicked ass. Always one step ahead. Always got the solution to the problem. Always so smooth."

"You better stop, girl. You're gonna swell my head."

"I could say something really dirty about that," she said, laughing, "but I'm serious. You were great. Maybe the best I've ever seen."

Her praise sounded so sincere, for a minute, he almost believed it. "That's the only way you get invited to catch a ride on the private plane," he said, loving the offer.

"It's about time," she said. "Now maybe you can finally join the Mile High Club."

"I am a charter member of the Mile High Club," he said, sitting down beside her. "Besides, private jets are for punks. Anybody can do it when there's nobody else around. The challenge is to get it done on the red eye to L.A."

She put down her drink and moved a little closer to him, reaching for his zipper without taking her eyes off his face. "If this goes well, you should make me a partner."

She pushed her hair behind her ears, as

he spread his arms across the back of the love seat. This was shaping up to be a perfect morning.

"Sometimes I don't know if you're sexually insatiable or just wildly ambitious," he said.

"How about sexually ambitious and wildly insatiable?"

"Works for me," he said, wondering if she really thought her pussy was worth a partnership. It was good, he wouldn't deny that, but no pussy is that good.

"So do we have a deal?"

There were times when truth was requested, but not required. This, Wes thought, closing his eyes, was one of those times.

"Baby, we got whatever you want, and then some!"

# ELEVEN:
# OUR MOST RECENT
# FAMILY FEUD

By four o'clock, the Rev still had not arrived and I was so nervous, I hadn't been able to eat a bite, even though I was starving. Sunday supper was always a buffet at Miss Iona's. Everybody served themselves and then found a place to perch wherever they could. Mr. Charles was good at putting a chair near every available surface so nobody had to balance a plate on their knees unless they wanted to. I had told my *can't talk about it yet* fantasy job lie so many times I was starting to think my nose was actually growing like Pinocchio's. It would have been bad enough if I had been lying to a bunch of strangers, but I had known some of these people all my life. They were my father's friends and parishioners and comrades in arms and here I stood, smiling and hugging and lying my ass off.

When Mr. Charles confided to me, as he sliced the perfectly pink honey baked ham in thin slices and arranged them on a big white platter, that the Rev was so proud he was about to bust, I fixed a shit-eating grin on my face and tapped my index finger to my lips to remind him that this was our secret. When Blue Hamilton turned those unbelievable turquoise eyes on me while his wife offered their congratulations, I was so grateful that their adorable two-year-old (christened Juanita, but known to all as Sweetie Pie) gave me an excuse to look away before he saw the truth.

I'm not sure I was so lucky with Miss Abbie, who gave me a really concerned look as I babbled about having to help Miss Iona and excused myself as fast as I could, since it's probably impossible to hide anything for long from somebody who makes a living looking through their third eye.

"This is driving me crazy." I burst into the kitchen like a madwoman, relieved to find Miss Iona alone making a pot of fresh coffee, but she held up a finger for silence. She was counting out the scoops and she didn't want to lose track and have to start again.

"He'll be here in a minute, sweetie," she said when she finished, guessing the wrong reason for my anxiety attack as she closed the coffee canister and flipped the switch to start the machine.

"I know that," I said. "That's not what I'm talking about."

"Well, one thing at a time, sweetie," she said, filling the silver sugar bowl. "I thought the Rev's arrival was your big one for today."

"Everybody thinks I'm going to work at the White House," I said, knowing I couldn't blame her, but wishing more and more that I could.

"We were just going on what you said. Honest mistake."

"What *you* said!"

"I was acting in good faith on bad information," she said calmly. "But the thing is, there's no use crying over spilled milk."

"They keep congratulating me," I said, sounding as miserable as I felt. "What am I supposed to say?"

She finishing pouring the sugar and looked at me. Her smile was meant to be reassuring. "We went over this, remember? You just say you can't talk about it until everything is confirmed. No biggie."

*No problem. No worries. No biggie.*

"I can't just keep lying all night." I sounded like a whiny six-year-old again. I cleared my throat and tried to get a grip.

"Okay, then I think you should tell them the truth."

"That I didn't get the job?"

Miss Iona nodded. "Exactly. Just spit it out."

"But I haven't told the Rev yet. I don't want them to hear it first."

She smiled at me. "Well, that takes us right back to our original plan."

I groaned.

"Oh, sweetie, just relax. Say hello to everybody and keep moving before they have a chance to ask you anything except how you're doin'."

"I'll keep moving," I said. "Right out the door and back to D.C. where I belong."

I wasn't kidding and she knew it. These all-is-forgiven moments never go the way you hope they will and I was getting more freaked out by the minute. Every time the doorbell rang, I jumped about a foot in the air. These people probably thought I had St. Vitus's Dance or something. In the last two hours I'd had plenty of time to consider how things could go wrong. What if he's still as mad as he was the last time we talked and as inflexible as my mother said he was the last time they did? What if he won't speak to me at all unless I apologize in front of everybody, which I couldn't possibly do and maintain a shred of self-respect so I'd have no choice but to defy him in front of everybody and show myself to be a rude and ungrateful child? What if he caught sight of me, turned on his heel, and just walked away? What if he couldn't even stand to look at me?

I figure that one is a lot less likely. The Rev loves words. Silent gestures are open to interpretation and the Rev likes to be clear, even if it might mean a public airing of our most recent family feud. I pinched the bridge of my nose again, a habit that provides no relief I can ever identify, and sighed. Even the smell of the peach cobbler that would be dessert as soon as the coffee was ready didn't soothe me. How could it? Mr. Eddie had already called to say he and the Rev were on their way. Now I'd have the White House lie, the current feud, and the Rev's reaction to worry about, all at the same time.

"Listen, sweetie," Miss Iona said, peering at me now with real concern. "Calm down. Right now, I know it seems like a big mess, but in less than an hour, it's all going to be over."

I was going to tell her that's exactly what I was afraid of when the doorbell rang. *Showtime.* Why had I ever agreed to this? I glanced at Miss Iona's back door, wondering if it was too late to make a run for it.

Through the kitchen door, I could hear greetings being exchanged and almost feel the energy level rise to meet the Rev's *boom* as he claimed the space, his voice rolling down the hallway in waves.

"Brother Larson, I hope you didn't let these Negroes start without me," he said. He was greeted by the laughter of people who had started and finished without him in the sure and certain knowledge that there was still plenty for their favorite pastor whenever he arrived.

I looked at Miss Iona, unsure of what I was supposed to do next. That six-year-old was in charge again and I was rooted to a spot between the stove and the refrigerator, waiting for instructions. Miss Iona didn't hesitate. She pushed open the door and called to him.

"Stop fussing, Rev, and come and get this plate I got in the oven for you," she said. "Eddie, you the guest of honor, so I'll bring you out yours."

That elicited more laughter.

"Look like you slippin', Rev," I heard Mr. Charles say. "You better learn how to grow somethin'. Otherwise, Ed got all your thunder."

"I'm growin' the future," the Rev shot back, his voice getting closer. "And don't you forget it."

I took a deep breath. I would have prayed, but at that moment the only prayer I could remember was the *Now I lay me down to sleep* one, which wasn't really appropriate. I didn't have time anyway. Miss Iona held the door open and my father stepped into her kitchen like the force of nature that he was. He had on a dark blue suit and a white shirt that still looked fresh even at the end of a very long day. Against the dark brown of his skin, his collar almost glowed. I couldn't see his shoes, but I knew they were shined to a high gloss, just like I knew Mr. Barlow had cut his hair yesterday morning like he did every Saturday. Even in the midst of all those good cooking smells, the Rev's Old Spice held its own and all that mattered was that he was still my daddy, and I was still his little princess, no matter what my mother said, and no way we were ever supposed to let a crowd of fast-talking Chicago Negroes come between us, even if they are undeniably fabulous. Politics is one thing, but even in Obamamerica, blood runs thicker than water.

"Now what's all this about me having to eat in the . . ." He started to tease her, but his eyes fell on me and he froze, speechless, which was probably a first. Then he did the

one thing that hadn't occurred to me during the last two worry-filled hours: *He wept.*

# Twelve:
# A Bunch of
# Dinosaurs

Figuring her work was done, at least for the moment, Miss Iona eased out of the kitchen, rejoining her guests with promises that cobbler and coffee were on the way and leaving me to walk into the Rev's open arms with a few tears of my own. We just stood there for a minute or two, grinning and crying and generally making a spectacle of ourselves. I laid my cheek against the vest of his Sunday suit and he squeezed me tight enough to make up for the ridiculous five months we'd been apart.

"Welcome home, daughter," the Rev was saying over and over. "Welcome home! Welcome home!"

Finally, he gave me one more hug and stepped back to give me the once-over that began when he first counted my fingers and toes and continues unabated whenever we lay eyes on each other whether it's been forty days or forty minutes. Without taking his eyes off me, the Rev took out a big snow-white handkerchief and blew his nose with a majestic honk.

"I've been missing you," I said, grinning like a maniac as he folded up the handker-chief and put it in his back pocket for the next wash.

"Five months it takes for you to miss me?" He looked at me and shook his head in mock exasperation. "You are as stubborn as your mother."

"Coming from you, that can only be a compliment," I said.

He laughed, but not the great public *boom*. This was just a father/daughter laugh, filled with memory and melody and all those things he never lets me see as much as I want to see them.

"He thinks admitting to being human makes him look weak," my mother said once, pacing around the house after they had argued. "He insists on equating leader-ship with infallibility, which is an extremely patriarchal notion."

Down the hall, we could hear laughter, the hum of conversation, the clatter of plates being stacked and cleared away for the next course.

"How have you been, daughter?" My father's voice was gentle.

"I've been good," I said, glad I had worn my pearls so I looked settled and solvent.

"Well, you look good."

"Thanks."

"You let your hair grow out."

"A little."

He nodded approvingly. "I'm glad you came."

"Me, too."

Still doing his visual inventory, he folded his arms across his chest, and for some reason, I did, too.

He smiled. "So can I take this visit as a formal apology?"

*He just couldn't resist.*

"You can take it as a truce," I said slowly. "A temporary cease-fire."

"Are we at war, daughter?" A small frown.

"No, Daddy." I shook my head. "We're family."

"Fair enough," he said, smiling again. Like me, content for the moment to let sleeping dogs lie. "How long can you stay?"

So great was my relief at how well our reconciliation was going that my White House lie had completely slipped my mind. I could see that the Rev caught my hesitation. Lying wasn't part of our deal, never had been, and I was almost certain any attempt to introduce it now would be foolhardy. I looked for neutral ground.

"I'm not sure," I said. "I'm going to be starting a new job soon, but the details haven't been worked out yet."

That was true. I hadn't found the job yet, but it would definitely be new. I wasn't lying so far.

"The details?"

I nodded, hoping he wouldn't press me. I knew I had to tell him the truth, but not standing in the middle of Miss Iona's kitchen. If I had to disappoint my dad, and dash my own dreams, at least I wanted to do it with a little dignity.

"You know, the exact date I'll be starting and all that," I said, trying to buy some time with a bright smile. *And all what?*

The Rev smiled back. "I have to confess to you, daughter, that Iona shared your good news with me although you pledged her to secrecy. Discretion is not one of Iona's many fine qualities."

He got that right. *Think fast!* "I . . . I wanted to tell you myself, but we weren't . . ."

"And you will tell me, daughter, of course you will, but I know now is not the time."

"Yes," I said. "You're right."

The Rev leaned over and put his big hands on my shoulders lightly. "I just want you to know I'm very proud of you. Maybe your president has more sense than I thought."

And he kissed me right in the center of my forehead. Coming from the Rev, this was high praise indeed. Too bad this change of heart was based on something that wasn't even true. I felt like my Pinocchio's nose grew another couple of inches.

"So how long before you know . . . *the details?*" the Rev said.

"A couple of weeks," I said, hoping that was true. "A month on the outside."

The Rev frowned a little and I wondered if my lie was too specific or not specific enough. I wasn't very good at this and I didn't want to be. Not most of the time anyway.

"What's the holdup? Doesn't that Negro want to pay you?"

My father called the president *that Negro* like it was his Secret Service code name. *That Negro is headed for the Rose Garden. That Negro is on his way to the press room.*

"It's not like that," I said quickly. "The vetting at this level is just really rough. They check everything."

At this level. *Listen to yourself,* I thought. *You're better at this lying thing than you need to be.*

The Rev leaned against the counter and

tried to sound casual like he always did when he asked about my mom. "What did your mother say when you told her?"

My parents have been madly in love since the second they first laid eyes on each other when she was teaching a feminist theory class at Spelman and asked if she could sit in on one of his New Testament classes and then stayed afterward to ask whether he thought people would have more readily believed the Easter morning cries of "He is risen!" if a group of men had found the rock rolled away rather than a group of women. He had never considered the question before so he invited her to join him for dinner at Paschal's and by the end of the evening, he would say when he still liked to tell this story, *he was smitten.*

That was, of course, a long time ago. These days, they can't be in the same room without disagreeing about something. Even with two thousand miles between them, they can still find ways to drive each other crazy.

"You know Mom," I said. "She told me to make sure I was getting paid as much as the boys and to give 'em hell."

The Rev threw back his head and roared. The *boom* was back. She had, of course, said nothing of the kind. I hadn't shared my fantasy with her like I had Miss Iona so all she knew was that I had my fingers crossed.

"That woman never lets up, does she?"

"Not last time I checked," I said. "But she is a little upset about that interview you did in *The Constitution* the other day."

The element of surprise was in my favor. He raised his eyebrows. "She told you about that?"

"I saw it online."

The Rev is so old-school that he's still amazed that I can read any paper in the world online. To my knowledge, although he has a brand-new computer in his study at home, he has never sent or received an email in his life.

"This is not an excuse," he said, "but your mother is as responsible for that foolishness as I was."

"She'll be surprised to hear that," I said. "How do you figure?"

"She had called to read me the riot act about something she'd seen me say on the Internet somewhere, I don't even know if I really said it, but she was convinced I did. She really got under my collar going on and on about how out of touch I was and — what's her favorite word?"

"Patriarchal."

"That's the one! She said we were all a

bunch of dinosaurs. Me, Jesse, Jeremiah —
all of us. She said we ought to step aside
while we still had a shred of dignity left and
go to the beach somewhere."

The rumble of his voice rose ominously
and I could see how offended he was, but I
heard myself giggle before I could stifle it.
The image of all of those bigger than life
men sitting around in trunks and T-shirts
grumbling about the goings-on at 1600
Pennsylvania Avenue was pretty funny. My
mother was fearless, but when the Rev shot
me a look, I caved immediately.

"I'm sorry, Rev," I said. "Go on."

"After she hung up, I probably should
have walked around the block to cool off,
but the reporter came early . . ." He shook
his head and looked at me. "Your mother is
still the only person who can make me lose
my cool."

Before I could add my *amen* to that, Miss
Iona stuck her head in and smiled at us
brightly.

"Sorry to interrupt," she said, "but folks
out here are demanding their cobbler, plus
Flora's getting ready to talk nice about Ed
and you know he can't stand being praised
for more than about ten seconds so if you
don't come on right now, you'll miss it."

"What about my dinner?" the Rev said.

"You used up your eating time talkin'," she said, taking his arm and winking at me. "You Negroes take too long to kiss and make up."

"Nobody told me there was a time limit," the Rev said, allowing himself to be led down the hallway with me following close behind.

While the Rev and I had our little reconciliation in the kitchen, Flora had gathered everybody in the living room and Aretha had propped a couple of the garden photographs up on the mantel for a little atmosphere.

"I'm not going to make a big deal out of this," Flora said as Mr. Eddie stood beside her, quiet and dignified as ever in a dark suit. He caught sight of us sneaking in from down the hall and gave me a smile and a nod. I waved back and blew him a congratulatory kiss. The Rev stood beside me, beaming at his friend. "We all know our guest of honor doesn't like a whole lot of fuss."

"He just likes to pretend he don't like it," Mr. Charles said. "Otherwise, how come he got on his best suit?"

There was gentle laughter as Miss Iona moved over to shush her husband. Flora just smiled.

"We also know that the Booker T. Washington High School garden will be celebrating their second harvest this year and we know the part Mr. Eddie has played in making that happen."

"We couldn't have done it without you," Lu said, "so we just wanted a chance to say thank you and to present you with a set of these pictures that Aretha took."

We all nodded approvingly, at Mr. Eddie, at Lu, at the pictures.

"Mr. Eddie has promised to be at the assembly next week, but he has made it clear he doesn't want to be one of the speakers," Flora said. "So we also wanted to give him a chance to say anything that might be on his heart, since we're all family here tonight, one way or another."

Mr. Eddie shook his head, but everybody applauded and Peachy Nolan started saying, "Speech, speech," until finally Mr. Eddie smiled and held up his hand again for quiet.

"All right, all right," he said. "You know I do appreciate all this, but I'm not much of a speech maker."

"The Rev hasn't rubbed off on you yet?" Mr. Charles said.

Mr. Eddie ignored him, cleared his throat, and shared a little smile with Lu. "When Lu came and asked me to help and we first got started up, people kept trying to get me to give it a name. Call it after this one who did this. Or that one who did that. Then they wanted me to name the stuff we were growing. Coretta Scott King carrots and Ralph Bunche broccoli. Obama okra." He shook his head. "But I never would do it, and I wouldn't let the kids do it either. Because the thing is, this is a garden, not a political statement. There's a lot of people worth honoring, I can't deny that, but somebody who never heard of W.E.B. DuBois or Malcolm X or Maynard Jackson can still grow enough vegetables to feed his family if he pays attention to what he's doing. And if he doesn't bring that attention, then his garden ain't gonna bring a harvest no matter how many names you give it."

"Ain't that the truth of it?" said Mr. Charles, nodding.

"Well, I'm glad you approve, Charlie, because I think I'd like to change my mind, with your permission."

"Shoot, go on man, you know ain't nobody going to stop you in this house."

"Amen," said the Rev. "Take your time, Ed!"

"Thank you, Rev," Mr. Eddie said. "Because what I want to say is about you."

Every head turned toward the Rev, standing in the back beside me. "Then make it plain," he said, with a small bow to Mr. Eddie. "Go on and make it plain."

"I just want to say," Mr. Eddie's voice was so quiet that we got quiet, too, "that sometimes, when we have true greatness in our midst for a long time, we get used to it. We start to take it for granted just a little bit. We start to expect greatness from certain individuals. It becomes a part of what they do, or who they are, and after a while, we forget to stop and acknowledge it, to recognize exactly who they are and what it means to have them here as part of our family."

"Ain't that the truth?" someone up front said softly.

"Amen."

"Sometimes we don't remember to say thank you for all that until they're gone, when it's too late to let 'em know, so I want to say my *thank you* today, the same way you're thankin' me, except I want to thank the Rev because he don't always get the credit for the part he played . . ."

"Still playing it!" the Rev said. "Don't send me out to pasture yet!"

And everybody laughed at such an unbelievable idea.

"No chance, Rev," Mr. Eddie said. "You got too much more work still to do, but for everything so far, as my leader and as my friend, I'd like to name this garden after you, with your kind permission, and let it be known as The Reverend Horace A. Dunbar Community Garden at Washington High School."

"That's a mouthful," the Rev boomed out from beside me. "And I accept!"

Flora started the applause as the Rev made his way up to Mr. Eddie, who embraced his genuinely surprised friend. The Rev waited for quiet and then stood with his arm around Mr. Eddie's shoulders.

"So does this mean I get all my produce free now?"

More laughter.

"You have to ask Lu about that," Mr. Eddie said. "She handles the business end."

"Then I'm home free," the Rev said, as Lu gave him a big thumbs-up.

"Well, good for all y'all." Peachy Nolan leaned around Mr. Charles to look at Miss Iona pleadingly. *Now can we have our cobbler?"*

"Coming right up," she said, laughing. "Lu, put some music on if these Negroes are through talking and don't let Charlie start playing that low-down blues!"

"The Lord ain't said nothing against no

137

blues, Iona, and you know it!" Mr. Charlie said.

Miss Iona took my hand as she started to the kitchen. "Come give me a hand while the Rev and Eddie indulge in their mutual admiration society."

"My pleasure," I said as the sound of Aretha Franklin singing the gospel music that was her birthright joined the group.

"You were right," I said as she added some napkins to the tray.

"Of course I was," she said. "About what?"

"About everything being over in an hour."

"Over?" That really made her laugh.

"What's so funny?"

She handed me a big pan of cobbler and pointed me toward the door. "Sweetie, we're just gettin' started good."

# THIRTEEN:
# KNEE-DEEP IN
# COLLARD GREENS

By the time the Rev and Mr. Eddie quit posing for pictures and Blue and Regina took their little girl home, Peachy and Miss Abbie headed back to Tybee because he had a convertible and liked to ride at night with the top down so Abbie could count the stars, even in February. The princess was fast asleep on Miss Iona's bed and Aretha had been talked into letting her spend the night. Flora and I waved away Miss Iona's attempted refusal of our offer to help with the cleanup and made her go join Mr. Charlie and Lu in the living room, still congratulating the Rev and Mr. Eddie on a job well done.

Miss Iona's kitchen was as well organized as everything else she did and as we put things right, Flora and I had a chance to talk a little more.

"So who is going to take over at your gardens?" I said, loading the dishwasher carefully according to the hostess's instructions.

"That is the big question," she said, spooning collard greens into a large Tupperware container. *Why do greens always taste better when you reheat them the day after?* "You're not looking for a job, are you?"

Before I could say *Make me an offer,* she held up her hand with an apologetic smile. "Of course you're not." She lowered her voice just like Miss Iona had. "Congratulations."

I cringed. *Here we go again.* Nothing like a big fat lie to get a friendship off on the right foot. "Thanks," I said, lowering my voice, too. "I . . . I can't really talk about it right now, you know, until everything is confirmed."

"I totally understand," she said. "Hank's job was like that, too. Couldn't hardly talk about it until it was all tied up with a bow. Maybe it's a Washington thing!"

"Are you excited about moving?" I said, moving away from my job prospects to her upcoming relocation. I couldn't read the expression that flitted across her face well enough to name it, but I can definitely say she didn't look overjoyed at the prospect.

"To tell the truth, I'm a little intimidated,"

she said. "Being involved in politics like Hank is . . . it's a real fast track."

She was right about that. Also treacherous, complicated, ruthless, passionate, and nonstop.

"But he's really good at this stuff, so D.C. is the place to be right now, I guess."

"What does your husband do?"

"He was a prosecutor in Detroit. When the crack dealers firebombed our house, he brought me and Lu down here to stay with Blue."

"Somebody firebombed your house?"

She nodded. "Luckily nobody got hurt, but Hank was worried. He knew we'd be safe here."

"Is that when you started working with the gardens?"

"I was actually the one who had the idea," she said with a self-effacing smile. "I had never done any kind of gardening before, but I just had a feel for it. By the time Hank wrapped things up in Detroit and came to get us, Lu and I were pretty much dug in, no pun intended!"

"Good one though," I said, enjoying her story.

"He wanted to move to D.C. right then, but Lu begged him to wait until she finished high school and he couldn't tell her no.

She's always been a real daddy's girl. Then he ran for City Council, so he'd have something to do, I guess, and got elected, which meant he had *plenty* to do, but he's not going to stand for reelection because of this new job."

She still hadn't told me exactly what the new job was and I suddenly wondered if Hank's job was as ephemeral as mine. I hoped not. I liked Flora and something told me we'd be good friends if we were ever in the same spot longer than a minute.

"What's the job?" I said.

Flora shook her head and laughed. "Which is what I started out to tell you in the first place. My mind is gone! You know all that stuff that came out from the Republicans during the campaign? Voter fraud, robo calls full of misinformation, scare tactics. All that stuff? Well, they're still doing it, but I don't have to tell you that, do I?" She smiled that *your secret is safe with me* smile again.

"They love that stuff," I said.

"Exactly. So what Hank does is help the Democratic National Committee manage the ongoing efforts to keep that mess under control."

From Detroit crack dealers to Republican saboteurs. The man clearly liked a challenge.

"That's great," I said. "At least the Republicans won't throw a firebomb through your window."

She laughed. "So far, so good!"

"I'd love to come by and hear more about what you're doing," I said as Miss Iona came through the door, unable to trust us alone in her kitchen for one more minute.

"Stop by any time," Flora said. "I'll be there all day tomorrow."

"Don't let her get you in that office," Miss Iona said, shaking a warning finger. "It's a force field. First, she gets you in the front door and next thing you know, you're knee-deep in collard greens and seed catalogues."

"There are worse things to be knee-deep in," Flora said, laughing and untying her apron. "Your timing is perfect. How'd we do?"

Miss Iona nodded slowly, looking around at our handiwork with a practiced eye. "Nice job. If you do windows, we've got a deal."

"Not a chance," Flora said. "Give me back my child and I will say good night."

"She's waiting for you up front and so is your dad," Miss Iona said.

Flora glanced at her watch. "Good grief! How did it get to be midnight already?"

"Time flies when you're having fun," Miss

Iona said as we headed down the hallway, where we all sort of migrated to the door in a big happy circle of good nights and great evenings and see you in the mornings and even a final welcome home or two. When the dust cleared, Miss Iona and Mr. Charles had gone inside to bed, Flora and Lu had accepted Mr. Eddie's offer of a ride home, and the Rev and I found ourselves alone on the sidewalk in front of Miss Iona's house.

The air was February crisp, but not cold, and the sky was clear enough to count the stars. The Rev looked at me and offered his arm. My father has been offering me his arm since I was tall enough to take it.

"Well, daughter," he said, turning us toward home. "Shall we ramble?"

# FOURTEEN:
# TILL YOU HEAR
# FROM ME

Me and the Rev took the long way home.
This had been our habit since I was a kid.
It's only two blocks to our house, but we
never went there directly. We *rambled.* My
father liked to be a visible presence in the
lives of his parishioners so we'd stroll home
through the neighborhood so they could see
him and call a friendly greeting or ask him
about one of the zillion meetings he was
always on his way to, or compliment him on
a great sermon the Sunday before. We'd
pass Blue Hamilton's house so we could
admire the giant magnolia tree in his front
yard. Or we'd turn at the corner so we could
check on the progress of Mr. Eddie's garden
or smell the honeysuckle that grows so thick
in his backyard that the sweetness can make
you giddy if you stay too long.

I had seen Mr. Eddie's son, Wes, kissing a
girl in their back porch swing once when he
was about twelve or thirteen. I was taking a

shortcut across their yard and as I slipped through unnoticed by the lovers, I wondered if it was Wes or just the smell of the honey-suckle that made her want to surrender to his dubious charms.

"Your father is getting sentimental in his old age," the Rev said as we strolled down Peeples Street. "Hope I didn't embarrass you bawling like that in the middle of Iona's kitchen."

It was a warm night for February and even though we both had our coats on, it wasn't too cold for us to fall into the easy rhythm of our ramble.

"You weren't bawling," I said, squeezing his arm. "You shed a few very dignified tears is all."

He patted my hand. "Thank you for that, daughter."

Sometimes we would talk while we rambled. I would tell him about school or work or my latest run-in with Mom. He would listen for a few minutes and then advise me on a course of action with such certainty that I rarely questioned it. Then he would talk to me about the events of the day. From local politics to world revolution, the Rev had a wealth of information about questions it would take me years to even articulate, much less understand. So I didn't try. I'd just walk along beside him and let the words wash over me. Sometimes I could follow the course of his thinking and sometimes I'd get lost in it, but just listening to his voice, feeling his courage and commitment, made me proud to be his daughter.

But tonight, neither one of us said a word. I know the Rev had more to say about his interview and I sure wanted to come clean about my White House fantasies, but it had been a very long day and I was exhausted. There was plenty of time tomorrow for true confessions. Tonight, all I wanted to do was ramble my tired ass home to a long hot shower and a good night's sleep in my bright pink baby girl bed.

When we got to the house, the Rev opened the big front door that he never locked and we stepped inside.

"We'll talk tomorrow," he said, leaning over to kiss my cheek and give me another hug.

"I'm all yours," I said, wondering why I thought it would be easier to tell him the whole truth in the morning than it was right now.

"Then I am a very lucky man," he said. "Good night."

I started up the stairs as the Rev hung his coat, but I felt bad. How could I lie to this man? Was I crazy? Why not just spit it out and get it over with? I took a deep breath. "Daddy?"

"Yes?"

Then I lost my nerve. We had just started talking again and here I was about to let him down big-time. What's the hurry? I thought. Tomorrow morning was soon enough.

"Nothing. Good night."

But as I turned around, the Rev called me back. "Daughter?"

"Yes?"

Something in his eyes was suddenly serious. "I need to ask you something important and I want you to give me a truthful answer."

I tried to look calm. "Okay."

"Do you think I'm the reason those Obama people haven't closed the deal on this job with you yet?"

I now felt officially awful. My father was feeling guilty because he thought his being persona non grata was keeping me from sitting at the right hand of *you know who.* I thought so, too, but I couldn't look my father in the face and say that, so I just leaned down from that third step and kissed his cheek. "No, Rev. It doesn't have anything to do with you."

"Are you sure? These are some grudge-holding Negroes, Ida B, and they have a very long reach."

"Everything is on track," I said. "Don't worry about it."

The relief that flooded his face made me feel even worse for keeping the lie going between us.

"Good," he said. "Then please forgive me for being such a foolish old man."

"Watch it," I said, "that's my dad you're talking about."

I stayed in the shower until the hot water steamed the stress out of my shoulders and I was able to convince myself that the Rev would understand. After all, I hadn't outright lied. It wasn't my fault that Miss Iona had told everybody about my slight exaggeration. Of course all that was neither here nor there at this point. What I needed was a way for the Rev to let the folks he'd been bragging to about me know I didn't really have a White House job without him having to actually *say* I didn't. As soon as I could come up with a strategy to save his face and mine, I could relax a little. But for now, all I could do was sleep on it.

I stepped out into the hallway wrapped up in the big terry cloth robe Miss Iona had given me after she came by a couple of

Christmases ago and found me wearing my high school robe, because I still loved it even though it had seen better days. Downstairs I could hear the Rev playing our old upright piano. He had a beautiful baritone voice and he and Mom used to sing all the time when I was growing up. She was never very religious, but she loved to sing hymns, spirituals, freedom songs from every major American social movement, Christmas carols, and a fairly impressive repertoire of pop tunes from the fifties and sixties.

My father was a gifted musician who had a very brief career around Macon playing saxophone in after-hours clubs until his mother found out and sold his horn, which she regarded as an instrument more suited to secular environments, and invested in a used piano. Some of my favorite childhood memories are of the nights when my parents' voices would wake me up and I'd slip out of bed and crouch at the top of the stairs, listening to them singing together. When my mom told me she was moving out, I remember not being surprised. They had stopped singing months ago.

But tonight, the Rev wasn't singing. He was just down there playing his ass off. I recognized the tune, but I couldn't remember the lyrics. I walked down the hall in my bare feet and sat down at the top of the stairs in my same old place to listen. At the end of the song, the silence in the house was so perfectly peaceful that we both sat still and let it play out. Then the Rev's voice floated up to me like we were already in the middle of a conversation.

"Don't you worry about a thing, daughter," he said, starting to play again softly. "For now, we'll just keep our own counsel. How does that sound?"

It sounded great, even though I wasn't really sure what he meant. "Okay."

His fingers paused on the keys. "Do you trust me, daughter?"

"Of course I do."

"Well, just don't forget it."

"I won't."

He started the song again. "Good night, then."

"Good night." I stood up, but first I had a request. "Daddy?"

"Yes, daughter?"

"Can you sing the words?"

"Of course."

It was an old Duke Ellington tune. One of my mother's favorites. As soon as he started singing, the words all came back to me in a rush. I headed down the hall to my room, half expecting to hear my mother's voice join in the way she used to, but all I heard was the Rev.

"Do nothin' till you hear from me,
Pay no attention to what's said . . ."

Which was, of course, easier said than done.

# FIFTEEN:
# SERIOUS
# SOUL-SEARCHING

At 3 A.M., the Atlanta airport has a ghostly quality. Most of the arrival gates are empty. Departures are sporadic. The stores, newsstands, and last-chance-to-tank-up-before-the-flight bars are closed until morning. Cleaning crews move like wraiths through the largely deserted concourses, lost in their own thoughts or talking furtively on their cell phones, sneaking a personal moment on company time. That was one of the things Wes liked most about being his own boss. He didn't have to ask permission to do a damn thing. It wasn't always easy, but it was always worth it.

The plane had touched down on a small runway, far removed from the giant carriers that disgorged hundreds of people at a time. Wes had been on private planes before, but not enough to get tired of them and never one as nice as this. It had six huge seats covered in soft gray leather, a giant flat-screen TV, complete with computer hookups, and a small bedroom with a shower. The towels were monogrammed HGM after the plane's owner, Herman Gilmore Murphy, an oil tycoon who saw Barack Obama's election as the worst single moment of his lifetime, not because of race, but because of what Herman called the new president's "Socialist agenda."

Wes thought Herman was a classless buffoon who wasn't half as smart as his millions made everybody tell him he was, but that didn't mean he'd turn down an offer to fly like the rich guys do all the way to Atlanta. They sent a car for him at ten thirty and by eleven thirty, he was settled comfortably in the lap of the kind of luxury to which he hoped to soon become accustomed. It was the most relaxing flight he'd ever had.

When they arrived in Atlanta, Wes thanked the flight crew, and thanked himself for arranging an early check-in at the Four Seasons. Wes was officially staying at his father's house, but he was a firm believer in one of his mother's favorite expressions: *It's a sorry rat ain't got but one hole.* Camping out in his old room was fine for strategic purposes, but he needed a neutral base of operations with high-speed Internet connections, twenty-four-hour room service, and a comfortable, private place to meet with other as-yet-unknown members of the team he'd pull together to get the job done. One of the mini suites at his favorite midtown hotel was just the ticket. Whether or not he ever actually slept there was beside the point.

At the bottom of the escalator, Wes joined other early risers waiting for the train to the main terminal: two guys in business suits and BlackBerrys and a young woman in Army fatigues with elaborate cornrows and world-weary eyes. Years ago, before security got so tight, Wes remembered an old man in faded overalls and a tattered straw hat who used to stand beside the train doors, holding a homemade sign that said "Repent" in big block letters. Wes wondered if anyone had ever been moved to do so by the man's silent witness. He doubted it. That kind of decision didn't usually manifest in airports. *Airplanes,* maybe, especially when flying through bad weather, but once people got back on terra firma, they tended to be better able to keep the serious soul-searching at bay until the next crisis.

The ride was only a few minutes and when the train hissed to a stop and deposited him at the bottom of the final escalator that would drop him off at rental car row, Wes spotted a tall, stocky brother in a dark blue suit holding a neatly hand-lettered sign, but this one bore not a spiritual command, but his name: "W. Harper." He smiled to himself. *A private plane and a private car? These guys are really trying to make a good impression,* he thought.

"I'm Wes Harper," he said to the driver.

"Welcome to Atlanta," the man said pleasantly, reaching for Wes's bag without being asked. "I'm Julius."

"I wasn't expecting anybody to meet me, Julius."

"Yessir," Julius said, without offering an opinion. He was in the business of agreement, not speculation.

Wes waited until Julius settled in behind the wheel. "I'm headed for the Four Seasons on Fourteenth Street," he said.

"Yessir."

It was a gray day, but not too cold. In New York, they were expecting six inches of snow. In Atlanta, it looked like rain.

"Take the streets through town, would you?" Wes said as the stadium loomed up ahead. "I haven't been home in a while."

"There's been lots of changes," Julius said, easing the car off the exit ramp at Andrew Young International Boulevard. "But you know what they say about Atlanta."

"What's that?"
"Nothing changes but the changes."

# Sixteen:
# Tavis Smiley
# Syndrome

There was something about that bed. As soon as my head hit the pillow, I was down for the count. Even after my extended nap and relatively early bedtime yesterday, by the time I opened my eyes, the Rev was already up and rattling around downstairs. He grinned at me when I presented myself at the kitchen door a few minutes later. He was, of course, wearing his usual dark blue suit, starched white shirt, and a pale yellow tie. The clock on the microwave said 6 A.M.

"Good morning, daughter," he said as two pieces of toast popped up from the toaster behind him.

"Good morning," I said, glad he had already made coffee. "What are you doing up this early?"

"On my way downtown for a breakfast meeting," he said, buttering the toast and putting it on two plates, one for him and one for me.

I poured myself a cup of coffee and reached for the sugar.

"Then over to Athens for lunch and a talk at the university. Tomorrow I'm headed for Macon all day."

"Was it something I said?" I teased him, taking the chair I always sit in next to the Rev, who was, of course, at the head of the table.

He leaned over and gave me a kiss on the cheek. "I wish you'd told me you were coming. I'm all over the state for Black History Month and it's too late to cancel anything."

February was always a whirlwind of speeches, sermons, rallies, and remembrances. Why should this historic *first ever with a brother in the White House* February be any different? Miss Iona's contention that the Rev couldn't find an audience anymore didn't seem to have any basis in fact.

"Don't worry about it," I said. "I've got a bunch of stuff to do and I'll probably go roam around the neighborhood for a while to see what you all have been up to without me."

"I'll be back before dinner," he said, sipping his coffee and checking his watch. "I'll fix you something nice."

I shook my head, savoring the buttery

perfection of the toast. "How about I'll fix *you* something nice? I haven't completely lost my touch."

The truth was, I hadn't cooked a meal in months and on my best days, I wasn't that great, but as long as you keep it simple, cooking is like sex and bike riding. Once you start, everything comes back pretty quickly.

"It's a deal," he said, obviously pleased at my suggestion. "Want to ask Eddie to join us?"

"Absolutely," I said. "I didn't have a chance to talk to him enough last night."

The terrible sound of the Rev's front doorbell blasted through the toast-scented air. I jumped about a foot in the air, but the Rev just smiled, stood up, and deposited his cup in the sink. "Good, then go on and ask him while I go grab my briefcase."

Like a lot of the older men in West End, Mr. Eddie liked Lincolns. When I opened the front door, he had parked his gleaming black Town Car out front and was standing there, tall and elegant in a charcoal gray pin-striped number and a dark gray homburg. I knew from years of traveling with him and the Rev that his overcoat was neatly folded on the backseat until they reached their destination, but he always wore his suit jacket. It used to cover his holster. Now it was probably just habit.

In the bad old days, Mr. Eddie was armed when the Rev would go around to these little towns like Moultrie and Americus, trying to let people know they hadn't been forgotten; that they were a part of this great rush toward freedom, too, the same as anybody in Atlanta or Montgomery or Birmingham. The small towns were the most dangerous, but they had always been the Rev's special constituency. He was as close as most of them would ever get to a Martin Luther King Jr., or a Malcolm X, and when he raised that magnificent voice of his from the pulpits of these tiny churches at the edge of some isolated two-lane road, he made just the possibility of freedom *irresistible.* I've heard my father give a hundred speeches, preach a thousand sermons, and at the end of every one, I wanted to jump up and join something, march somewhere and demand something. At the very least, I was ready to shake my finger in somebody's face.

These days, all he was asking people to do was register to vote and the person who still made sure he got there on time to deliver that message was Mr. Eddie. When he saw me, he immediately took off his hat like the gentleman he always was, even when I was just a little girl. He's the first man who ever pulled out a chair for me at the dinner table. He still does it.

"Well, good morning! The Rev didn't tell me you were going to be joining us today!"

"I'm joining you two for coffee only," I said, giving him a hug. "After that, you're on your own."

He put his hat on the table by the door where we always toss our keys and followed me into the kitchen. "The Rev will be right down."

I knew Mr. Eddie drank his coffee black, so I poured him a cup. He leaned against the counter and took a long sip.

"You doin' all right?"

I nodded. "Can't complain."

"We're all very proud of you."

*Would it never end?* "Thanks, but nothing definite yet."

He looked puzzled. "What do you mean?"

Maybe I should have some cards made up that I can just hand to people with a picture of the White House in a red circle with a red line through it.

"Well, it's going to take some time before anything's official."

Mr. Eddie frowned. "It's official *now,* isn't it? They swore the man in *twice,* what more do they have to do?"

That's when I got it. He wasn't talking about my job working for the president. He was talking about my role in *electing* the president.

"Nothing," I said, smiling and patting his arm. "Not a thing. I misunderstood you."

Relief flooded his face. "All right, then! For a minute there, I thought we were going to have to march on Washington *one more time!*"

I laughed. "They don't want that!"

He grinned at me and sipped his coffee. "Not if they know what's good for them. Me and the Rev don't cut the mustard so good anymore, but we can still spread the mayonnaise."

Mr. Eddie was the calm ballast to the Rev's more volatile personality. Think Dean Martin and Frank Sinatra, without the women and the gangsters and the booze.

"The Rev told me about the schedule for the next couple of weeks. Aren't you ever going to slow down?"

He shook his head. "Not likely. Your father thinks he's got to show up at every one hundred percent church in the same month. I told him, that's a great idea, but there are one hundred of them and only twenty-eight days in the month. We gonna do four or five of 'em a day? And you know what? He actually stood right there and thought about it. Like we could physically hit one hundred churches even if we went eighteen hours a day!"

I had an image of my father and Mr. Eddie looking like two sped-up cartoon characters, tearing up and down the road in a cartoon car that lengthened out like a long black train as they barreled from Macon to Moultrie, Savannah to Statesboro, barely stopping for sustenance as the shortest month of the year blew by in a sepia-toned rhetorical rush.

"How'd you talk him out of it?"

"I didn't." Mr. Eddie laughed. "You see me standing up here at the crack of dawn, don't you? I might as well be back on the Crescent if I'm gonna be keeping these hours."

Mr. Eddie was a Pullman porter and then a sleeping car attendant for over forty years, and by his own account, really loved his work, although he never liked having to regularly rise before the sun came up to get things ready before his passengers slid open the doors to their tiny roomettes, yawning and sniffing the air for coffee.

Glancing at his watch, Mr. Eddie frowned slightly. "Speaking of which, we need to get

164

out of here if he's gonna make this breakfast on time. He'll be the main one fussin' if they start without him."

The food reference reminded me. "You're invited for dinner tonight when you two get back," I said. "I'm cooking."

He shook his head. "Too late. I've already got plans for dinner, and so do you."

"I do?"

"Wes is home. You and the Rev are invited to my place."

It'd been years since I'd seen Wes Harper. I had a massive crush on him when I was a teenager, but he left West End for boarding school in the wilds of New Hampshire when I was eight and he was twelve. Aside from catching him kissing on his back porch, my most vivid memory of him was at the going-away party his parents threw to let the community express their collective pride in his achievement. He spent most of the evening looking alternately bored and restless while people who had known him all his life pressed envelopes into his hand with Hallmark cards and hard-earned twenties enclosed to help him on his way. He had seemed to me then to be one of those people who think they deserve better without ever realizing that *everybody* deserves better.

"Great," I said, actually a little relieved that I didn't have to deliver on my well-intentioned promise to have a meal waiting when the warriors returned from the road. "Do you want me to bring something?"

"Just your own sweet self," he said. "I've got some lovely catfish fillets I'm gonna bake with some lemon. We'll make out okay."

"Make out okay on what?" the Rev said, carrying his briefcase, wearing his coat and hat like he was already halfway out the door and could therefore not be accused of holding up progress.

"You're both invited for dinner," Mr. Eddie said, putting his cup in the sink beside the Rev's. "Wes is staying at the house for a couple of days."

"At your house?" The Rev looked surprised. "Who's he hidin' from?"

"He didn't say. You can ask him yourself at dinner."

"Well, if you don't, I will," the Rev said, giving me a quick peck on the cheek and heading for the door. "Come on, then. Let's hit the road."

When she used to be the receptionist at *The Sentinel,* Miss Iona would finish every exchange by telling the caller to "do something for freedom today," and that's exactly the way the Rev lived his life. Come hell or high water, the Rev was going to do something for freedom every day God sent him. I watched them head down the walk, laughing and joking like they always did, and all of a sudden, I wanted to go, too, but before I could throw up my hand, the Rev put his coat in the backseat beside Mr. Eddie's, opened the passenger-side door, and got in without looking back. He never saw me there, standing in the doorway, waiting for a wave.

I watched the car until it turned the corner, fighting back a powerful rush of déjà vu, and then realized my phone was ringing. I dashed inside and snatched it off the key table. "Hello?"

"Where the hell are you?"

My mother was not known for her flowery salutations. It was a trait she shared with Miss Iona, but even for her, this was a bit abrupt.

"I'm in Atlanta," I said. "What's wrong?"

It was four o'clock in the morning in San Francisco. My mother was an early riser who did group tai chi in the park every morning at six, but nobody calls this early unless there is a crisis.

"Nothing's wrong. What are you doing down there?"

"I'm spending a couple of days with the Rev," I said, trying to sound casual. "Why are you calling me so early?"

"Why didn't you tell me?"

"I'm telling you now," I said. "It's no big deal. Now why —"

"I'm in D.C." She sounded annoyed. "I was trying to surprise you and when I got to your place, your landlady was kind enough to tell me you had gone to Atlanta. Imagine the egg on my face!"

"It was a spur of the moment kind of thing."

"You saw it, didn't you?"

There was no use pretending I didn't know what she was talking about.

"I saw it."

"That's why you're there, isn't it?"

Both my parents could have second careers as mind readers.

"Don't deny it," she said. "Tacos and sangria! Has he lost his mind? I hope that's what you went down there to ask him."

"His mind is fine," I said. "What are you doing in D.C.?"

"National Women's Studies Association. Big doings."

"Yeah?" My mother loved to gossip with me about the latest goings-on in the rarified world of feminist scholars even more than

168

she liked to critique my dad.

"Can you keep a secret?"

She was forever swearing me to secrecy about things I had so little interest in or information about, I probably couldn't have remembered them under torture.

"Absolutely."

She lowered her voice conspiratorially. Sometimes with all the sotto voce going on, I felt like I was surrounded by spies. "I'm on the short list for the Director of the Women's Research and Resource Center at Spelman."

I was shocked. Not that Spelman, a women's college with a nationally celebrated Women's Studies program was looking for a new leader to replace their founding director, who was retiring, but that my mother would even consider moving back here. The only thing that made possible the uneasy peace between my parents was the fact that my mother had had the good sense to relocate herself two thousand miles away when she left the Rev. Spelman College was smack in the heart of West End. It was literally in the Rev's backyard.

"Surprised, right?" my mother said. "That I would even allow myself to be considered."

"You know they're going to offer it to you," I said. "Are you going to take it?"

"Why shouldn't I?" she said, as if I had questioned her right to do so. "It's a great program and it would be an amazing opportunity to build on a strong foundation."

"That's not what I mean," I interrupted her before she could launch into her spiel. "And you know it."

She sighed loud enough for me to hear. "The problem is, it's not like I'd be across town. I'll be right up the street."

"You don't have to live in West End," I said, glad the Rev wasn't here so I didn't have to lower my voice, too. I wasn't prepared to be the messenger on this one if I could possibly help it.

"I love West End," my mother said. "I helped create West End. Why should I come back to Atlanta and not live in West End?"

My mother is capable of arguing all sides simultaneously so I cut to the chase. "Does the Rev know?"

"I certainly haven't discussed it with him," she said, sounding restrained and self-righteous, difficult to pull off, but she executed it flawlessly. "But you can tell him if you like."

I did that bridge of the nose pinching thing again. Still nothing. "Are you trying to make this as stressful as possible for me, or is it just something that comes naturally?"

"This doesn't have anything to do with you," she said, as if she was amazed that I would think such a thing.

"Exactly," I said. "So why are we talking about it again?"

"I just thought you might like to know I'm being considered," she said. "Aside from all that other stuff."

"They would be lucky to get you."

"I'd die to have it, if it wasn't for the Rev being right there, but even with that, I'll have to give it serious consideration."

That meant she was going to take it. It never rains but it pours.

"What's your father doing these days anyway, when he's not making a complete fool of himself all over the Internet?"

"Uplifting the race, of course. It's Black History Month, remember?"

"You're not riding around with him handing out flyers, are you?"

"Not this time." I didn't tell her *almost.*

She sighed. "I think the thing I could never forgive your father for is that he's so good when it comes to race and such a fucking Neanderthal when it comes to gender."

I wondered if it was too soon to hang up. I didn't want to hurt her feelings, but this conversation was bringing me down and the day hadn't even gotten started good yet.

"Listen, Mom, I've got to go."

"Me, too, but Ida B?" She lowered her voice again. "Is he really okay?"

This was for a fine line. My mother's concern was real. I knew that. But I also knew that anything I said could and probably would be used in future heated exchanges with the Rev without regard to pledges of confidentiality.

"There's nothing wrong with him," I said. "That interview was a fluke. They caught him at a . . . bad moment."

No need to tell her he laid the blame for that moment at her feet.

"Well, you keep an eye on him, that's all. How long are you going to be down there anyway? Don't they need you to help run things up here?"

"I think they'll be able to muddle through without me for a couple of days."

"Have you heard anything yet from the Great God Obama?"

Both my parents voted for the man and in their hearts, they realize how lucky we are to have him, but it's almost like they can't admit it, even to themselves. *Tavis Smiley syndrome.* Easy to recognize. Impossible to argue.

"Not yet."

"Then what are you doing down there?

Shouldn't you be up here lobbying on your own behalf or something?"

"Haven't you heard that absence makes the heart grow fonder?"

"Haven't you heard that out of sight is out of mind?" she said. "Don't forget to tell your father about Spelman." And she was gone.

# Seventeen:
## Between the Lines

"How does she look to you?" the Rev said when the breakfast gathering was over and he and Mr. Eddie were back in the Lincoln, headed for Athens.

Mr. Eddie shrugged and set the cruise control on sixty-five. "She looks great. A little tired, maybe, but she just helped elect a president. She's supposed to look a little worse for wear."

"She's too thin."

"Well, you know a lot of young women these days prefer travelin' light."

"I'm not talking about how much luggage she brought. I'm talking about her health. She looked worried."

"Listen to yourself! All you do is worry. The girl is fine. She looks fine. She sounds fine. She's here to spend some time with you before she moves into the White House. She's probably just a little preoccupied. Why don't you relax?"

"Why don't you slow down? You're going to get us a speeding ticket."

"Have I ever once gotten a speeding ticket?"

"There's always a first time."

Mr. Eddie looked at the Rev and kept his voice neutral. "Why don't you just lean back and gather your thoughts?"

"My thoughts *stay* gathered," the Rev said. "I don't have to do any special gathering."

"Good, then how about some music?"

Mr. Eddie liked blues, and Albert King's voice filled the car with a tale of unmatched, unmitigated woe.

"Cut off my lights this mo'nin',
They set my furniture out doors . . ."

"Now, *that* is a Negro with some bad luck," Mr. Eddie said, falling in behind a cream-colored El Dorado with Florida vanity tags that said: *4UEthel.*

"What's Ida B got to be preoccupied about?" The Rev turned down the music.

"Every human bein' has got a right to be preoccupied when they want to," Mr. Eddie said. "She's a grown woman, after all."

The Rev, like many fathers before him, knew this to be a fact, but he didn't have to like it. "It's all my fault."

Eddie glanced over at his friend. "What is? That's she's a grown woman? How's that got anything to do with you? Time passes."

"That she might not get that job at the White House."

"I thought Iona said she already got it."

"That's exactly what Iona said, but from what Ida B told me last night, your president is doing some more fancy backtracking."

"Did Ida B use the words 'fancy backtracking'?"

"That's not the point."

"What exactly did she say?"

"She said they are still going through the vetting process and she ought to know something in a couple of weeks, but I can read between the lines."

"That doesn't sound like backtracking to me," Mr. Eddie said. "It sounds like being thorough."

The Rev snorted. "Thorough? She's got no kids, no household employees, no back taxes. It doesn't have anything to do with Ida B. It's about *me*."

"You still worryin' about that Jeremiah Wright business?"

"I'm not *worried* about it. I'm *conscious* of it. I know how vindictive these Chicago Negroes can be."

"You think they're not going to give Ida B a job because you're her father?"

"It's not outside the realm of possibility."

Mr. Eddie passed a truck with a camel painted on the side, running so fast its big pink tongue was hanging out and trailing behind it and the words "Humpin' to please!"

"I can't argue that, Rev," he said, calmly, "but I will say that if they didn't trust you, why would they have asked for your assistance in a matter that we know means a whole lot to them?"

The Rev considered the question, but unable to still his worried mind, he changed horses in midstream.

"You don't think they sent Ida B here to keep an eye on me, do you?"

Mr. Eddie just grinned and turned up the music. "Shoot, man, they already got *me*. How many eyes you need on you at one time anyway?"

# EIGHTEEN: THE OLD NEIGHBORHOOD

It was only seven thirty and our street was still quiet when I stepped outside to take a look at the old neighborhood, so I turned toward West End's main commercial drag, where the day had already officially begun. I grew up here and even with all the changes, the things that defined this neighborhood for me are still intact. The five colleges of the Atlanta University Center anchoring things at one end and the Wren's Nest, Victorian Home of Joel Chandler Harris of Brer Rabbit fame, holding down the other. In between, the churches, from St. Anthony of Padua to the Shrine of the Black Madonna, the bookstore, the park, the tattoo parlor next to the braid salon.

There was Watkins Funeral Home; the twenty-four-hour beauty salon; the flower shop that stays open until midnight; the gardens every couple of hundred feet; Miss Iona's house; Mr. Eddie's backyard; and all those bright blue front doors that had sprouted after I left. Aretha had painted them because she had read that turquoise on the front door was supposed to ward off all manner of evil spirits. Maybe I'll see if I can get some of that paint to take back to D.C. with me.

I turned off Peeples Street and onto Abernathy on my way to the West End News, hoping to score a *Washington Post* and maybe a cappuccino. I knew I'd already had two cups of coffee, but there are worse ways to die than an overdose of caffeine. I remembered in the pre–Blue Hamilton days when the West End News was a dingy little storefront that sold a few newspapers, but specialized in dream books for lottery plays and porno magazines so foul that patrons had to go into little cubicles to make their selections. I went in there once as a young girl looking for a copy of *Jet* magazine because there was a picture of my father in it. I remember the heads of the men in the little penlike enclosures all swiveled from whatever giant breasts or welcoming vaginas they had been contemplating for purchase, to see me suddenly standing in their midst. The man behind the counter handed me the *Jet* and showed me the door.

When Blue rescued the neighborhood,

one of the first things he did was buy the place, gut it, and turn it into a real newsstand and coffee shop, featuring over one hundred international publications and a gleaming antique cappuccino machine that looked like a prop from *The Godfather.* The place was always crowded in the morning with equal numbers of students on their way to class and commuters on their way to the MARTA rapid rail station a block away. When I stepped inside, careful not to let in any cold air, there were two young women ahead of me, and one man standing at the counter, clutching a five-dollar bill and waiting patiently for his order.

I took my place in line and inhaled deeply. The place smelled great. Coffee and newspapers, my two drugs of choice. When it comes to newspapers, I'm old-fashioned. I read lots of stuff online, but I like to hold my newspapers in my hand. I picked up *The Washington Post* from a rack beside the door and reached for *The New York Times.* That's when I saw Flora waving from a tiny corner table. I waved back. She grabbed her coat off the back of the chair and headed toward me.

The West End Grower's Association was two doors down the street and I had planned to stop in before I went home.

That's the other thing about this neighborhood. You don't have to look for anybody. All you have to do is step out the front door.

"You're up early," Flora said.

"The Rev and Mr. Eddie hit the ground running before the sun came up," I said. "They didn't come by your house, too, did they?"

She laughed. The large man behind the counter had finished the cappuccino order and was now pouring two cups of the house blend for the two girls in front of me, who were giggling over a text message and pushing a neatly folded dollar bill into the tip jar.

"If they did, they missed me," she said.

"Actually, I was planning to stop by your place a little later."

"I was hoping you would say that," she said, sounding genuinely pleased as the texting twins got their coffee and stepped aside, rolling their eyes at each other over the response they'd just received. "Hey, again, Henry!"

"You need one to go?"

"I do," I told Henry, deciding to forgo the cappuccino for a faster option. "How about a large coffee, cream and sugar?"

Flora held up her hand. "I've had my limit."

"Just the coffee and the papers," I said. "Oh! And let me get a *Constitution* and a *Sentinel.*"

She smiled. "You and Hank and your newspapers."

"I'm addicted," I said, paying for the order and leaving a tip in the jar. "But I'm trying to cut back."

"You all need an organization," she said, walking beside me to her headquarters, "like alcoholics or dope fiends. *Hi, I'm Ida Dunbar. I'm a news junkie.*"

I liked Flora. She took everything seriously except herself. We had only met the night before, but she already felt like an old friend.

The West End Grower's Association boasted the most colorful front window on the block. It featured a brightly painted scene of a community garden filled with impossibly red tomatoes, dark purple eggplants, a few tall stalks of pale yellow sweet corn, and double wide rows of dark green collards. In the center of the garden stood a man and a woman, two little kids, and a grandfatherly guy who looked a little like Mr. Eddie to me. In big red letters painted in sort of a semicircle around the garden were the words "West End Grower's Association, Est. 2000."

"I didn't know you'd been here ten years," I said, following her into the storefront and looking around while she flipped on the lights.

"Well, we've *existed* for almost ten years," she said, "but we've only been in this spot since 2004. Before that, I just sort of ran it out of our apartment. I think you were already away at school then. When did you move to D.C.?"

"Well, I went to Smith first, in Northampton. That was in ninety-two. After that, I went to graduate school and then I started doing some consulting and working with campaigns. It's actually been seventeen, eighteen years since I lived here."

The number startled me. Eighteen years? *How was that possible?*

"All right," I said. "Why don't you tell me about these famous gardens?"

# NINETEEN:
# NO SURPRISES

The house hadn't changed at all. Or if it had, the changes were so minimal as to be invisible to all but the most careful observer. Wes had no interest in the details. He knew every inch of this house. There were no surprises here. The carefully arranged living room suite, his mother's pride and joy, was still holding court in front of the fireplace. The badly framed photographs documenting his youth and later successes still covered the wall just inside the front door, along with pictures of his parents at all manner of dances, picnics, house parties, community gatherings, and a wedding or two. The Rev was well represented in this gallery, including one photo with Wes on the day he left for Phillips Exeter, leaving the world he'd been born into and stepping into the one he'd chosen. *And not a moment too soon,* he thought.

Wes took his bag upstairs to his old room

and quickly unpacked. Unlike some people who enjoy the nostalgia of spending a few nights in a former bedroom, Wes regarded the space as he would a hotel room. The artifacts of his adolescence held no more fascination than a brochure welcoming him to one more Holiday Inn. He had already hung up two suits and a week's worth of shirts before he noticed the paper taped to the center of the mirror above his dresser.

"Welcome, son," it said in his father's spidery hand. "I'll be back around five. Rev and Ida B coming for dinner. Make yourself at home because you are."

He had known the Rev would show up fairly quickly, but Ida B. Dunbar? He sat down on the edge of the bed. The house had fooled him. This was a surprise all right. He hadn't expected to find her here. Not that she was working necessarily, but he didn't believe in coincidences and if his guys were after the list, the Obama people probably had it, or had sent the Rev's baby girl down here to get it. Wes smiled to himself. He loved a challenge and this shit was about to get interesting.

There had been a couple of times when he'd come across her name during the campaign. The first time, she was looking into some shit he and Oscar had done in

Santa Fe and she got too close for comfort. They had to shut it down fast or risk big exposure. The next time, same thing in Pennsylvania. She was good, but his cover was so deep that he doubted she even knew he'd been involved at all.

His phone vibrated in his pocket and Toni's voice greeted him on the other end.

"So how does it feel to be playing in the big leagues?"

"The eagle has landed," he said. "All systems are go."

"You're mixing your metaphors, aren't you?"

"Probably, but guess what? I think the Obama people have already got somebody down here."

"Doing what?"

"Same thing I'm doing, probably. Trying to get hold of that list."

"Which is where all those years of singing in the boys choir are going to come in handy, right?"

"She's closer than that."

"It's a woman?"

"The Rev's daughter."

She laughed. "You're kidding. You know her?"

"All my life. She used to have a big crush on me, as I recall."

"You think everybody has a crush on you," Toni said. "So what are you going to do?"

"I'm going to charm her with my winning ways."

Toni laughed and he could imagine her running her fingers through her hair. "Works for me," she said. "Go get 'em, tiger!"

# TWENTY:
# TWO BIRDS WITH
# ONE STONE

Between the time I walked in, and three hours later when I walked out, Flora told me everything about her gardens. I say "her gardens" because it was very clear that her vision had shaped the thing, from the very first rows of collards and tomatoes that she and a few volunteers had planted on a couple of empty lots, to the multifaceted organization she was now overseeing. Way more than just a few neighborhood plots, the Association, which Flora sometimes called WEGA, included a network of almost a hundred gardens, including fifty of the Coretta and Martin Luther King Peace Gardens, which, she said, focus on flowers instead of vegetables and are located across the country; the school garden project, which Mr. Eddie sort of ushered in by allowing himself to be drafted into Lu's dream of growing tomatoes for her high school cafeteria; and a distribution operation that not only supplies the neighbor-hood's amazing well-stocked grocery store that could give Whole Foods a run for the money, but all the restaurants in West End.

She also ran a website, responded to inquires from urban gardeners all over the place, and maintained a free library, offering an eclectic selection of books where gardens or gardening or farming play some role in the lives of the people, including a complete set of the Laura Ingalls Wilder Little House on the Prairie series, the usual seed catalogues, and a bunch of "how to grow it better" books.

While I was there, a steady stream of people trooped in and out, and to each one, she offered her full, calm, attention. As we talked, I could see that WEGA was standing at that classic make or break crossroads that all small, nonprofit organizations reach one day. Their founding charismatic was leaving at a moment of growth, innovation, and increased national visibility. The question was, would they continue to thrive without her? As we talked, I could see how passionate she was about the project, but I knew the question that was keeping Flora up at night was not could the organization survive without her, but could she survive without the organization. I thought I could probably help her on both counts, but first I had a bone to pick with Miss Iona.

When I stepped up on her porch, I could hear the vacuum cleaner. She came to the door wearing a pair of brown slacks, an orange sweater, and a pair of brown leather flats. Her hair was covered with a brightly colored silk scarf and gold hoops were swaying in her ears. This was as casual as Miss Iona ever got.

"I've been calling you for hours," she said. "I thought all you big-time professional women had cell phones permanently attached to your ears."

"I went over to the Grower's Association," I said. "Flora wanted to show me what they're doing."

"She's a jewel," Miss Iona said, closing the door behind me and pushing the vacuum cleaner over to one side. "I don't know how they're going to survive without her."

"That's what she's worried about, too."

She cocked her head at me. "Now, there's a thought. Why don't you take it?"

I looked at her. "I'm not here looking for a job, remember? I'm here to respond to an SOS from someone who said my dad was going off the deep end."

She smiled and took my arm, guiding me

over to the couch. She had a little fire going and the room was cozy. "And so he was," she said, poking the fire gently, before taking a seat next to me.

"And now?"

She spread her hands and smiled brightly. "And now he's back. Aren't you glad?"

"Of course I am, but I just need to know if you were really worried about him or if you were just trying to get us back together."

She looked disappointed. "You saw that video."

"Yes."

"Did you ask him about it?"

"Of course I did."

She raised her eyebrows. "And?"

"He said it was all Mom's fault."

She looked at me for a second like maybe she hadn't heard me right and then she burst out laughing. "Oh, Lord! Those two are going to be the death of me!"

"If they don't kill each other first!"

"You don't need to worry about that. They're going to grow old together."

Now she was the one with the obvious mental lapse. "What are you talking about? At this very moment, they're not even speaking to each other."

"Mark my words," she said. "This is all foreplay."

"So can I go home now?"

"You are home, darlin'. That's what I keep trying to tell you."

A timer dinged in the kitchen and Miss Iona glanced at her watch. "I've got a pound cake in the oven," she said. "Want a piece?"

"I haven't had my lunch yet," I said.

"Good. Then come on in the kitchen. I'll make us a couple of sandwiches. *Then* you can have a piece."

I didn't realize how hungry I was until I bit into the leftover turkey sandwich Miss Iona put in front of me. She poured us each a glass of ice tea and sat down, nibbling her own sandwich delicately around the edges.

"Listen, Ida B," she said. "I need to tell you something."

Her voice was so serious. I swallowed hard. *Here we go.*

"I was telling the truth about being worried about the Rev, but it wasn't just that video that made me call you."

"What's wrong?"

"A couple of weeks ago," she said, "one of the reporters down at *The Sentinel* started working on a story about how the Republican party never shut down their dirty tricks operation after the election. They just sort of went underground."

I put the uneaten part of my sandwich

down and took a sip of ice tea. "Go on."

"Somebody told this guy that they've got a plan to use the old Civil Rights warriors to attack the president so they can begin to erode his support in the community."

"That will never work," I said. "Black folks haven't loved anybody like we love Barack Obama since Dr. King died."

"*They* think it will. They plan to target the ones they know already feel left out after the whole Jeremiah Wright thing. Even they recognize Alan Keys and that crowd don't have any credibility, but if they can get some of the guys who actually walked with Dr. King, some of the *icons,* like your dad . . ." She looked at me and shook her head impatiently. "And with the Rev they'd be getting two birds with one stone because of that damn list."

"The Rev would never do anything like that," I said.

She shook her head and frowned. "I never thought he would either, and I don't think he would now, if he was thinking straight."

"What makes you think he's not?"

She raised her perfectly plucked eyebrows. "Tacos and sangria?"

There was no denying he had behaved badly, but the idea that the Rev would ever sell out the race, for any reason, was simply not within the realm of possibility.

"Did you tell him what you heard?"

"He practically bit my head off. Accused me of being disloyal, paranoid, not trusting him. All sorts of good things."

It was hard for me to imagine the Rev accusing Miss Iona of anything. She and Mr. Eddie had been the ones who always had his back, through good times and bad. They were always there.

"What do you want me to do?" I said. "The Rev and I haven't had much luck talking about politics lately."

"I know that, but this is what you do, right? Find the dirty tricks before they can play them?"

"That wasn't the part I was involved in," I said. "I bumped up on a couple of things, but the campaign is over, remember?"

"So you mean to tell me after all that time you spent with these people, day after day, for two years, you don't have anybody you can call, just to check it out?"

She was right, of course. All I needed to do was make a couple of calls and I'm sure I could put Miss Iona's mind at ease.

"Okay," I said. "I'll see what I can find out."

"Thank you, darlin'," she said, sounding relieved. "I don't think the Rev has any idea how many people would love to get their hands on that new voters list he keeps bragging about. Or what they're prepared to do to get it."

"He seemed to know *exactly* how valuable it was last time I talked to him about it," I said. "Don't forget, this is the Rev we're dealing with here."

She took a deep breath, pulled the scarf off of her head, and shook her hair out a little. Never at a loss for words, she seemed to be trying to figure out the right ones and not having much luck.

"What?"

"See, the thing is, Ida B, getting old is a lot harder than any of us thought it would be. It's like becoming invisible a little at a time, and that's the one thing these guys don't know how to be." She smiled almost to herself. "They used to face down the baddest white men in America, I'm talking about stomp down crackers with guns on their hips, and the cameras made sure the world was watching. Now they sit around at Paschal's, drinking coffee and talking about the old days and there's not a camera in sight. Once Black History Month is over, how many speeches you think the Rev's got lined up?"

I hadn't thought about it, but I know a

rhetorical question when I hear one so I didn't say anything.

"All those guys thought they were going to die in battle. In a blaze of glory." She shrugged, picked up her sandwich, put it back down, and looked at me. *But they didn't.*

# Twenty-One:
# Weak for You

Sitting at the kitchen table, watching his father strip the husks off of several ears of fresh corn and listening to the sound of Nancy Wilson floating in from the front room, Wes realized he didn't need to worry. His father seemed genuinely happy to see him and their greeting held none of the awkward stiffness that Wes had been dreading. Mr. Eddie had come home from a day of driving the Rev with a bag full of fresh produce for dinner, a six-pack of Heineken, which he knew was Wes's favorite, and a couple of pounds of the most beautiful pink catfish fillets Wes had seen in ages.

They'd greeted each other warmly and moved to the kitchen so they could catch up a little while Mr. Eddie got dinner started. As was his habit, Mr. Eddie removed his jacket, rolled up his sleeves, and wrapped a big black kitchen apron around his middle, but he didn't change his suit.

Mr. Eddie liked to cook in street clothes, especially when he was cooking for company.

Wes took a long swallow of the cold Heineken he was drinking as Mr. Eddie rinsed the corn in cold water and set it aside.

"You remember Ida B?"

"Sure I do," Wes said. "She used to have a crush on me."

Mr. Eddie ignored that. "I'm surprised you two haven't run into each other," he said, reaching into the refrigerator for the catfish. "She worked in the Obama campaign."

"You know I stayed out of that one, Pop," Wes said, the lie rolling easily off his tongue. "Too many die-hard Clinton folks on my client list."

Mr. Eddie nodded and laid the pale pink fillets out on the counter gently. "Well, they better get over it. The best man won and he needs all hands on deck."

Wes took another sip of his beer and didn't answer. Mr. Eddie salted and peppered the fillets and added a spicy mixture of his own concoction.

"You look good, Pop. Retirement agrees with you."

"Shoot, I'm working harder now than I ever did working for those white folks. The

Rev is about to run me ragged. I'm thinkin' about askin' the president to suspend Black History Month next year. I'm gettin' too old for this mess."

Wes grinned at his father. "That's not what I hear."

"What you hear about what?"

"About two old guys in a big black Lincoln, tearing around the Georgia countryside, registering fifty thousand black folks to vote, *just because they could.*"

Mr. Eddie looked at him and grinned. "You heard that, huh? All the way up there in New York City?"

Wes grinned back at his father. "That's what I heard. Any truth to it?"

"More like one hundred thousand," Mr. Eddie said, turning the fish and drizzling each piece with olive oil. "You can ask the Rev when he gets here."

*Bingo!* Wes thought. He had now officially hit the mother lode in less than twenty-four hours and without ever having to leave the house.

"Congratulations, Pop," he said, raising the green glass bottle in a salute. "That's an amazing accomplishment."

"It's all because of the Rev," Mr. Eddie said, still drizzling. "I've never seen him work so hard or so long as he did to get

199

these Negroes registered in time to cast a vote for Obama. The Rev was all up in people's faces, scaring them half to death about being on the wrong side of history. They had no choice but to get themselves down to the courthouse."

"I saw the picture online of him standing on somebody's front porch with a clip-board."

"Young people call that old-school. What they don't know is, that's the only school we know!" He laughed. "What did your mother used to say? *If it ain't broke, don't fix it.*"

The front doorbell announced the arrival of the other dinner guests. Mr. Eddie was placing two slices of lemon on each piece of catfish and reaching for the dried parsley.

"Go let 'em in, will you, Wes? You can see if Miss Ida B's still weak for you."

# Twenty-Two:
## Full Disclosure

"Whatever happened to that nice young man you brought around during the campaign?" the Rev said, apropos of nothing, as we stood waiting on Mr. Eddie's front porch. We had been talking about his trip to Athens and how much more politically active the campus had become since the election. Many of the students had voted for the first time and they were anxious to find a way to stay involved. His question took me by surprise.

"Archie?"

I had crashed at the house with another campaign staffer one night when a line of serious storms grounded all the Atlanta planes headed west and there were no hotel rooms to be had for miles. Archie was an egotistical asshole and sometime sexual partner who spent the whole night trying to talk me into giving him a blow job in my baby girl bedroom. The degree to which even the possibility excited him sort of creeped me out and I don't think he said ten words to me or the Rev before we pulled out early the next morning.

"What makes you ask about him?"

"Ed tells me Wes is single again," he said and actually gave my arm a conspiratorial little squeeze. "You never know."

"Never know what?" I said, but before I could bust the Rev down on his matchmaking, the door opened and there was Wes, smiling and, according to the Rev, free as a bird, looking exactly like I remembered him from glimpses over the years when he'd be home for the holidays and we'd bump into each other at church after he had shed his adolescent chubbiness for the new body he was still carrying around.

"Welcome, welcome," he said, holding out a hand in greeting, which the Rev pumped enthusiastically. "It's been too long!"

"Longer than that," the Rev agreed. "You remember my daughter?"

"Of course," Wes said, leaning over for a quick peck on the cheek. "Good to see you."

"You, too," I said and I blushed.

*Okay.* In the interest of full disclosure, I'm sure my memories of him are much more vivid than his of me. Wes Harper was one of my favorite masturbation guys from about fourteen to seventeen. *Not that there's anything wrong with that.* At fourteen, which I think is the age I was the last time I saw him, eighteen can be a legitimate object of sexual fantasy. Fortunately, I don't think he ever returned my imaginary affections, since at eighteen, lusting after a fourteen-year-old is not only creepy but illegal, although I think some southern states still have some weird child-bride loophole. I'll ask my mother the next time I see her. That's the kind of stuff she keeps in her head just in case the topic ever comes up in otherwise pleasant conversation.

"There's my girl!" Mr. Eddie emerged from the kitchen carrying four wineglasses and a bottle of something. He was wearing an apron identical to the one Mr. Charles had been sporting last night. I wondered if all the men in West End had now taken to cooking, the way they had to driving those big black Lincolns.

I hugged him and handed him the pound cake Miss Iona had pressed on me when I told her we were coming for dinner.

"That woman thinks nobody knows how to make dessert but her," he said, turning to the Rev. "I don't need to say anything to you. How many times a day can a man say *hey* anyway?"

"I'm not studyin' you," the Rev said. "I'm here to have dinner with my godson."

"Then let your godson pour you and Ida B a glass of that high-priced wine he's always sending me and I'll be right back."

"It would be my pleasure," Wes said as we followed him into the living room. "Red all right?"

"Fine with me," said the Rev. "My doctor said I can't drink bourbon anymore, so it's all the same to me."

"Well, maybe that's just because you haven't been drinking the good stuff," Wes said, opening the bottle and pouring four glasses. "Try this."

The Rev took a swallow and wrinkled his nose. "This is the good stuff?"

Wes laughed. "It better be, as much as they're charging for it."

It was good wine. Not that I'm a connoisseur or anything. I tend to be a one margarita and I'm done kinda gal. A lot of places don't carry a wine list, but every bartender alive can make a decent margarita. I sat down next to the Rev and smiled at Wes, who smiled back. The Rev was beaming, probably already picturing us walking down the aisle at Rock of Faith after we had promised *'til death do us part.*

"How long are you in town for?" Wes said.

"Couple of days," I said, refusing to be distracted by the slide show of fantasy flashbacks playing in my head. "Maybe a week. I was hoping to spend some time with the Rev, but he and Mr. Eddie have the busiest calendar in West End, so I may be here a little longer. See if he can work me in."

The Rev smiled at me like he hoped I'd stay until Christmas and turned back to Wes. "And how about you? To what do we owe this visit? Business must be good."

"Never been better," Wes said. "I'm actually thinking about opening an office here in Atlanta. I'm here to check some things out before any final decisions are made."

Mr. Eddie came in wiping his hands on a dish towel, picked up the wineglass Wes had poured for him, and joined the conversation. "I told him you were the one to give him the lay of the land."

"I don't know how true that is," the Rev said, picking up his wine, deciding it still had not morphed into a glass of Jack Daniel's on the rocks, and putting it back down. "I'm sort of out of the loop these days."

"I can't believe that," Wes said. "Any man who put fifty thousand new voters on the rolls . . ."

"One hundred thousand," the Rev corrected him.

Wes smiled. "Exactly my point. Any man who put one hundred thousand new voters on the rolls *is* the loop."

The Rev laughed his big public laugh. "That's what I keep trying to tell these Negroes, but you think they're listening?" He shook his head. "Not likely."

"What's the name of your group again?"

"BAC-UP!" The Rev's voice supplied the exclamation point.

Black Activist Clergy United for Progress. How could he forget that?

Mr. Eddie put down his glass and disappeared back into the kitchen. "I always thought that was a gutsy name for a group of preachers," Wes said. "I'm glad you hung on to it for this latest campaign."

"Why wouldn't I hang on to it?" the Rev said. "It was my idea."

"I should have known that." Wes nodded. "It's genius. When you hear it or read it, your mind immediately gives you the unspoken word, so you internalize it as *back the fuck up* even though you never say the word."

"We better not!" The Rev laughed.

Wes looked over at me and smiled apologetically. "Excuse my French!"

When was the last time you heard anybody

actually say that? Especially anybody under seventy-five? I just looked at him.

"That was exactly my intention," the Rev said. "And here comes that fool from *The Constitution* asking me if it meant we were there to provide *backup* to some other Negroes who were actually leading the charge. And what Negroes would that be? I asked him. Have you seen any of them around here lately?"

"It's the age of the Internet," Wes said. "Everybody gets to be a reporter."

"I should be glad they even sent somebody to talk to me," the Rev said. "It's like pulling teeth for me to get any coverage these days."

"From what Pop tells me, you're drawing standing room only crowds everywhere you go."

"Well, if that's who you're trying to meet, I've got you covered, but folks who fly in on private jets aren't usually looking to talk to the usher board at the First Baptist Church of Moultrie."

I couldn't tell if my father was signifying or just stating a fact. The hardworking people the Rev could always count on didn't usually show up as a desirable demographic no matter who compiled the list.

"The people who own that jet don't want

to talk to them either," Wes said. "They want to sell them something."

And that, I thought, is the big difference between politics and business. If they're constituents, you have to actually go out there and speak to them. In business, all you have to do is take their money. Suddenly, I had a question.

"Whose jet is it?"

Wes turned and looked at me the way people do when you ask them how much money they make, which, of course, only makes you more curious. "Just a client of mine," he said. "Company out of Texas. They had a plane coming to Atlanta so I caught a ride."

"Now, that's a state I never wanted to take a drive through," Mr. Eddie said, coming back in and picking up where he left off. "Too big and too flat. You can go for miles in Texas with no place to turn off if you need to."

"Too many mad white folks," the Rev said.

"Can't fault 'em there," Mr. Eddie said. "If I lived in Texas, I'd be mad, too."

Beside me, the Rev's stomach growled so loud that I heard it. He grinned at me and patted his stomach. "That catfish smells done to me. What do you think, Brother Harper?"

Mr. Eddie stood up and put down his glass. "I think that's good enough for me. Dinner is served."

As we headed to the kitchen for the feast Mr. Eddie had prepared, Wes fell in next to me.

"Oil," he said, still smiling. He was taller than I remembered, or maybe just not as heavy.

"Excuse me?"

"My client with the plane," he said. "He's in oil."

When we got to the table, he pulled out my chair.

# TWENTY-THREE:
# A MORNING IN HELL

They ate every piece of catfish, devoured every ear of corn, and waved off Mr. Eddie's apologies for the store-bought tomatoes that couldn't match his own home-grown. They lingered for a few more minutes, enjoying coffee and Miss Iona's pound cake. Over the course of the meal, Ida B and Wes had successfully established an easy familiarity that acknowledged their past interaction, but didn't hold it against each other.

Wes felt like he knew a lot of women like Ida. Smart, attractive, sexually active, and unattached. She said she was "between jobs," which usually meant frantically looking for one, but he assumed she was just being evasive. She answered his questions about her campaign involvement pleasantly enough, but when he confessed that he had decided to sit it out, for business reasons, she just smiled and changed the subject. It was the same look he had gotten from his friends who had seen action in Iraq or Afghanistan whenever he ventured an opinion about the war. It was the way you would look at a five-year-old trying to talk about the stock market. No chance of understanding, so why bother to engage?

That was, of course, exactly how he wanted her to think of him. As an ambitious young businessman, prepared to sit out the election of a lifetime in order to avoid offending his clients, but not above taking advantage of the new racial space that was Obamamerica. Her question about the owner of the plane was to be expected. It had just caught him off guard because he had been so focused on the Rev. His initial feeling had been right on target. The Rev was still feeling the blowback from the whole Wright episode and his exclusion from the new president's national orbit was as painful as it had been when he realized he had not been invited to the inauguration.

"Can you believe that?" he had asked at dinner. "I still can't believe it. Who the hell do these Negroes think they are?

Wes noticed that when the Rev started slamming the president, Ida B kept her eyes on her plate or on her cup; anywhere but her father's face.

"The thing he's got to understand," the Rev was saying, "is that this can't be about a cult of personality. It has to be bigger than loving Obama. We can't keep building our movements around one man."

Mr. Eddie shook his head. "You can say that if you wanna, Rev, but most people figure if they get the right man, he'll bring the right idea."

"So that means we've got to find somebody new for them to love every time there's an election?" the Rev said. "What if there's nobody lovable willing to run? Then what?"

"Then you get John McCain," Wes said. Ida B rewarded him with a grin.

"Half the people we registered went to the polls thinking they were voting for an Obama/Dunbar ticket," Mr. Eddie said.

"That would have been Dunbar/Obama." The Rev laughed. "And don't forget it!"

Ida B laughed, too. She was prettier than Wes had first thought. Maybe because she had been a little tense when they first got there. He had watched her slowly relax, laughing at his father's jokes, shaking her head at the Rev's life on the road stories, and eventually turning toward him, her gaze intelligent and unblinking, not at all like the shy, skinny kid who never seemed to be able to look him in the eye. She wasn't a kid anymore. She was almost as tall as he was and slender without sacrificing her womanly curves. Wes was old-fashioned. He liked a woman with a little meat on her bones. Not jiggling and juicy, but enough to give a man something to grab on to when the spirit moved him. He wondered what she liked to grab on to when the spirit moved her.

The Rev yawned and turned to Ida B. "Well, daughter, it's getting late. Time for us to take our leave."

"Can I help with the cleanup?" she said.

"Not a chance." Mr. Eddie shook his head. "You need to get this old man home so he'll have energy enough to drive himself to Macon tomorrow."

"You're driving yourself?" Ida B sounded surprised. "Why?"

The Rev stood up and looked at Mr. Eddie. "My right-hand man here is being honored at an assembly event over at the high school. Too late for me to reschedule, so I'm on my own."

This was too easy, Wes thought. He almost felt guilty about what he was getting ready to do. *Almost.*

"We can't have that," Wes said, standing up, too. "I'd be honored to drive you."

The Rev looked surprised. "To Macon?"

"All the way down and all the way back," Wes said. "It'll give me a chance to bend your ear about my new office. What do you say?"

"I might just take you up on that," the Rev said slowly. "Can you be ready at six?"

Mr. Eddie was smiling and nodding, obviously pleased that Wes had stepped up without being asked.

"Absolutely."

That's when Ida B spoke up, sounding concerned. "Aren't you going to the assembly?" she said, looking at Wes with a small frown.

Before he could answer, Mr. Eddie spoke up in his defense. "I didn't invite him. You know I don't like a whole lot of fuss around me."

Wes turned to his father. "What's going on?"

"Flora Lumumba's daughter got me doing a garden with the kids. It worked out pretty good so they want to thank me. I told them to name it after the Rev, but Lu said they still want to give me a plaque or something."

Wes wondered whether his father really didn't want him to come or if he was just giving him a way out if Wes didn't want to be bothered. *And he truly didn't want to be bothered.* Sitting in a high school auditorium listening to a bunch of kids talking about how growing a patch of collard greens changed their lives was his idea of a morning in hell.

"Well, since Pop didn't invite me, I'm going to take him at his word that he's got no particular need to see my face in the place." He turned to his father, who nodded, looking relieved.

"But I also think," Wes turned to Ida B, "that he might not mind having somebody around just to . . . handle the media."

She smiled. "I think I can arrange that. How about it, Mr. Eddie? Can I be your press secretary for tomorrow?"

Mr. Eddie's grin alone was worth the price of admission. "Now you're talkin'."

# Twenty-Four:
# Grown Man Fine

Wes Harper was the kind of man whose charm fools you into trusting him when your brain is telling you to run for your life. He was fine, too. There was no denying that. Not *pretty boy fine,* but grown man fine. My type, if someone as deprived as I've been lately can even be said to have a "type." And he had a great smile. I say all that so that the degree of discipline necessary to make what I'm about to say *truth* instead of wishful thinking will be clear. *I did not conduct any testing once I got home to see whether or not Wes was still able to perform the function he had executed so reliably during the three or four years that he was in my fantasy guy stable.* It seemed a little inappropriate to go from having dinner at his father's house to asking his fantasy doppelganger to lick this, or squeeze that, or slow down, *or whatever.* What would Mr. Eddie say if he knew?

Or maybe it's just that it's hard to bring

those masturbation guys back once you retire them. I mean, I had a lot of good moments with Keith Sweat, too, back in the day, but that doesn't mean I'm ready for an encore. That's the way I feel about Wes Harper. That was then and this is now. If there's going to be any fooling around between us, I'd rather he was along for the ride.

That morning, he arrived bright and early to pick up the Rev and thanked me for standing in for him at the assembly. I thanked him for hanging out with the Rev and for a moment, we became a mutual admiration society, bonding over what good children we were. He said he hoped we'd have a chance to talk again soon and I said me, too, but then the Rev presented himself, briefcase in hand, and they were out the door before we got to exchange any specifics. That wasn't really a problem, of course. We were staying less than two blocks from each other. If he wanted to see me, I was pretty easy to find.

The good thing was, the Rev wouldn't be traveling alone. Wes was practically family, which made my recent train of thought perilously close to incest, but be that as it may, he was an appreciative audience and an attentive ear. I had watched the Rev bloom like a rose the night before at dinner while Wes flattered him shamelessly. He was good at it, too. He was a great listener and I admit the first few times he turned that *tell me everything about yourself* smile on me, I told him more than he probably wanted to know. Good thing I wasn't going to be there long enough to get myself into trouble. Serious trouble anyway.

Booker T. Washington High School was farther than I wanted to walk, so I drove over. The parking lot was full, even though I was a half an hour early, so I parked on the street. Students with backpacks and low-slung pants were walking toward the school in twos and threes, along with a few others, like me, who were there to support Mr. Eddie. Miss Iona was standing out front in a light blue coat with a faux fur collar and navy blue pumps, talking to a woman I didn't know. When she spotted me, she detached herself and headed in my direction.

"Have you heard anything back?" she said, giving me a quick hug and looking for an update about the plot.

"I haven't had a chance to call anybody yet," I said. "You just told me yesterday."

She looked at me. "I hope you are taking this seriously, Ida B. Your father could ruin a reputation he's spent a lifetime building into something we can all be proud of. This can't wait!"

I took her arm and steered her toward the front entrance, past the life-size sculpture of Dr. Washington pulling back that veil of ignorance. When we were kids, we used to say he was really pulling it back down, but never in front of the Rev. He admired Booker T. Washington and W.E.B. DuBois for their very different, but equally impassioned positions on how to uplift the race. No disrespect to either one was allowed.

"I'm taking it very seriously," I said. "I'll see if I can scare up my guy this afternoon and find out what's going on. I promise."

"Don't do it like it's a favor to me," she said, still a little miffed at what she perceived to be my foot-dragging. "He's your father, not mine."

*But he's your hero,* I thought.

"You've known him longer than I have," I countered. "Looks like you would have raised him better."

"You better bite your tongue, girl," she said, smiling again. "When I met the man, he was already fully formed."

I'm sure that was true. The Rev probably arrived on the planet wearing a suit and tie.

The auditorium was filling up, but Mr. Eddie had left instructions that we were to be taken to the reserved section up front whenever we arrived. We followed the smiling usher, whose great big ears and gap-toothed smile made him look like a mischievous ten-year-old.

"Where's Wes?" Miss Iona said, her eyes scanning the room as we headed down the center aisle.

"Mr. Eddie told him not to come, so he's driving the Rev to Macon."

She stopped dead still. "You're kidding."

I shook my head. "They left at six. I'm supposed to be his proxy or something."

"That doesn't count," she said, as our young usher stopped at the second row and looked around for us. "You were coming on your own anyway, right?"

"Right."

"Well, then," she said, like that settled the matter.

"The Rev isn't here either," I said, feeling the need to defend Wes in the face of Miss Iona's disapproval.

Miss Iona sighed. "The Rev had a previous engagement. It's Black History Month, for God's sake! Plus, he was trying not to overshadow anybody. If the Rev walks in, it's all about the Rev. He was trying to give Ed his chance to shine."

"Maybe that's what Wes was trying to do, too."

"Please," she said, "that boy has never respected his parents. Even as a kid, he was always putting on airs."

I knew what she meant, but I just shrugged. "He seemed okay at dinner last night. Maybe he's turned over a new leaf."

"New leaf, my foot," she said. "You can't teach an old dog new tricks."

That seemed to be her last word on the matter, but we still weren't making much progress down the aisle because she kept stopping to speak to people. Our usher got tired of waiting and passed us on his way back to the door. Miss Iona never noticed him. She was too busy presenting me to people who remembered me and introducing me to people who didn't.

"You remember Ida B," she'd say, which always elicited a big hug and a question.

"Are you here for the Rev's Founder's Day sermon?"

"No," I said the first time somebody asked me. "I'll be gone before Founder's Day."

The next time, Miss Iona didn't wait for me to respond. "You remember the Rev's daughter, Ida B," she said to a woman about her age, equally stylish in a light gray coat and a spectacular knockoff of the hat Aretha

Franklin had rocked at the Inaugural Festivities. "She's here for Founder's Day."

The woman nodded enthusiastically and hugged me again. "We're all looking forward to it," she said. "Even more than we usually do because of everything being so historic this year and all. President Obama's first year in. Your dad's first year out. History everywhere you look!"

"Yes, ma'am," I said. The woman turned to greet another friend in the crowd and I looked at Miss Iona. "No way I'm going to Founder's Day. I won't be here that long."

"Of course you're going," she said calmly. "Hasn't he asked you yet?"

"Asked me what?"

"To introduce him."

We had finally arrived at our seats. Mr. Charles was already there, sitting next to Aretha, who was showing him a digital image on one of several cameras slung around her long graceful neck. I followed Miss Iona down the row, seeking clarification.

"What are you talking about?"

"He asked me if I thought you would want to do it."

"And, of course, you told him yes?"

"What other answer is there?" she said, sitting down next to Mr. Charles.

Before I could suggest a few alternatives,

Mr. Charles turned to greet his wife and I heard someone call my name.

"Ida B. Dunbar, is that you?"

Precious Hargrove looked exactly the way she had last time I saw her, which had to be almost three years ago. Her hair might have been a little grayer, and the laugh lines around her eyes a little harder not to notice, but otherwise she hadn't changed a bit. Over the past twenty years of her public life, she had created an outstanding record as a state senator by walking that fine line between social and fiscal responsibility. She had stepped in to rescue Mandeville Maid Service when their founder was convicted of running an underground prostitution ring (*don't ask!*), and stood by her son, Kwame, when he was involved in a high-profile murder case that went all the way to Blue Hamilton's doorstep, but no further (*don't tell!*).

Well respected and well liked, she was widely expected to be a serious contender in the next governor's race. A victory would make her the first African American *and* the first woman to hold the position. In spite of the Rev's recent falling out with her, I considered Precious a friend and a mentor. When we shared a brief hello hug, her cheek felt warm and smooth.

"Senator Hargrove," I said, honoring her title. "I didn't expect to see you here."

"I could say the same," she said. "Welcome home. Iona told me you were coming to spend some time with your father."

There was no use pretending not to see the five-hundred-pound gorilla in the room.

"Did she tell you how sorry I was about the Rev's *YouTube* debut?"

"You don't have to apologize," she said, quickly. "The Rev and I have had our differences before. We'll figure it out. It's just that all this new technology lets everybody else in on the *figuring* before we get it done."

She was right about that. The rise of social networking sites had changed the political landscape forever. It was too soon to tell what the long-term effects would be, but the change itself was a fact. She leaned over to speak to Miss Iona and Mr. Charles, but now they were talking to a man in the row behind us. In her next life, I think Miss Iona is going to be the social director on a cruise ship: the SS *Freedom Now.*

Precious leaned a little closer and lowered her voice. "Actually, I was going to call you this afternoon," she said. "But face-to-face is still the best."

"Old-school," I teased her gently. "What's up?"

"We're not sure exactly," she said. "But one of my guys told me the feds are quietly looking into some plans they've uncovered to illegally purge thousands of Georgia Democratic voters from the rolls before the midterm elections. They're particularly interested in new voters, all those folks your dad got registered."

It never rains but it pours, I thought. Atlanta seems to be like one of those ancient talismans Angelina Jolie is always searching for in the tombs she's raiding. All the good citizen energy floating around here attracts its opposite in all the bad guy energy that can't stand progress, even when they know it's inevitable.

"They never quit, do they?" I said.

She shook her head. "Nope, so neither can we. That's why I need to let the Rev know what we've heard so that . . ."

On the stage, a slender girl wearing the denim overalls that identified her as an active gardener stepped up to the microphone. "Will Senator Precious Hargrove please come backstage?" she said. "Our program is about to begin."

The students clapped and whistled their approval with the enthusiastic boisterousness that usually defines a pregame pep rally in the middle of a winning season.

Precious waved at the girl and smiled at me. "Showtime! Listen, I know the Rev won't call me, but Kwame has more information about this if he wants it. Iona's got the number."

I nodded. "I'll tell him."

"It might be nothing," she said, giving my hand a squeeze. "But he's got that list and we know they want it. Better to be safe than sorry."

As she moved away, I looked up toward the stage and there was Mr. Eddie, standing in the wings as cool as you please. Buzzing around him were four or five more kids in overalls, including Lu. I could also see Flora, sticking close to Mr. Eddie. As Precious joined the group to complete the lineup, I was glad to represent for Mr. Eddie's extended family, but Miss Iona was right. Wes should have been there.

# TWENTY-FIVE:
# MAKE IT PLAIN

By the time the Rev shook the last hand, kissed the last baby, and answered a kid's wide-eyed question about whether or not he had really met Dr. King with a long story about his frontline experiences with the man, Wes was exhausted. He was glad Atlanta was only an hour straight up the interstate.

"You sure you don't want to stay over?" the Rev said when Wes tried to stifle a yawn as they pulled onto the freeway. "Me and your pop never do these fast turnarounds anymore. There's a nice Holiday Inn at the next exit."

"I'm good," Wes said, easing into the passing lane. "I'm just wondering how you two keep this up every day."

The Rev laughed. "We pace ourselves. This day just got out of hand. I agreed to do one thing and then two and then that became three." He shook his head and looked out the window. Once they left Macon, there were long stretches of dark highway cutting through those famous Georgia pines. Wes put the car on cruise control.

"It's hard for me to say no sometimes," the Rev said. "Nobody else who's talking to them regularly is making any sense. They're looking for somebody to tell them what's going on and what they should be doing about it."

He took off his hat, smoothed the crown gently, then turned to lay it carefully on the backseat beside his briefcase. "I guess that's always been my job."

"Long as I've known you," Wes said. "And you know what, Rev? You're still one of the best I've ever seen."

The Rev turned back to Wes and grinned. "*One* of the best?"

Wes laughed. "The best! No contest. The absolute best."

"Make it plain," the Rev said. "Make it plain."

The truth was, Wes had shadowed the man all day and he wasn't lying: The Rev was a pro. He started the day at a prayer breakfast, met with a group of community activists who were mad at the mayor, spoke at a high school Black History Month assembly, had lunch with that same mayor, where he shared the activists' concerns and got a promise from the man to look into the matter and report back, then spoke at a dinner where he received a proclamation declaring it Rev. Horace A. Dunbar Day in Macon, in honor of his role in securing full citizenship rights for African Americans "across Georgia and throughout the world."

Wes smiled when he read that as he stood by, holding the framed parchment while the Rev did one final interview with a reporter from the local paper whose tape recorder seemed to need a charge. *Throughout the world.*

"So what now, Rev? Black History Month will be over in a couple of weeks. You going to kick back a little?"

"No time for that," the Rev said. "According to Charlie Larson, every month is now Black History Month, so I guess I'll have to just keep doing what I'm doing."

"More registration drives?"

The Rev nodded. "We've got a lot of momentum and I don't want to lose it. That's why I'm all over the state trying to keep those little churches activated and energized."

Wes's brain immediately reimagined that as a campaign slogan: *Vote for our guy! He's activated and energized!*

"It is my intention to register another fifty thousand voters before the midterm elections."

Wes could imagine how happy that would make Oscar. One hundred fifty thousand new voters to disenfranchise. The man might actually swoon with joy.

"That's pretty ambitious," he said. "You think there are fifty thousand folks left you didn't get the last time, even with Obama mania?"

"We're going to target new voters, the ones who are just turning eighteen, and people who aren't affiliated with any church. Lots of them still floating around, and we're going to add more churches because now they know the one hundred percent idea really works."

"You think it's replicable up north?" Wes said as they passed a huge McDonald's sign glowing at the end of the exit like a beacon, lighting the way home, one burger at a time.

"Absolutely," the Rev said, with conviction. "I've already looked at Detroit, Chicago, Cincinnati, Cleveland, and Baltimore. If I can get some boots on the ground by 2010, there'll be no stopping us."

Wes had immediate visions of following a passionate and clueless Rev across the country, purging voters and suppressing turnout from one end of black America to the other. He ought to get a nice bonus and a sizable long-term retainer for his firm if he pulled this off. This whole thing had just fallen into his lap. All he had to do was be cool and reel the Rev in.

"Listen, Rev," Wes said. "Can I speak frankly?"

"Of course." The Rev turned slightly toward Wes.

"I'm in a position to help you," Wes said, choosing his words carefully. "The truth is, we're in a position to help each other."

The Rev grinned. "You going to drive me to Albany, too?"

Wes grinned back in the darkness. "I think I can help you find a sponsor."

"A sponsor?"

"Someone to underwrite the expenses associated with a statewide registration effort. A corporation that could help you put those boots on the ground."

The Rev's eyes hardened in the dark brown of his high cheekboned face, but his voice didn't change. "What are you getting at?"

"You've got an active list of one hundred thousand people. Voting isn't the only thing they can do, Rev. They also eat potato chips and drink Coca-Cola and buy back to school clothes for their kids." He looked over to the Rev quickly and then back to the dark road. "My clients don't care about politics. They care about consumers. That list is worth its weight in gold."

The Rev didn't say anything and Wes wondered if he had made too big a leap.

"Nothing too heavy-handed," he said quickly. "But there would certainly be some interest out there in sponsoring, say, a tour for you around the state and, maybe later, something national." He smiled but kept his eyes on the highway. "In exchange for the opportunity to communicate with the people on your list about the goods and services my clients want to provide."

"Communicate with them how?"

"Email blasts," Wes said. "Social networking sites. The whole nine yards."

That's when the Rev let loose one of those great big boomers of a laugh. It was so loud in the closed space, the effect was what Wes imagined it felt like to hear a bullet fired in a car. *What the hell was so funny?*

"Wes, these people don't do email."

"What do you mean?"

"I mean, you been in the big city too long, boy. These folks don't own computers. A good percentage of them don't even have cable TV. Lord knows what they're going to do when the government makes them go digital."

"So how do you communicate with them?"

"We call them on the telephone. We send them letters in the kind of mail you put in a box. We place notices in their bulletins at church right beside the list of sick and shut-ins. We go knock on the front door and hope they invite us in for lemonade."

Wes felt like he was caught in a time warp. The Rev was carrying this old-school shit too far. "Don't you find it frustrating to have one hundred thousand names on a disk and not be able to send them an email reminding them that tomorrow is election day?"

"What disk?"

"Your mailing list."

The Rev shook his head. "It's not on any disk."

Through a time warp or down the rabbit hole. Wes couldn't decide. "You lost me, Rev."

"Our registration drive was hands-on. Door-to-door. Every person who registered filled out a card for us, too, with their name and address, phone number if they wanted to, age, church affiliation, and anything else they wanted to say."

"What do you mean?" Wes said, passing a truck with the Target logo on the side.

"Well, a lot of people we took down to register got really emotional about the whole idea of a black president so I told them if they wanted to put something down on the card for posterity, they could. Eventually, I'll get Iona to go through the cards and gather up all of what they said. Put it in a book or something. That's probably when we'll get somebody to type it all up."

Wes had a sudden, sickening feeling. *Type it all up?*

"Are you saying your list isn't typed up anywhere?"

"Not yet," the Rev said cheerfully. "I've been trying to get Iona to do it for me, but she says if she wanted to spend all day staring at a computer screen, she'd still be working at *The Sentinel.* I keep trying to tell her I don't want her to type it herself. I just need her to organize it for me, but you know I never could make that woman do anything she didn't want to do."

"It's all on cards?"

"Index cards," the Rev said. "Not the little ones. The five by sevens."

Wes took a deep breath. "Where are the cards now?"

"I keep them at the house," the Rev said. "Me and your pop just started stacking them in the big closet in my office and after a while, we had to take out everything else just to make room. They're stacked pretty much floor to ceiling."

"The cards?"

"The boxes."

Wes just drove in silence for a minute. Time wasn't a big pressure yet. They had almost a month and a half before this guy was leaving the registrar's office in April, but *damn*. He'd been thinking all he had to do was find a way to get the Rev to copy the disk for him, but of course that would be too easy. He couldn't even imagine how long it would take to type one hundred thousand names into a computer. He needed Toni to get her fine ass on a plane and get down here *ASAP*. She would know how to get it organized, because this wasn't a big problem. This was just some word processing shit. The hard part was already done. He and the Rev had picked up where they left off. All they were talking about now were logistics.

"Let me level with you, Rev. Old-school is fine, and you know I respect what you're doing, but this is the twenty-first century. If you're going to be a major player on the national stage again — and that's where you should be, Rev, we both know it — you have got to step up and show these people you know what you've got and you're not afraid to use it."

"By putting my folks' names on a computer that any fifteen-year-old kid can hack into and sell to the highest bidder?"

"Is that what you're worried about?" Wes said. "Security?"

"I'm not worried," the Rev said calmly, turning on the radio. The DJ was playing Betty Carter and the Rev turned it up. They were getting close to Atlanta. "I'm just enjoying the ride."

Wes was afraid he had pushed too hard, too fast. *Old-school* wasn't just an idea to the Rev. It was a code of conduct. A way of moving through the world that required constant vigilance and maximum control. Of course, his list was stacked in the closet where he could keep an eye on it personally. He knew what the Rev was thinking: *How much safer could it be?* Or was he?

"You know, Wes, a couple of days ago, my estranged wife called to tell me I was a dinosaur," the Rev said.

"Well, my ex-wives have come up with some pretty creative ways to insult me." Wes chuckled sympathetically. "But that's one

I've never heard before."

"She accused me and my whole sorry generation of Negro leaders, her words not mine, of outliving our usefulness. Said we need to go on a retreat and get our shit together. Again, her words, not mine."

"She's sounding more like my exes all the time."

"Well, I don't feel in any way like a dinosaur, but I guess in an age where everything happens in the blink of an eye, an old fool with a closet full of index cards must look a little ridiculous."

Wes relaxed. He obviously hadn't fucked up too badly. The Rev was talking to him man-to-man as they sped down the Georgia highway.

"When I said I could help you, Rev, I didn't know it then, but maybe this is what I meant." Wes stretched out the dino metaphor just a little longer. "Maybe I'm supposed to help you get out of the stone age and bring you into the modern world."

Betty Carter was scatting her ass off and the Rev was unconsciously patting his foot to the beat. "Shoe boxes and all?"

Wes laughed. "Shoe boxes and all."

It was time to close the deal, this phase of it anyway. The part where the Rev agreed to place himself in Wes's capable, almost-like-family hands.

"How about we do this, Rev, my assistant is coming down tomorrow. Let me see if we can put our heads together and come up with some ideas to get things moving."

The Rev seemed to consider Wes's offer as the sign told them they were only twenty miles from Atlanta. When he spoke, his voice was quiet, almost overshadowed by the music. "Can I ask you a question, Wes?"

Wes turned the music down a little. "Go ahead."

"What's in it for you?"

The directness of the question surprised him, but he was ready for it.

"A big part of how I make a living is trading in access and information," Wes said slowly. "Opening an office in my hometown is a lifelong dream, but this is a tough market. Being able to tell potential clients I've got an active list of one hundred thousand Georgia consumers will give me a leg up on any and all competition."

"Consumers or voters?"

"You can decide, Rev," Wes said. "I'm all about consumers because that's my bread and butter, but once we get things squared away so you can access it easily, that list belongs to you. You retain all the rights and you don't have to let anybody use it for anything you don't want. Including me."

The Rev smiled, but didn't turn his head. "All right, then," he said. "Me and your dad will be traveling this week, but Ida B can let you in so you can take a look at the card closet. See what you think. Then when I get back, we'll talk again."

"Good enough," Wes said.

They rode along in silence, each man with his own thoughts and then the Rev spoke up. "What's his name?"

"Whose name?"

"Your assistant. So I can tell Ida B."

"Toni," Wes said. "Toni Cassidy. She's a woman."

The Rev shook his head. "Sorry. My wife would call that a patriarchal assumption."

Wes chuckled at the modern American feminists' well-known propensity for argumentative naming of sexist phenomena.

"Don't worry," he said, merging onto I-20 and heading toward West End. "I won't tell if you don't."

# TWENTY-SIX:
## SUNFLOWERS AND ROSES

The Rev told me not to wait up for him, but of course I did. I had grown up accommodating the Rev's schedule. It was second nature to me and, truthfully, I liked having the house to myself. By the time I saw the car pull up out front, the fire had burned down and I was settled on the couch in what had been one of my favorite daydreaming spots as a kid reading a book Flora had given me. It was called *Along Martin Luther King: Travels on Black America's Main Street*. These two guys, a writer and a photographer, went all over the country for a year, talking to people and taking pictures on some of the six hundred and fifty streets named after Dr. King. The book is a record of what they found. After too many bad jokes by too many black comedians about the need to run for your life if you look up at the street sign and realize you're on one of those six hundred and fifty streets, it was great to see somebody take the whole idea of black America's main street and flip it another way.

I marked my place on the page where an artist who calls himself Franco the Great, the Picasso of Harlem, was explaining how he started painting murals on the metal riot gates that store owners use on 125th Street to secure their properties from thieves. When I went to open the door for the Rev, he was already coming up the front steps. Wes, idling at the curb, tapped the horn in friendly greeting. I threw up a hand as he pulled away.

"Welcome home," I said, kissing the Rev's cheek, and stashing his briefcase next to the hall table while he put away his coat and hat. "How'd it go?"

"It went long," he said. "I think I presented every child in Macon with an award for something."

"Well, I'm sure they deserved it," I said, poking the fire back to half-life. The Rev sat down in his favorite chair, loosened his tie, and sat back with a sigh. "They'll probably remember this day their whole lives. Like when I got that letter from Mayor Young for writing the best essay about Atlanta when I was ten? I still have it."

The Rev smiled at the memory. "Andy

was always good about communicating with constituents. Not as good as Maynard, but pretty good."

As the city's first black mayor, Maynard Jackson would always hold a special place in the hearts of Atlantans who were old enough to split time into before and after his election. As a young pastor, the Rev had worked to send Maynard to the mayor's office all three times, and as far as he was concerned, nobody had ever done the job better.

"Want some cocoa?" I said. "I got marshmallows while I was out today."

"How about a glass of red wine?"

I poured us each a glass and touched his lightly. "What are we toasting, daughter?"

"Us," I said. "You and me sitting by this fire. Isn't that enough?"

"Good enough for me," he said and took a long, grateful swallow of merlot. "How'd the assembly go this morning?"

"You would have loved it," I said. "The principal had Precious Hargrove there to introduce Mr. Eddie and Lu led the garden kids in this great poem about how growing things had changed them . . ."

"Did you have a chance to speak to the senator?"

I hesitated, wondering if this was the time

to pass on her concerns. "I did. She said . . . she was sorry you two hadn't spoken in a while."

"Those Chicago Negroes aren't going to let her speak to me."

"You should call her," I said. "She's got some information about . . ."

He didn't even let me finish. "If she's got something to say, my number hasn't changed."

I steered our conversation back around to Mr. Eddie. "Flora got a proclamation from Mayor Franklin and at the end of the program, they read it out and declared this Edward Harper Day in Atlanta."

The Rev laughed. "Well, ain't that nothin'? I guess I'm going to have to drive *him* down to Albany tomorrow instead of him driving me."

"How'd your second string handle the job today?"

"Wes?" The Rev chuckled and slipped off his shoes, stretching his legs toward the fire, wriggling his toes in their black thick and thins. "I wore that boy out."

"I'll bet you did," I said, picturing the two of them zipping around Macon all day. "You see I had the good sense to stay right here."

"He wants to find me a sponsor."

"A what?"

"A sponsor. He seems to think one of his clients might be willing to make a sizable contribution to BAC-UP! so we can keep our registration drive going."

"In exchange for what?"

The Rev looked at me and nodded. "Good girl. That's exactly what I asked him."

"And?"

"He said anybody doing business in Georgia would see the value of having access to the folks on our mailing list."

Miss Iona's warning whispered in my ear: *I don't think the Rev has any idea how many people would love to get their hands on that new voters list he keeps bragging about.*

"What kind of access?"

He shrugged. "I'm not sure. We've never had a sponsor before. I don't know exactly how it works."

"I do. They underwrite all your expenses and in exchange they put their name on everything."

"Is that such a terrible thing?"

"Depends on what they're selling. Coca-Cola's one thing. Pimp Juice is another."

"Pimp Juice?"

"It's an energy drink, like Red Bull. One of the rappers is backing it."

"Why in the world would they call it that?"

"I have no idea," I said. "It must be a man thing."

"No, daughter." He shook his head. "That's a *fool* thing."

"And a bad example," I said. "I'm sure Wes isn't working for anybody like that."

"If he is, I'll find out soon enough. I told him we could talk more about it again when me and Ed get back from Albany. He's going to bring his assistant by here tomorrow or the next day to take a look at some materials in my office. Let them in, will you?"

Before I could ask him to be a little more specific, he yawned and suddenly I could see how tired he was. I glanced at my watch. It was after midnight and the Black History Month Express was pulling out for South Georgia in the morning. They'd be gone two nights, which gave me plenty of time to see what Wes was up to.

"You better get some rest," I said. "How early is Mr. Eddie coming tomorrow?"

"Too early," the Rev said, finishing up the last of his wine and standing up. The fire was down to coals again. "You sure I can't talk you into riding down with us?"

The miles of open space and empty cotton fields between here and Albany were familiar to me. I had made that trip with the Rev three or four times as a kid and it always felt twice as long as it actually was.

"Not a chance," I said.

"All right, daughter. Don't say I didn't ask. You coming up?"

"In a little while," I said, holding up the book. "I'm reading about black America's main street."

The Rev looked at the title and nodded. "If Flora has her way, all those King streets will be lined with sunflowers and roses."

It was a wonderful image. All those neglected thoroughfares blooming under the loving hands of gardeners who saw the potential for beauty in their own backyards.

The Rev leaned down and kissed my cheek; then he looked at me kind of funny.

"What?" I said, smiling up at him. I was happy for these small moments in the midst of so much motion. This doing something for freedom can be a full-time job if you let it.

"I'd like you to do something for me, daughter."

"Yes?"

"You know Sunday is Founder's Day at Rock of Faith and I'll be preaching my first sermon as pastor emeritus."

"I'm surprised they let you back in there, as bad as you talked about their new pastor,"

I said, teasing him and immediately wishing I hadn't.

The Rev didn't miss a beat. "Pastor Patterson has a forgiving and compassionate heart, daughter. Not only has he invited me into his pulpit, but he has graciously agreed to allow me to pick the person who will introduce me. And that person is you, if you will do me the honor."

And he sort of bowed a little courtly bow, but I couldn't imagine introducing the Rev at Rock of Faith.

"What can I possibly tell them that they don't already know?"

He grinned and headed toward the stairs. "You can tell them something nobody knows but you."

"Oh, yeah? And what's that?"

"Tell them how it feels to be my baby girl."

I laughed and surrendered. "Why didn't I think of that?"

"Good night, daughter."

"Good night, Daddy."

"Don't forget to say your prayers."

# Twenty-Seven:
# A Few Juicy
# Whispers

After the Rev and Mr. Eddie rolled out of here at eight o'clock sharp, I put in a call to Joe Conner, a campaign buddy of mine in D.C. who I hoped could help me get to the bottom of that weird little feeling I had last night when the Rev was telling me about Wes's offer of support, even though Wes is the most apolitical person I've talked to in a long time. I figured it wouldn't hurt to just check it out. Miss Iona was right. This was no time to be careless.

Me and this guy went through three primaries together. After election day, he went back to teaching political science at Georgetown, his Obama campaign experiences told and retold as his favorite stories in a repertoire that also included a tour of duty in Iraq that he never talked about unless other veterans were present, and a nomination for a MacArthur genius grant, which he couldn't stop talking about, although that whole process is so secretive most people don't even know they're under consideration until they get the call.

From his book-crammed office in a quiet corner of the campus, he kept up with a far-flung network of political insiders, obsessive bloggers, and conspiracy theorists of all kinds. His information was usually reliable and he had a lot invested in being able to get to the bottom of the rumors that always swirl around D.C. like autumn leaves. He probably had two or three moles deep in the RNC who could be queried with discretion and confidence. His voice mail answered on the second ring and the message was short and sweet.

"This is Dr. Conner. Leave a message."

"Good morning, Professor," I said. During the campaign I used to call him professor after discovering that we both love that scene in *The Philadelphia Story* where Katharine Hepburn's character is teasing Jimmy Stewart's character, whose name happens to be Conner, by calling him professor because he's a writer. "This is Ida Dunbar. I've got a question that I hope you can answer for me. I'm in Atlanta on some family business and folks down here keep hearing rumors about a move to enlist the help of well-known, but slightly disgruntled Civil

Rights pioneers in discrediting the president. It's making them a little nervous, especially since there are already a few juicy whispers about a major voter purge floating around. So, you know the drill. Find out what you can and call me. Later!"

No way he wouldn't call me as soon as he got the message. In the meantime, I was going to return Flora's book and stop by Miss Iona's to let her know I was on the case.

It wasn't even ten o'clock when I opened the door to the Grower's Association and found myself face-to-face with a poster-size photograph of Barack and Michelle Obama walking down Pennsylvania Avenue just after he got sworn in. He's smiling from big ear to big ear, and she's wearing that amazing chartreuse outfit with those fabulous green leather gloves and they look so happy and healthy and confident and *connected* that it's hard to believe they're heading to their new house in the 1600 block of that same street.

"Is it straight?" Aretha was standing on a chair adjusting the picture according to the dictates of Lu Lumumba and another young woman I didn't know.

"Down a little on that side," Lu said, pointing.

"Left or right?"

"Right," the two girls said at the same time.

Flora was sitting at her computer with a young man who was staring at the screen intently. When the little bell above the door announced my arrival, she looked up and smiled in welcome.

"Hey," she said. "Welcome back!"

"How about now?" Aretha said.

The girls cocked their heads in an identical motion and squinted their eyes.

"Perfect," Lu said, nodding her approval.

"I just love them," her friend said, gazing adoringly at the first couple. "They are so cool."

"You got that right," Aretha said, stepping down. "Too cool for school. How you doing?"

"I'm good," I said.

"Can you hang out for a second?" Flora said. "I won't be long."

"No problem." I took a chair near the seed catalogues.

Lu's friend winked. "I told you it wouldn't take him no time. Cornell is a genius."

"He's a nerd," Lu said, loud enough for Cornell to hear. "ShaRhonda Smith, this is Miss Dunbar."

"Nice to meet you," ShaRhonda said. "She's just jealous because I'm dating a college man."

"A college nerd," Lu said, rolling her eyes.

"I hope you know I can hear you," the boy behind the computer said without taking his eyes off the screen. "And that I know you are just jealous because you couldn't figure this out without my expert advice."

"For which we are always grateful," Flora said, laughing and intently watching what he was doing.

"That's such a great shot," Aretha said, adjusting the portrait slightly. "I wish I'd taken it."

"I wish you had, too," Lu teased her. "Then you'd be famous."

"I'm a legend in my own mind," Aretha said. "And don't you forget it. All right! I'm outta here!"

"We gotta go, too," Lu said. "Mom! Are you going to release the nerd anytime soon or should we go next door and get a cappuccino?"

The boy turned to Flora. "You got it, right?"

She nodded. "I got it."

"Then my work here is done."

The boy stood up then, or should I say unfolded. He was taller than I had guessed and lean without being skinny. He spread his long arms wide and smiled at Sha-

Rhonda. "I'm all yours."

"Not quite so fast, nerd boy," Lu said. "You've got to help me finish my project *first*. Then you and Miss Girl are on your own."

"Well, let's go," ShaRhonda said, taking Cornell's hand. "It takes you forever to do anything."

"That's because I want to do it right," Lu said, reaching for her backpack and blowing her mother a kiss. "We're going over to Tech. Be back in time for dinner."

"Of that I have no doubt. Be careful."

"Call me if you have any problems with that program," Cornell said, grinning and holding the door for the girls. "And don't worry, Mrs. Lumumba. I won't let the other nerds anywhere near them!"

Flora's laugh followed them out the door. "It's a madhouse around here today!"

"They seem like nice kids."

"They're great kids. She's from right outside West End, lots of family drama, so she came to live with us when she was eleven. Cornell is a second-generation computer whiz. His dad works in the registrar's office down at the county and he's a freshman at Tech. He's the one who keeps us up and running. We've been streaming video from the King Peace Gardens Tour and he just figured out how we can do it faster and with a lot better quality."

She smiled and shook her head. "Which is a good thing, but which is probably also adding to the general confusion around here. We've already got more email than we can handle!"

"Then the problem is to find somebody to answer it, not to cut back on the programs that are generating such a big response," I said, laying the book on her desk.

Her eyes widened. "You finished it already?"

"Last night," I said. "I started to call you, but it was after midnight."

"I'm a night owl," she said. "Especially when Hank's in D.C. You can call me anytime."

"Next time I will," I said. "I just wanted to tell you that the King Peace Gardens are a great idea."

Flora beamed. "I think so, too! I told Miss Abbie when she first said it. I've always thought it was terrible that we just let those streets go."

"The whole time I was reading it, I kept picturing all the M. L. King streets I was on during the campaign and almost all of them were horrible."

Flora smiled. "Nothing a few sunflowers

won't cure."

"Exactly," I said. "But since I'm not very good at growing things, here's what I can do for you."

"I'm all ears," she said.

# TWENTY-EIGHT:
# ALL MANNER OF
# MISINFORMATION

"He's hot for it," Wes said, sitting on the plane he'd flown in on less than a week ago, having a quick drink with Oscar, who was passing through on his way to a mission in New York he was being obnoxiously mysterious about. They could have easily met at one of the airport bars, but Oscar didn't want to be seen in the terminal. Something about not being in two places at one time. Arrangements had been made in advance and when Wes arrived, he was driven out to the plane on a golf cart.

The buxom blond flight attendant welcomed him aboard with a twinkle that was probably part of her job description, but Wes didn't have time to flirt.

"Good work," Oscar said, taking a sip of his Coke, the only thing Wes had ever seen him drink. "Sounds like you've got us within a cunt hair of our goal."

Wes smiled. *White boys say cunt,* he

thought. *Niggas say pussy.*

"The good thing is that the model can be replicated," Wes said. "He's already thinking about Detroit, Baltimore, Cleveland."

"You think we can activate a purge in all those places?"

Wes shrugged. "Even where there is no possibility of purging, we'll have a way of communicating all manner of misinformation."

Oscar smiled. "You're still the best."

Wes accepted the compliment, knowing it was his due. He had worked up several mailers for urban populations (read: African American and Latino) aimed at making people afraid to show up at the polls. It wasn't hard. Tell them they'd get picked up for back child support or unpaid traffic tickets and you can clear out a whole precinct.

"How long you figure it will take to actually get your hands on a copy of that disk? Our guy in the registrar's office is getting a little antsy, so time is of the essence."

"We'll have no problem getting it done by your target date," Wes said. "Piece of cake."

"We need to move that up a little if we can."

*There's always one more thing.* "How far up?"

"March first."

"That's less than three weeks from now!"

"Is that going to be a problem?" Oscar said, sounding surprised. "I thought you said we were within a cunt hair."

Wes was beginning to really hate that expression. He wanted to say: *How many times do I have to tell you? Pussy, muthafucker. Niggas say pussy.*

"There is a logistical challenge that may make that difficult."

"Nothing we can't fix, I'm sure."

"There is no disk to copy," Wes said. "There is no master list of any kind. The names — all one hundred thousand of them — are on index cards in shoe boxes, stacked in the Rev's closet."

Oscar looked confused. "What do you mean?"

"What word hung you up?" Wes snapped. He didn't want to rush the Rev. In gaining trust, timing was everything. "These guys don't trust technology so they don't use it."

"Ever?"

"Not if they can help it."

What had the Rev said: *You been in the big city too long.*

"This is insane," Oscar said, looking like he wanted to get up and pace, his best thinking move, but the space was too compact for that. "How can these people do business like this?"

"They're not trying to do business. They're trying to get free, remember?"

Oscar looked at Wes and gave him a tight smile. "Certainly an admirable goal, but what the hell, Wes? Our guy in the registrar's office is really getting antsy. He's so paranoid he sees feds in the trees. We can't afford to let him slip through our fingers because of a bunch of backward preachers."

This was not the time to remind Oscar that these backward preachers had just elected a president. Wes made his voice sound soothing.

"Nothing is slipping through our fingers, okay? This is a logistical problem. He already trusts me to have his best interests at heart. All he's got to do is agree to let me pick up the boxes and we'll get it done."

"How long?"

"Hard to tell until we actually see what we're working with," Wes said. "Do you want me to talk to this guy?"

"That might be a good idea. Just cool him out a little." Another tight smile. "You know, *brother to brother.*"

Wes put his glass down and stood up without smiling back. "What's his name?"

"Estes. Major Estes."

"I'm on it."

# Twenty-Nine:
## Sugar for Sex

Miss Iona called to tell me that Mr. Charles had left that morning to spend two weeks with his daughter by his first wife, who had just delivered his third grandchild, but that wasn't the first thing on Miss Iona's mind when she opened her front door just as I was reaching for the bell.

"Have you heard anything?"

"I left a message for my guy," I said, knowing I'd get my greeting later. "I'm just waiting on him to call me back."

"That's my girl!" She sounded relieved. "Good morning."

"Good morning," I said, pointing at her coat. "Are you coming in or going out?"

"I'm on my way to the market. I'm restocking my refrigerator for two weeks of being a solo act," she said.

"Want some company?"

"I'd love some," she said, stepping outside and turning up her collar like she always did. She was pulling one of those little wire carts that old ladies use to carry their groceries home and she still looked stylish in her red coat and black boots.

"How'd the Rev survive without Ed for one whole day?"

"He did just fine," I said. "I think Wes spent the day making him feel like a rock star."

"The boy is such a little ass kisser. Always was."

"You really don't like him, do you?"

She shrugged. "I don't trust him. Do you?"

I wasn't expecting her to turn the question back to me, so I stumbled a little over my answer. "I don't trust him or not trust him. He just doesn't seem as bad to me as you think he is."

"Suit yourself," she said, looking at me like I was hiding something. "Where are you on your way to?"

"I've been where I'm going," I said. "I was over at the Grower's Association pulling some stuff together for Flora."

"What kind of stuff?"

"Things she'll need to tell whoever replaces her. Everything from history to services offered to job descriptions."

"You're going to help her do all that?"

"It won't take long," I said. "That's what I used to do before the politics. It's mostly just helping her organize her thinking about what comes next."

She looked at me admiringly and I realized she had probably never known exactly what I did before the campaigns. "I like Flora."

"Me, too. What time does Mr. Charles's train get in?"

"Not until eight o'clock. He'll call me." She sighed a little. "I hate to admit it, but the truth is that man has made himself such a permanent place in my days, from the way I eat to what side of the bed I sleep on. Two weeks without him seems like a very long time."

"You're my role model," I said. "Whenever I think I might never find the right one, I think about how long it took for you and Mr. Charles to get together."

She laughed. "That wasn't because I was being picky. He had a wife and I had a beau. We weren't looking for anybody."

Miss Iona's love affair with the late Louis Adams, founding editor of *The Sentinel,* was the stuff of West End legend. She had been a close friend of his beloved wife who died young after giving birth to their son. Out of loyalty to her memory, they never formalized their decades-long union, and to my knowledge, never apologized for it to anyone either.

"Now you're just bragging," I said. "I can't find one good man and you've had two."

"Are you looking?" She sounded surprised.

I was in the habit of thinking I was, but was I? Looking for a job. Looking for a man. That was what women my age were supposed to do, weren't we? The trees were bare and the branches were stark against the bright blue February sky. I hooked my arm through Miss Iona's.

"I think I've given up looking." That was the truth, but it sounded weird to hear it out loud.

"You're too young to give up on anything," she said, patting my arm encouragingly.

"It's just hard to meet any good men," I said, echoing the lament of a whole generation of smart, high-achieving black women. At the corner, we headed down Oglethorpe. The route we were taking was a quieter walk than cutting over to Abernathy, which was fast becoming West End's noisy *up South* version of Harlem's famed 125th Street. It was hard to have a private conversation in the middle of so much sidewalk commerce and vendor sweet talk.

*"Sister, sister, I got lovely incense today! Guaranteed to keep your man at home!"*

*"Sister, sister, I got Obama tees, two for one!"*

On Oglethorpe, you could hear yourself think.

"Good for sex or good for life?" Miss Iona said.

I laughed. "Do I have to choose?"

"Of course you have to choose." She bumped her cart gently over a giant tree root pushing up through the concrete. "Almost nobody is good at both and a pitiful few can lay legitimate claim to either one."

Two fat squirrels chased each other around a big tree and I tried to answer honestly. "I know I'm supposed to say for life, but . . ."

"Truth is the light, girl. If you're looking for a life partner, I'd suggest you go see Abbie. She'll be able to tell you about your past lives and your next lives and whether your true love is headed this way or dawdling somewhere down the cosmic road."

That sounded a little mystical for me. "What if I'm looking for sex?"

"Then I can help you," she said, smiling. "There is just one simple thing you must do to ensure that offers of sex will present themselves faster than you can decide yea or nay."

Just one thing? I thought. What could it be? A Brazilian wax? A huge inheritance? A voice like Mary J. and a body like Beyoncé?

"What is it?"

"All you have to do," she said as we turned left at Peeples Street, "is take a vow of celibacy."

Either Miss Iona was losing her hearing or I had not made myself clear. "I'm already celibate."

She shook her head. "No, sweetie. You're *deprived,* the unfortunate result of forces that are almost always beyond our control. Celibacy, on the other hand, is a conscious choice to close up shop for a while so you can take inventory."

I liked the sound of that. It sounded so industrious. "So making the choice *not* to have sex is going to allow me to have sex?"

"Not *allow* you, but present you with an unexpected option or two."

"Just because I'm not supposed to be interested?"

"Exactly."

That sounded like a strange way to address the situation, but I had nothing to lose. My history with Wes notwithstanding, masturbation can only go so far. What does that Johnny Cash song say: *Flesh and blood needs flesh and blood?*

"How long does it take to work?"

"From my experience, pretty fast. I'd say, within a month."

"You tried this?"

"Right before me and my Charlie got together."

"Can I count the time I've already been . . ." I couldn't bring myself to say *deprived.* "Alone?"

"Sort of like time served?"

I nodded.

"How long has it been?"

"Nothing since election night." And I really shouldn't have counted that one. Anybody who couldn't get laid the night Barack Obama won the presidency just wasn't trying.

Miss Iona thought for a minute. "No, I don't think you can. First of all, if you do, my within a month prediction is immediately shot to hell, and second, because you still haven't made the choice, so the clock isn't even running."

Why was Wes Harper's face floating around in my mind's eye like he was waiting for his cue?

"But if it works and I do have some options presented to me, I'm allowed to change my mind, right?"

She slowed down and looked at me, cocking her head like a bird. "We're not talking about Wes Harper, are we?"

*"I'm not,"* I said, as if he was the furthest thing from my mind.

She didn't believe me for a second. "Well, there's nobody keeping score, sweetie, but I would venture to speculate that if you go into it with the intention of not following through, it probably defeats the whole thing. Changes the energy or something."

I knew she was probably right. Besides, why was I looking for a loophole? There weren't any real prospects remotely on the horizon, unless I counted Wes, which I was not prepared to do. Not in front of Miss Iona anyway. Who knew how deeply she was into the mind-reading portion of her psychic training under the tutelage of the West End visionary amazons?

We turned onto Abernathy and suddenly the smell of Krispy Kremes filled the air with sweetness. In the store window, the famous sign was flashing: "Hot Donuts."

"All right," I said. "For the next month, I'm substituting sugar for sex, starting right now."

She laughed. "I like a woman with the courage of her convictions!"

# Thirty:
# A Fair Shake

The Rev had been acting funny all day. Distracted, irritable, impatient. Mr. Eddie clocked it, but didn't comment until they had finished a late dinner and retired to the Rev's room for a nightcap. At home, they had both resigned themselves to red wine and a beer every now and then, but on the road, they allowed themselves a little more leeway. For those moments, Mr. Eddie always carried a small silver flask with just enough cognac to taste it, but not enough to get themselves into trouble.

The Rev took off his jacket and sat down on the edge of one of the room's two double beds without loosening his tie. Mr. Eddie, who had his own room right next door, poured them each a splash in the paper cups the Best Western provided and pulled out the desk chair. Neither one reached for the remote control, and the room was quiet. They often sat this way, comfortable in each other's silences. Everything couldn't be put into words easy. Sometimes even the Rev needed a minute to find the right ones. Eddie wasn't worried. Words were what the Rev did best. He looked over at his friend and poured himself another shot.

"So what's on your mind, Rev?"

The Rev held his cup out for a refill, too. "I need to tell you something, and you're not going to like it."

Something in the Rev's voice made Mr. Eddie know that what he had suspected but hadn't said to a living soul was true. A father knows his child. He stood up and walked over to the window, pulled back the curtains. The parking lot had filled up quickly, including two Georgia state patrol cars. There was a time when that would have given him pause, but not anymore. He turned back to his oratorically gifted friend who suddenly seemed lost for words.

"It's him, isn't it?"

They didn't know how to lie to each other. After all these years, what was the point?

The Rev nodded. "Yes."

They just looked at each other for a minute and then Mr. Eddie came back and sat down.

"That motherfucker," he said softly, almost as if he was talking to himself. "That motherfucker."

"He's still your son," the Rev said quietly.

Mr. Eddie looked at his friend. "You think it's because I let him go up there with those white folks when he wasn't nothin' but a kid?"

"He wanted to go. You know that."

Of course he knew that. He remembered the night he told them he was leaving.

"Let him go," his wife said. "He's not like us. Let him find his own."

Driving back home from the train station, she took his hand and held it tight like she knew their son was never coming back. But he did come back. Like a thief in the night. Working against his own people. Betraying his own family.

"When it all goes down, are they going to arrest him?"

"I don't know," the Rev said. "We just have to let things run their course. The Justice Department will decide who gets charged with what."

"There's a brother over that, too, isn't there?" Mr. Eddie poured the last of the cognac, wishing he'd brought a bigger flask.

"Yes. Eric Holder is the attorney general."

"Then he'll get a fair shake, I guess."

"He hasn't committed any crimes yet," the Rev said, going over to where his suitcase sat unopened on the luggage rack. He unzipped it, and as if hearing his friend's unspoken request, pulled out a flask of his own. "Maybe he won't go through with it."

Mr. Eddie allowed the Rev to top him off, and felt the beginnings of a buzz. "He'll go through with it."

The Rev didn't argue. They both knew there were only two choices: warn Wes and blow the whole operation or keep quiet and let the chips fall where they may.

"Does Hank know?"

The Rev nodded. "There could be jail time coming out of this, Ed. Nobody can blame you if you need to step away. *He's still your son.*"

Mr. Eddie rolled the cup gently back and forth between his palms. The sweetness of the familiar smell was as comforting as the warmth that was slowly spreading through his veins.

"Remember when Mrs. Hamer came up to Atlanta, sixty-three I think it was?"

The Rev knew he was talking about Fannie Lou Hamer, the fearless civil rights pioneer and founder of The Mississippi Freedom Democratic Party. "I remember."

"She had just gotten out of jail and she didn't want her family to see her 'cause she looked so terrible. She was beat up so bad she couldn't hardly walk. Her face and her arms were still all swollen and there were so many bruises on her I thought she had on some dark stockings, but it was just from where they had abused her so."

The story she told of having to endure brutal beatings at the hands of black male prisoners, who themselves were being threatened with beatings by the white guards if they refused to obey, had brought tears to the eyes of the small group that had come together to offer her whatever support they could.

"I remember," the Rev said softly. "She was a brave woman."

Mr. Eddie nodded. "None braver. I remember speaking to her afterward and telling her I couldn't think of nothin' anybody could do to make me beat her like that, but she wouldn't say a bad word about those men. She said nobody knew the conditions they were livin' in and that they just didn't have no choice."

He swallowed the last of his cognac. "Now, I didn't argue with her. Lord knows I didn't have the right or even the inclination, but I always thought she was wrong about that." He looked up then to meet his friend's eyes. "Everybody always got a choice."

# THIRTY-ONE: DO THE MATH

Toni got in at noon. Wes booked her a room at the Four Seasons and told her to call him from the hotel. She was ordering room service when he arrived and she came to the door with the phone in her hand. She was wearing beautifully cut navy blue pants and a white silk shirt. Her jacket was flung across the bed, but she was still wearing her pumps and a double strand of pearls. She looked good and smelled even better. Anybody who thought a man could work with a woman fine as Toni and not think about fucking her was a faggot or a fool.

"Do you have Pellegrino?" she was saying. "Yes, the big one. And some lime. How long will it be? Fine. Thank you."

She closed the door behind him and put the phone down, wagging a reprimanding finger.

"What?" he said, smiling back. Five minutes to flirt and then they had to get down to business. Oscar was being a hard-ass about time all of a sudden and Wes didn't want any shit.

"I'm here to save the day," she said. "I thought you'd meet me at the gate with an armload of roses and a marriage proposal."

"I told you I'm not a marrying man," he said, giving her a quick kiss on the cheek. But he had to admit, if he was, she would definitely have been in the running for wife number three. "You look great."

"Bullshit," she said. "But I plan to clean up real nice later."

She walked over to the small couch, sat down, and crossed her legs. "Now tell me what's going on."

That's one of the things he liked about this woman. She could tell the difference between work and play time.

"We've got permission to go by and take a look at the Rev's closet tomorrow."

"The closet at his house?"

"That's what he said. Floor to ceiling. Nothing but cards."

"Would it be rude for me to ask him what century he's livin' in?"

"You have to wait until Monday. Right now he's in Albany with my dad."

She wrinkled her nose slightly and did his favorite movie star hair toss. "Is that really a place? It sounds like the fuzz that grows on top of old Chinese takeout."

"Don't be so bourgie. Your folks haven't been in Connecticut that long."

She grinned at him. "Four generations long enough for you?"

Wes let that slide. He wasn't in any position to win the whose family's been free the longest contest. His ancestors probably greeted the news of their emancipation with deep panic. Who was going to look out for them now?

"His daughter's going to let us in so we can get a better idea of what we're up against."

She looked at him. "Why are you tripping on this so hard? It's time-consuming, sure, but otherwise it's nothing but data input. Straight up typing, okay?"

"How long you figure it will take?"

She shrugged. "Can't say until we actually see the cards. Are they written in pen or pencil?"

"What the hell difference does it make?"

"Pencil is a lot harder to read, especially if these are old people. They don't press down hard enough."

Out the window, he could see traffic snaking down 14th Street. There was a siren in the distance, getting closer. He sighed. "I don't know what they're written in, okay? All I know is Oscar's all up in my ass about getting everything done by the first of March instead of the first of April."

"That still gives us a little more than two weeks, right? Hand me a piece of paper." ·

Wes passed her a legal pad and a pen. She started scribbling numbers. "Okay. Let's say we get twenty girls."

"Twenty girls from where?"

"From a reputable secretarial service. Where do you think? We're not transcribing military secrets, Wes. It's not illegal."

"Go on."

"Twenty girls and one hundred thousand cards. That's five thousand cards per girl. Let's say they work eight hours a day, give or take . . ."

Wes took that to mean Toni would allow them a few minutes for lunch. She scribbled a little more.

"They could probably do five hundred a day easy." She drew a line and turned the scribbles in his direction triumphantly. "We should be able to have it all done in ten days, leaving you plenty of time to meet your deadline even if some of the typists are a little slow."

He was impressed. Sometimes Toni's fineness made him forget how good she was at her job. She could, of course, be counted upon to remind him. He felt his stress level receding.

"What if we get more girls?"

"More girls, more cards per hour. Do the math, Einstein."

"So how long will it take you to put together the secretarial pool?"

"I'll line it up this afternoon."

"Get a price on round-the-clock security while the cards are in our possession, too, will you?"

"Nice touch, boss," she said, made another quick note and tossed the legal pad aside. "Feel better?"

"I'm getting there."

"Good," she said. "Now can we have sex?"

Before he could answer, there was a light tap on the door. *"Room service."*

He grinned at her and stood up. "No time, babe. I'm having drinks with Oscar's contact in the registrar's office. I'll call you later."

"My offer to christen your boyhood rec room is still good," she said, standing up, too.

"We don't have a rec room, remember?"

"There was something else I wanted to tell you," she said, reaching for the door.

"What's that?" He could smell her burger through the door and realized he was hungry, too.

"Oscar offered me a job," Toni said, opening the door to the young waiter who was holding her lunch aloft on a big silver tray. She smiled and stepped aside.

"What job is that?"

"Spying on you," she said, watching the waiter putting down her meal carefully.

"Did you take it?" he said as she reached for the check, added a generous tip, and scrawled her signature.

"I'm here, aren't I?"

# Thirty-Two: The Heart of Darkness

I was studying the Grower's website when Joe Conner called me back from D.C. So far, I'd counted five full-time jobs under Flora's personal umbrella along with several others she farms out to her dedicated cadre of volunteers. Unlike most of the nonprofits I've ever worked for, WEGA doesn't have a budget problem. They have an organizational problem. If all I did for Flora was write up each job description separately so she could see exactly what she was up against, that would be a good start.

"Professor," I said. "How goes it in the academic world? You keeping current?"

"I could ask you the same question, my far-flung friend." He laughed. "You are woefully out of the loop."

"Which is the reason I'm calling you," I said. "Enlighten me."

"Well, there might be something to the purging voters thing, but that targeting the icons plot is yesterday's news. Political urban legend."

"Where there's smoke, there's usually fire," I said. "You don't think there's any truth to it at all?"

"Not a scrap. It came up about a month ago, right after the inauguration, and I checked it out all the way back to the heart of darkness."

That's what we always called the Republican National Committee.

"I came up with nothing, nada, zip, zilch. It only sounded plausible for its fifteen minutes because nobody could believe the way these brothers kept going off on Barack. Andy Young said he wasn't as black as Bill Clinton, Jesse Jackson wanted to cut his balls off, and Jeremiah Wright almost did."

He chuckled, although how that could ever be amusing is a mystery to me.

"Black folks would rather believe it was part of an evil Republican plot instead of a bunch of angry, egotistical old men without a new battle plan."

He had reduced the lives of three courageous, if recently somewhat confused, race men to four scornful words: angry, egotistical, old men. He had also dismissed the idea of an ongoing race-based plot as naïve. They deserved better, and so did I.

"Well, I'm going to be down here until Monday," I said. "If you hear anything else, let me know."

"Sure, kid, but this Obama train is picking up speed. You need to get back up here as fast as you can."

*Kid?*

"Take care, Professor."

But as I hung up the phone I knew that what I needed was a new contact.

# Thirty-Three:
## The Good Old Days

When they pulled into Moultrie a few minutes early for the mayor's prayer breakfast, their route to City Hall took them right past the church where the Rev was scheduled to speak later that evening. To publicize his appearance, they had hoisted a large hand-lettered sign written in bright red on what looked like a king-size bedsheet. "See Living Black History Before It's Too Late!!! Rev. Horace A. Dunbar, Tonight Only, 8 P.M."

It was the three exclamation points that elicited the first smile of the day from Mr. Eddie. After their discussion last night, it had been a quiet morning. The Rev knew his friend needed time to think. He also knew there was no appropriate advice to give, so he didn't offer any. Instead, he put in a Shirley Caesar CD and let her call in the spirit on Ed's behalf.

"Stranger on the road,
The road seems long . . ."

The sheet flapped gently in the wind as Mr. Eddie slowed to a stop at the sign.

"They must figure you not going to be around much longer," he said.

"How you figure that?"

"*Before it's too late.* What do *you* think it means?"

"Maybe it means before I decide there might be better ways for me to use my time than trying to get these Negroes to make something out of themselves."

"Like what?"

"Like writing a book."

"A book about what?"

"About my life."

Mr. Eddie turned the corner and headed for City Hall. "How you gonna write about it when you still livin' it?"

"Lots of people write about their own lives," the Rev said. "None of them waited until they died."

Mr. Eddie didn't say anything for a minute then he frowned slightly. "So that's what we're going to do? Sit around Paschal's with a bunch of guys talking about the good old days?"

At the other end of the parking lot, closest

to the entrance, the Rev watched two large women in elaborate church hats emerge carefully from their immaculate sky blue Fleetwood. He knew where they were going. To have breakfast with some living, breathing black history, *before it's too late.*

"Maybe that's just what we ought to do," the Rev said, sounding suddenly weary.

Mr. Eddie eased the big Lincoln into a space marked *reserved* as per their instructions from the mayor's staff, and turned off the car. "Well," he said slowly, "I ain't gotta figure nothin' out. Once we get this month done, I'm gonna put this car in the shop for its annual checkup and get my gardens ready for spring planting. Then I'm gonna see if I can get Iona to give me the recipe for her peach cobbler and beat Charlie at checkers until I get tired. I might even go down to Tybee and see what they got new on the menu at Sweet Abbie's. I might go visit my boy."

When he mentioned Wes, his voice was steady, but his eyes held all the questions he couldn't answer.

"Then when you figure out that all we're supposed to be doing is exactly what we been doin', you call me, and I'll check the tires, get my suit pressed, and show up at the designated hour to take you where you need to go."

The Rev didn't know which he admired more in his friend, his calm or his clarity. "Just like always?"

Mr. Eddie took out the keys and reached for his hat on the backseat. "Nothin' changes but the changes."

# Thirty-Four:
# Two Grown Men
# Doing Business

Hotel bars are the site of such a dizzying variety of rendezvous, assignations, meetings, trysts, dates, liaisons, and all manner of affairs, conducted by all manner of people just passing through, that it was difficult to surprise the bored-looking bartender, but Major Estes managed it the minute he appeared in the small, dark paneled room and looked around. He was wearing a long dark overcoat, a black hat pulled down low, and sunglasses. He didn't step in so much as he sidled, glancing around furtively, looking for all the world like a cartoon spy on an impossible mission.

Wes briefly considered pretending not to be himself and leaving the fool to fend for himself, but he hadn't made the choice so he couldn't override it now. It was still early and the place hadn't filled up yet with travelers seeking happy hour, but too weary, or too wary, to venture outside the hotel's protected confines. There was one couple at a corner table with a laptop set up between them, talking quietly, and one man alone, working his BlackBerry and sipping a gin and tonic between texts.

Wes raised his hand without waving it and Major scurried over, but didn't sit down. The bartender stayed where he was, waiting for this strange new arrival to light somewhere before offering him a libation. The waitress was late so he was filling in. Reluctantly.

"Are you Harper?"

Wes looked at him. "Why don't you sit down, Mr. Estes? Take off your coat."

The man repeated the question. His voice a little more insistent. "Are you Harper?"

"Why the hell else do you think I was waving at you?" Wes said calmly.

Satisfied, Major slid into the chair across from Wes. The bartender headed their way, slowly, but Major made no move to remove his coat and hat. Wes sighed. This cloak-and-dagger shit was getting on his nerves already. When he had volunteered to try to cool this guy out, he had no idea he was a complete nut job. Oscar was slipping.

"Can I bring you something, sir?"

Major shook his head. "No. Nothing. Thank you."

"He'll have a beer," Wes said, smiling the way people do when a member of their party is acting weird to let the stranger or the server know that the person is harmless. "Heineken."

The bartender went to get it and Major frowned behind his sunglasses. "If I had wanted a beer, I would have ordered one."

Wes looked at the man and suddenly wanted to kick his ass. Then he wanted to go find Oscar and kick his ass. *Twice.*

"You look ridiculous," he said quietly. "We are two grown men doing business. That's all. No matter what you think, or what anybody told you, that's all."

He paused to let his words sink in as the bartender brought the beer and retreated. "You've got some questions and I'm here to help you figure out some answers. That's what I do, so relax. Whatever's wrong, I can fix it."

The man leaned forward, his eyes still hidden behind those Nicole Richie shades. Wes wondered if he'd filched them from his wife.

"That's what they always say," Major hissed at Wes, "and then somebody ends up going to jail."

The smell of fear was rolling off this guy in waves.

"What are you talking about?"

"I told Mr. Thames, and I'm telling you. I can't do time."

Major's voice rose slightly and the man with the BlackBerry glanced their way briefly. Wes realized he had to get control of the situation or risk this guy having a public meltdown right there in the hotel bar.

"Listen to me, Mr. Estes," Wes said firmly, "I understand your concern, but you are going to have to get hold of yourself."

"I'm not . . ."

Wes held up his hand and the man stopped in mid-sentence. "The first thing you are going to have to do," Wes said and it was an order not a request, "is to take off all that spy shit and drink your beer like you've got some goddam sense so we can figure out how to make you feel better. Do you understand me?"

The man didn't blink. Wes didn't either.

"Or you can take your ass on home and call those guys at the casino to tell them why you still can't pay back what you owe."

The man just sat there for a minute then he stood up and took off his coat and hat and laid them on the empty chair. When he sat back down, he slid the sunglasses off, folded them slowly, and slipped them into his breast pocket. When he looked up at Wes, his eyes were haunted and sad. Wes pushed the beer closer and Major took a long swallow.

"I used to be lucky," he said, quietly. "Then something happened. I couldn't catch a break no matter what I did. So I started borrowing from these guys and now they're hassling me, and my kid needs tuition . . . you know how much it costs to send a kid to Georgia Tech?"

Wes didn't know and didn't care. This guy's troubles were beyond banal. All he had to do was throw some money at them and Major Estes would be his friend for life.

"That's why this operation is as important to you as it is to us," Wes said, soothingly. "And that's why the first thing you have to do is calm down."

Major took another long swallow of beer. "I can't go to jail."

"Mr. Estes, nobody's going to jail," Wes said.

"Call me Major."

When Oscar had first told him the guy's name, Wes thought he was a military man, but that wasn't the case. The man was simply one of those unfortunate black folks saddled with a name chosen to trick white people into having to address a black man with a title of respect because it was his Christian name. There were lots of them:

*General, Mister, Junior, Major.*

Wes smiled. "Look, Major, all you have to do is exactly what you've been doing. Have you had any problems so far?"

He shook his head.

"Then what makes you think you're going to have any problems now?"

"My supervisor's secretary," he said. "Me and her ride the same casino bus to Biloxi once in a while and she told me that the feds have been asking questions."

"Did she say what kinds of questions?"

"She didn't know, but she said they were there twice."

"In how long?"

"Couple of weeks."

This was definitely not a good sign. The new Justice Department had a significant interest in protecting voting rights, especially the voting rights of citizens who would most likely vote Democratic. He'd let Oscar know, but at the moment, job one was cooling out this skittish civilian who was playing politics at a level where the stakes were almost as high as gambling with gangsters. Maybe higher.

He motioned the bartender for another round. "Okay, here's the deal, Major. As I see it, you got two problems. One is a political problem, which means I'll handle it. The other is a financial problem, which means . . ." Here he stopped and smiled at Major like they were old friends. "I'll handle it."

Major looked confused. Their drinks arrived and Wes waited until they were alone again. For somebody who didn't want a drink, Major was sure knocking back the brews.

"We both know that when we pull this shit off — and we will pull it off, I can promise you that," Wes said, exuding confidence, "these white folks are going to hand both of us a sizable piece of compensation for our services."

He had now introduced two powerful elements into their discussion: racial solidarity (any reference to "white folks" harkens back to a brotherhood as old as slavery), and money (the universal sweetener).

Major rose to the bait. "What do you mean, you'll handle it?"

"I mean our boys in D.C. will make the Justice Department find someplace else to stick their noses so there's no chance of them looking over your shoulder and you can be about the business at hand."

Major looked hopeful, but not convinced. "You can make that happen?"

"There hasn't been time for this new

crowd to replace everybody yet. It works from the top down and we're ahead of the curve."

Major nodded slowly. Washington politics were a mystery to him. When the friend of a friend had first come to him four or five years ago to see if he might be of assistance, he couldn't remember even asking what party the guy was in. His kid was getting ready to start college and times were tight. Accidentally wiping some voters off the rolls only meant there would be a lot of confusion on election day and then they'd just have to register again. Seemed to Major that was no big deal. It wasn't like it was still a death-defying act or anything. Besides, he needed the money. He still did.

"What about the other?"

Wes didn't blink. "How much do you need to buy yourself some breathing room?"

Major wasn't quite sure what that meant, but he liked the sound of it. "Breathing room?"

Wes nodded. "This whole operation will be over soon and you can take care of everything once and for all, but I mean, just to kind of cool things out for a minute, catch up a little so the guys aren't leaning on you so hard."

When Wes had called him out of the blue

to set up this meeting, Major had hoped this would be one of the outcomes. If he could get five thousand dollars in his hand, he could relax a little, stop looking over his shoulder all the time.

"Five grand?" It was a question, but he whispered it like a prayer.

Wes reached in his pocket and pulled out an envelope, his judgment vindicated again, as if he needed any further proof that he knew what the fuck he was doing. He slid it halfway across the table toward Major and stopped, tapped it with his finger. "I've got ten in this envelope."

Major's eyes widened like a kid who wakes up on his birthday and sees a pony in the backyard with a big red bow around its neck.

"It's not part of any arrangement you have with Oscar. It's because you're a vital member of this team and I can't afford to let you fuck everything up because you're distracted about a couple of dollars."

Major's eyes flickered down to the envelope. If he could have figured out how, he would have picked it up, stuffed it in his pocket, and made a run for it before Wes changed his mind, but he wasn't that fast or that crazy.

"I won't fuck it up," he said softly, scared

to say more. "I'm cool."

Major Estes was many things, Wes thought; bad gambler, loving if distracted father, computer genius, but cool was nowhere on the list.

"Because if you do fuck anything up," Wes said, his smile nowhere in sight now, "jail will be the least of what you'll have to worry about. Do you understand me?"

Major nodded, although he didn't really have a clue. "Yes."

"Good." Wes slid the envelope across the table and stood up. This meeting was over. "Take care of the check, will you?"

Major restrained an impulse to withdraw the bills and fan them out like a winning hand, but even he knew better. Time for that later.

"Yes," he said. "I will."

Wes rewarded him with one last smile. "Don't forget to leave a tip."

# THIRTY-FIVE:
# A SISTER IN
# TRANSITION

The Rev and Mr. Eddie had checked in from South Georgia, and my next appointment with Flora wasn't until tomorrow night. I had called Miss Iona to tell her my D.C. contact had said we didn't need to worry about the plot, as she was heading out to her book club meeting. She had invited me to join them for their Black History Month discussion of *The Hemings of Monticello,* by that black woman lawyer who confirmed once and for all that Thomas Jefferson had a complex, long-term, sexual relationship with one of his slaves, Sally Hemings, without ever freeing her.

"And she's got the DNA to prove it," Miss Iona said, which only conjured up a picture of the author striding up to the front door of Monticello, holding up a little vial of DNA, and demanding an explanation and an apology, not necessarily in that order. Tempting as it sounded to spend another evening trying to figure out the strange workings of wealthy white men's minds, I declined.

"Suit yourself," she said, leaving me officially on my own. I decided to try the new burger joint that people kept telling me about. It was just a few blocks away, so I grabbed my coat and headed over there. I could see the flicker of the evening's cop shows or medical dramas at the houses where nobody had shut the drapes yet. It's a mystery to me why people are drawn to shows featuring sex crimes and terminal diseases, but to each her own. I missed the Rev's company on my ramble, but walking alone gave me time to try to sort out some things in my head.

Even though I wasn't sure I could trust Joe Conner's easy dismissal of the anti-icon plot, I knew he was right on the money about the loop. Things always move fast in Washington political circles, but with the twenty-four-hour news cycle, it's gotten ridiculous. A day is a week and a week is a lifetime. The longer I was away, the less I could claim to have the most accurate reading of those two most critical constituencies: the people and the press.

On the other hand, if I could come up with a good reason to be spending time here, something not connected to the Rev, or having to go to any kind of rehab, it could be a plus. Consulting with Precious Hargrove, for example, would be a perfectly respectable reason to leave town for a minute. Precious was a rising star in national Democratic politics. Helping her get elected wouldn't be like being in exile. It would be like being in the vanguard. But working with Precious meant coming back to West End just in time to meet my mother at the airport and get sucked back into the latest saga of the reluctant soul mates and that was not an option.

I could see the neon sign for Brandi's Burgers & More on the front of what used to be Montre's, a notorious West End strip club that claimed to be the first to offer a five-dollar lap dance. Those days were long gone now. Someone had given the place a complete makeover, and nothing remained of the past except a small stage and the new owner, Brandi herself, who had once been a featured dancer here in the bad old days. She greeted me, fully clothed, and took me to a table near the tiny stage.

"This is our karaoke night," she said, handing me a menu and an extensive list of songs I could choose from should the spirit move me. I smiled back and shook my head.

"Not me, but thanks."

"I heard that," she said. "I don't do it either, but these fools love it. Soup tonight is Chef's Choice vegetable. American beer is two for one until the music starts."

I wondered if her spotlight on American beer reflected patriotism or the preferences of her regulars.

"I'll take a Beck's," I said.

"Coming up."

I was amazed at how good the place looked. Not that I ever saw the inside of it before. Strip clubs were never my cup of tea, even when a lot of my girlfriends started going just for a hoot. No way I wanted to tuck a dollar bill into the G-string of a woman who was probably just trying to feed her kids. There were tables up front, booths in the back, and lots of framed photos of Atlanta's music business luminaries, many signed to Brandi herself, and some of which included her standing beside them, grinning like a Cheshire cat.

I wondered how she had made the transition from her old life to her new one. However she had done it, she seemed to be thriving, which is, of course, all I wanted to do: *thrive.* The question was, *where.* If it wasn't D.C., where was my place? I needed a sign. Something to push me in the right direction. I didn't think that I was asking too much. After all, this was West End, home to mystical women from Abbie to Iona. Seemed like the least the sisterhood could do during my moment of transition.

I opened the menu and turned to the offerings of every kind of burger you could think of, including veggie burger, turkey burger, and a four-pound beef behemoth that you got free if you could finish it in an hour. Health food or heart attack, at Brandi's, it was your choice. I had just about decided on a classic cheeseburger, when I glanced up and saw Wes Harper walk in the door. *Did somebody order a sign?*

# THIRTY-SIX: SECOND-GENERATION BALLBUSTER

He couldn't believe he had left his briefcase at his father's house. Trying to wrap his mind around that closet full of cards and get a handle on Major Estes's spy versus spy act had distracted him. Wes Harper was not a man who forgot things. A firm believer in a place for everything and everything in its place, he had once broken up with a woman because he loaned her his car and she lost the keys.

He hadn't even missed the damn briefcase until he went back up to his suite after he left Estes and realized it wasn't there. He had been working on a proposal for another client last night after his father went to bed and when he closed his eyes, he could see his Coach case, sitting there in his boyhood room, looking sleek, expensive, and out of place, like a Maserati in the Kmart parking lot.

He intended to spend the night in midtown, but he still had a few things to finish up on that proposal, not being a man to put all his eggs in one basket, so he decided to drive across town, pick it up, and get back in time to give Toni some very special room service. He cruised past the Rev's house, half hoping to run into Ida to confirm their appointment for tomorrow, but the place was dark and nobody seemed to be around. Then he turned onto Abernathy and saw a woman he was almost certain was her disappearing into something called Brandi's Burgers & More. On a whim, he circled the block, pulled into the lot, and stepped inside. Even if it wasn't her, he hadn't eaten all day and his stomach growled loudly.

She was sitting alone at a table near the tiny stage, studying the menu like it was a practice test for the SATs. She looked smaller than she had the other night and softer. The hostess, who looked somehow familiar, greeted him pleasantly, but before she could offer him a table, Ida looked up and smiled in his direction. He smiled back and she waved him over.

"Hey," he said. "Small world."

"Smaller than that," she said. "If you promise not to sing, you can join me."

"I beg your pardon?"

"Karaoke night," said the smiling hostess,

304

handing him a menu and the night's playlist. "You say it, we play it. American beer two for one until the music starts."

"Jack Daniel's," he said. "On the rocks."

"Coming up."

Wes took off his coat, pulled out a chair, and looked around slowly, trying to remember. "Didn't this place used to be a strip joint?"

She nodded. "Montre's, home of the five-dollar lap dance."

"That's where I've seen her before," he said, looking in the direction of where Brandi was pouring his drink. "She used to be a dancer."

"So you've been here before?" Her voice was suddenly icy.

*Oh, hell,* he thought. "No, not here," he said quickly. "Of course I drove by it, but I saw her dancing at a bachelor party a couple of years ago. A buddy of mine from back in the day. She was good, too," he added admiringly.

Brandi sent a waitress over to bring the drinks and take their food order. They both opted for the traditional cheeseburger. He took the fries and Ida got the onion rings, but the whole time he could tell she was waiting to jump on his ass for saying he'd seen Brandi doing her thing. He saved her the trouble of having to bring it up.

"I hope I didn't make you uncomfortable," he said, wondering why he felt the need to explain. "Nothing happened. We never had sex or anything."

She raised her eyebrows. "It's none of my business if you had."

He sipped his drink and smiled. This was just what he needed. A little verbal jousting with a second-generation ballbuster. Next to lying, it was his favorite kind of foreplay.

"I just meant," he said in a tone he hoped sounded conciliatory, but not obsequious — feminists can smell fear — "if we had a mutual friend who was a hell of a basketball player and you'd never seen his jump shot, I would probably mention that, too."

"Why?"

She wasn't going to make this easy, but he was up to the task. "Because when somebody is excellent at something, whatever that something might be, attention must be paid."

"Even dancing naked on a silver pole?"

He counted that as a point for his side. She'd said the word "naked," always a step in the right direction. "You ever try it?"

"Not that I can recall. Have you?"

He wished she was drinking something stronger than beer. He smiled a little wider.

"No, but I'm sure it's harder than it looks."

"It looks impossible."

"Well, there you go," he said. "Our hostess is the best I've ever seen at a seemingly impossible task. I think a well-deserved shout-out is perfectly in order."

"She's not the hostess. She's the owner."

*Okay, hard-ass,* he thought. *Here's a little obsequious, just for you.* "Which means in addition to her dancing abilities, she must also be a hell of a businesswoman."

And he raised his glass, a risky move because what if she didn't raise hers. But she did. *Bingo!*

# Thirty-Seven:
# A Post-Campaign
# Wave of Paranoia

There was no denying he was charming as hell and what he said kind of made sense. *Kind of,* but it was an asshole's argument and we both knew it.

"What exactly are we toasting?" I said.

"How about my willingness to totally change the subject if you'll just give me a second to pull my foot out of my mouth and offer my sincere apologies for being a big, fat chauvinist pig."

I clinked my glass against his and grinned. How long had it been since I had heard anybody except my mom and her girls even use the words "chauvinist pig"? "I'll drink to that," I said, and I did.

He did, too. "Your mother would probably have thrown me out the door."

"You remember my mother?"

He shook his head. "It's not so much that I remember her growing up. My first wife was a big fan. In fact, it was after one of your mother's lectures at NYU that she found the courage to leave me."

"That must have been during her *monogamy is the death of love* phase. I'm sorry."

His smile never wavered. "Don't be. I wasn't very good at marriage or monogamy."

I've never understood the guys who think it's appealing to tell you what a failure they've been with the other women they've had sex with. Who wants to be in that number?

"Is that why you tried it again?" I said. "See if you could get it right?"

"Something like that," he said.

"How'd that work out for you?"

He laughed. "Not so hot. I think two's my limit."

"Well, you know what they say."

"What's that?"

"Three's the charm."

He laughed. "I'll keep that in mind."

"You do that."

"I'm glad I ran into you," he said. "Did the Rev tell you I'm coming by tomorrow to take a look at his cards?"

"What cards?" The Rev had said *materials*. That was all I knew.

"The cards he's got stacked in the closet."

I must have looked as confused as I felt.

"The Rev told me you and your assistant were coming by, but he didn't say anything about cards in a closet."

He sat back, surprised. "You've never seen them?"

"I don't know what you're talking about."

He took a swallow of his drink and folded his arms on the table. "When your dad registered all those people to vote, in addition to the official application, he had them fill out an index card with their name, address, precinct, and anything else they wanted to say on it."

"To say about what?"

"The historic moment, voting for the first time, whatever."

That sounded like the Rev. Always trying to translate and transcribe that intangible moment when people first decide to stand up. "Go on."

"Well, they'd give their application to the registrar and the Rev would keep the other card for himself. By the time they were done, he had one hundred thousand cards with new voters' names on them."

It was dawning on me that this was the mailing list. The same one that had come between me and the Rev just a few months ago. Was Wes telling me that the well-guarded, much bragged about list was still a handwritten hodgepodge of index cards stacked in an office closet? I couldn't help but smile. All the time we were arguing over what he should or shouldn't do with it, it never crossed my mind that first it would have to be typed.

"My dad put the *old* in *old-school*," I said. "Are those the *materials* you're coming to look at tomorrow?"

He nodded, smiling in a way that could only be described as rueful. "I'm hoping he'll agree to let me organize the list for him. Put it in some kind of useful form."

There was that little prickle again. "Useful to who?"

"To him, first of all, and then to whoever he decides to share it with."

"Including you?"

The place was starting to fill up. I wondered if it was the burgers or the coming karaoke.

"Absolutely including me," he said. "Look, I don't do the kind of courageous work your father does or help make history like you just did. I market barbeque sauce and potato chips, soft drinks and the occasional malt liquor, which is not to say I don't have some principles. I just turned down a campaign for a casket maker who was looking to crack the inner city market, no pun intended, because I'm not a ghoul, no matter what you've heard."

I wondered where he thought I would have heard that, but I just kept listening.

"However, in addition to my other fine qualities, I would love to be able to tell my clients I could give them statewide, targeted exposure for their goods and services. In my business, a hit like that is worth a lot. I can help the Rev come into the twenty-first century and he can help me sell all the canned collard greens Moultrie, Georgia, can stand."

I had never tasted canned collard greens and hoped I never would, but I got the drift. His motivations were clear: One hand washes the other. Nothing more nefarious than good old-fashioned capitalism. Maybe Miss Iona and I were just riding a post-campaign wave of paranoia that saw enemies around every corner. Maybe he wasn't a villain at all, but a good godson come to help the Rev regain his footing and come back strong. Even I knew that no politician can resist a mailing list like that, or the genius who gathered the names in the first place.

"Well, I'll tell you this," I said, as the waitress emerged from the kitchen and headed our way bearing burgers and a mountain of fried sides. "That list isn't going to do anybody any good where it is. If you can help him get it together, you have my blessings."

"Good enough," he said, as the food's arrival took precedence over any further conversation. "Help yourself to the fries."

Which, of course, I did.

# THIRTY-EIGHT: ME AND MRS. JONES

They were both hungry and the burgers were as good as everybody said they were. Now that they had settled on a time for tomorrow's visit, Wes was free to enjoy the evening and he ordered another round of drinks as the waitress whisked away their empty plates. Toni wasn't going anywhere and things were moving along so well with Ida, he ventured a stroll down memory lane.

"Do you have any growing up memories of me?"

She sipped her beer. "As a kid, you mean?"

"Yeah. I guess we saw each other a lot, our parents were back and forth all the time and your house is right around the corner, but I can't call up a memory of us together."

"I was only eight when you got that scholarship to Exeter," she said. "You were twelve. Practically a grown man."

"To hear me tell it, a full-grown man."

She smiled. "I caught you making out on

314

your back porch once," she said.

"Making out?"

"Right there in broad daylight."

He laughed. "With who?"

"I didn't know her, but it was right before you went away. I was cutting through your yard as a shortcut, I knew your dad wouldn't mind, and you were sitting on the back porch swing with this girl."

"What were we doing?" He was loving the way this conversation was going.

"I told you, making out."

"Can you be more specific?"

She shook her head and he would have sworn she blushed a little. "The usual, I assume. I wasn't trying to commit it to memory. I was on my way to a Brownie Scout meeting."

"Now, I should remember you in a little Brownie uniform."

Brandi was directing a couple of guys about how to set up for the karaoke. Wes smiled to himself; she was still in show business.

"You know what I actually remember most about you?"

"What's that?" he said.

"How much you hated being here."

The absolute truth of what she said took him aback. Had it been that obvious? Even at twelve? Before he could confirm her observation, or lie and deny it, Brandi took center stage and called for their attention.

"All right, y'all! You ready to show me what you got?"

The crowd, gathered at every available table as well as clustered two deep at the bar, yelled in one voice. *"Yes!"*

"Okay, then here's how we do it. You come up here and give your selection to Deejay Do Right over here."

A short, muscular young man sporting a head full of dreads and one arm full of tattoos, waved his non-inked hand at the crowd, who chanted his name in affectionate greeting. "Do Right! Do Right! Do Right!"

"He'll hook you up with your lyrics and then it's on you!"

More applause. Brandi held up her hand for quiet. "Now, those of you who been here before know we got a tradition here at Brandi's. We ain't been here but a minute, but a tradition gotta start somewhere, right?"

"Damn right!" somebody called out from near the bar.

Brandi frowned slightly, but never stopped smiling. "Watch your language there, brother. This is a family place now!"

Laughter and some good-natured shouts of "That's right!" echoed around the room.

Satisfied, Brandi turned toward Wes and Ida B still sitting near the stage finishing their drinks. "The tradition is, whoever is in the first seat, at the first table, gotta do the first number." She held the mic toward Wes. "That's you, baby!"

The crowd laughed and applauded. Ida B grinned at him and shrugged like it was out of her hands. On the stage, Brandi was twinkling at him with an *I dare you* smile and he wondered suddenly if she remembered him, too.

"Come on, brother! Show us what you got!"

He grinned at Ida B. "Well, at least this will give you a more current memory to draw on!"

Then he stood up very slowly and pushed back his chair dramatically to the delight of the crowd.

"Go 'head, brother! Do yo' thang!"

He walked over to Deejay Do Right, made his selection, and accepted the mic from Brandi, who moved over to watch from the edge of the stage. It had been years since he'd done anything like this, but he thought he could still pull it off. Too late now if he couldn't. The tiny light that in the old days had probably shone on hundreds of bouncing brown breasts was now shining on him. And there was his cue, the first few unmistakable bars of the R&B infidelity classic "Me and Mrs. Jones." The crowd, recognizing his selection, roared their approval. As he stepped forward, he saw Ida B laughing and clapping, too. He gave her a wink and hit it.

*"Me and Mrs. Jones, we got a thing goin' on . . ."*

# THIRTY-NINE:
# CONSIDERING THE
# QUESTIONS

"I can't believe you did that," I said, still laughing, as we headed outside. Wes had offered to give me a ride and I accepted. I was so amazed by his karaoke performance, I welcomed a chance to compliment him as we drove the few blocks home.

Wes grinned. "I wouldn't have done it if I wasn't good at it."

Good doesn't begin to describe it. He had a great voice and very sexy stage presence. He was no Blue Hamilton, of course, the standard against which we West Enders measure every R&B singer, amateur or professional, but he was head and shoulders above anybody I'd ever seen in a karaoke bar and the crowd loved him.

"I'm surprised your fans let you get away with just one song," I said, enjoying that golden moment known to all groupies of snagging the lead singer.

"That's the key," he said. "Always leave

them wanting more."

The streets were pretty empty. It was too cold and breezy to be out strolling around. Everybody was hunkered down somewhere for the night. Everybody except us.

"I'm glad we had a chance to talk," he said, when he pulled up in front of the Rev's house and put his rental car in park.

"Me, too," I said, wondering if I should ask him in or take his advice and leave him wanting more. Neither of us said anything for a minute, but the air was clearly charged.

He smiled. "Why does this feel like high school all of a sudden?"

I laughed, relieved that he felt it, too. Wondering if there was a possible post-karaoke exception clause in my celibacy oath. "It does, doesn't it?"

He turned toward me as fully as he could and leaned in just a little. "Yeah, except that if it was high school, I'd be trying to talk you out of a good-night kiss."

"Except that I don't kiss on a first date," I said. *Like fun I don't.*

"But it wasn't technically a first date since we didn't actually *plan* it."

I nodded, as if considering the questions. "You're right. Nobody asked anybody to meet anywhere."

"Exactly, it was just a fortunate coincidence, which means your reputation remains above reproach."

"Good," I said, enjoying the game, anticipating the smooch. "A girl can't be too careful."

And as I closed my eyes and leaned in to seal the deal, his cell phone rang. The first few bars of the *Mission: Impossible* theme. We both froze, opened our eyes, waited. The ball was in his court. He shrugged apologetically, reached for his phone, glanced at the caller ID, and said the words I surely did not want to hear at that moment.

"I need to take this."

# FORTY:
# ROCKET SCIENCE

"What the fuck do you mean next week?" Wes said as he watched Ida B open her front door and disappear inside. *Damn!* Toni was still a sure thing, but new pussy was always welcome. Oscar's timing was lousy. "I just talked to the guy!"

"Obviously you didn't talk hard enough."

"I handed him ten grand to cool the fuck out and wait for instructions. Is that hard enough for you?"

"Well, he said if we can't give him the disk on Monday so he can run it that night, he's out."

*"Monday?"*

"That's what he said. Somebody from the supervisor's office called him when he got home, one of his gambling buddies or something. Totally spooked him."

Wes pulled away from the curb. Any hope of wrapping this up and then seeing if he might still collect on that kiss was out the window.

"So now he's all freaked out worse than he was before. He says it's got to be Monday or no-go."

"What I'm saying is it's not doable, Oscar. It's flat out not doable."

There was silence on the other end of the line. Wes waited. *Monday!* That was only five days from now. How the fuck was he supposed to make that happen? He was good, but he wasn't a miracle worker.

"Listen, Wes." Oscar's voice was quiet, but firm. "We need this to happen."

He remembered that old joke about the Lone Ranger turning to his faithful sidekick in a moment of peril and saying, "We're going to die, old friend. We're surrounded by hostile Indians." And Tonto saying, "What you mean *we,* white man?"

"There's still a lot of finger-pointing going on, you know that," Oscar said when Wes remained silent. "Everybody's playing the blame game and nobody's in charge. Steele is a joke and Limbaugh is out of control. If we can make this happen — you and me — if we can put Georgia solidly back in our column for 2010 and 2012, nobody's going to forget that, Wes. Most of all, I'll really owe you one, buddy. I'll owe you one big-time."

Wes turned into the driveway of his father's house. The motion-activated security lights flooded the yard and he squinted in spite of himself, feeling suddenly exposed. Oscar needed this *personally,* he thought. That's why he was begging so hard. He'd heard a rumor around the campfire that Oscar had been slipping. From the desperate sound in his voice, Wes could only guess that Oscar was within *a cunt hair* of being shown the door.

Wes sighed loud enough for Oscar to hear him, like he was resigned to helping, but not enthusiastic about it. "What am I supposed to do? This guy's list is still in a stack of shoe boxes in his closet. He hasn't even given me permission to move them, much less make copies."

"This isn't rocket science, Wes. What the fuck do we always do when somebody's got something we want and they don't want to give it up?"

It was a rhetorical question. "We go get it."

"Exactly."

# FORTY-ONE:
## FREEDOM HIGH

Wes's phone call had saved me from indulging a moment of weakness and I was grateful. What was I planning to do anyway? Climb in the backseat? Sneak him up to my baby girl room and hope the Rev didn't decide to come home early? Exactly the kind of bad decision from which the celibacy oath was supposed to protect me. I thanked the goddess for her electronic intervention, hung up my coat, and went to take a look at the Rev's stash.

I turned on the overhead light, opened the closet door, and there it was: *the list.* Thousands of cards in boxes, stacked up neatly from floor to ceiling, waiting patiently to be called into service by the man who had collected them. Wes had said they supposedly had the usual information and then a space for personal reflections. Unable to resist taking a look at what people might have written, I pulled out a box that wasn't wedged in too tight, lifted off the top, and pulled out the first card.

*Mattie Jenkins,* it said, *Madison, Georgia.* No phone or email listed, but under comments, she had written. *I am seventy-two years old and have never voted for president before. I sure do hope he wins.*

That made me smile. I replaced it and pulled out the next one.

*Mrs. Hugh Barnett,* it said, *Albany, Georgia.* No phone or email on this one either. Her comment was: *Come together, black people! Yes, we can!*

I pulled out two or three more and they were all so hopeful and determined, it made me remember how people would come in the headquarters, asking what they could do to help, offering time or money or homemade chocolate chip cookies. Then I looked at all those boxes and I thought about all the hard work and love and faith that had gone into getting all those people to register. I thought about how great it feels to be *freedom high* and how hard it is to keep that feeling going when things get crazy and I thought about how long the Rev had been getting up every morning, rain or shine, doing what needed to be done. I thought about how much I owed him for it.

Even if he did miss a birthday party or

two, and even if he was stubborn and defiantly *old-school.* Even if it was sometimes hard to get a word in edgewise. The Rev had given me and all of us a gift that no one could ever take away, *our freedom.* That's when I knew I didn't have to write a big long elaborate introduction for Founder's Day. All I had to do was say two words on behalf of everybody who would be there: *Thank you.*

# FORTY-TWO:
## HEART AND SOUL

Wes and his assistant weren't due at the Rev's until late that afternoon since I had promised Flora I'd come by her house this morning so we could talk "off site." That's just fancy *consultant speak* for getting the subject of the interview out of their everyday work space for a few hours, which theoretically frees up their mind and allows them to see the long-term possibilities more clearly. I actually did my meditation, ate some Cheerios and the last banana, checked to make sure the downstairs bathroom was ready for company, and headed on over to Flora's.

She lived about five or six blocks from us on Queen Street, but West End blocks are short so it only took me about ten minutes to get there, as the crow flies, but of course I *rambled.* I stopped at the West End News for two cappuccinos and when I came out, Aretha blew her horn at me in greeting as she headed down Abernathy in her bright red truck. Across the street at the grocery store, folks were already taking advantage of Wet Wednesday, when all seafood was half price.

I love walking through West End. It's about the only place I know where things only change for the better. Too bad there's no way to clone Blue Hamilton and send him to inner city communities from coast to coast to replicate the model. The problem is, some models can't be replicated. Some models require such a specific set of skills or such a specific group of people or a specific visionary at the helm, that as hard as you try, it's not possible to grow it anywhere else.

I think West End is like that. Newark, Chicago, St. Louis, Detroit, New Orleans, and Oakland will have to come up with their own way of figuring out how to get control of the men and renew the hope of the women and make these kids act like they got some sense. In the meantime, it was good to know there was still one place where you could ramble any hour of the day or night without looking over your shoulder.

When I balanced our two cappuccinos in one hand and rang Flora's front doorbell, I couldn't hear the sound it made because someone was playing *The Sound of Music* so loud I could hear it standing on the front porch. A lifelong movie musical fan, I recognized the scene where the lovely governess, Maria, comforts her charges during a thunderstorm by sharing a few of her favorite things. My mother loved the song. So did the Rev, although he was partial to the John Coltrane version, not the one Julie Andrews made famous.

Flora opened the door and hurried to turn down the DVD. The Von Trapp children continued to pile into Maria's big featherbed, but now we couldn't hear their voices or their seven-part harmony. "Come in! Come in! Is it ten o'clock already?"

"On the nose," I said, handing her a cappuccino. "Didn't know if you'd already had your coffee."

"Bless you," she said, taking my coat. "I didn't even go by there this morning because I knew I'd find myself at the office and once I'm in, I can never seem to get out."

"That's why I thought we should meet over here," I said, taking a seat on the couch.

"Well, I'm glad you did." She took the rocking chair next to a large basket of bright orange and yellow yarn with two giant knitting needles sticking out of it. "My favorite chair," she said, reading my mind, but her voice cracked just a little. "Good grief," she said, raising her cup to her lips and taking a small sip.

"I've been weepy all morning. My hormones are all over the place. I keep trying to get a jump on the packing, but everything makes me sentimental, so I stop to catch up on a little housework and then I start worrying about Lu graduating high school and dating and I wonder if I've told her everything she needs to know."

"Don't worry about that," I said. "My mother told me more than anyone had a right to know and I'm still clueless."

Flora smiled. "I'm going to be a basket case on moving day. I can see it now."

"You'll be fine," I said. "D.C. is an amazing place. Especially in the circles you're going to be running in."

"I know, I know," she said, not sounding like she knew anything of the sort. "It's just that we've had such a great life here. All our friends, the gardens . . ." And she teared up again. "Here I go! Don't tell Lu!"

I had come with a bunch of questions for Flora, but they could wait. She was in the midst of a big life transition, just like I was, and sometimes business just had to wait. Flora reached in her pocket for a Kleenex and blew her nose.

"You ever consider commuting?"

Flora shook her head. "No way. I had enough of that mess when me and Lu were here and Hank was going back and forth to Detroit for a year and a half. It drove me nuts."

Clearly, she was one of that small percentage of very lucky women in this world who are crazy about their husbands.

"Besides," she said, with a shaky smile, "I've heard there are some predatory sisters up there in our nation's capital and a good man is hard to find."

"You got that right," I said. "I told Miss Iona yesterday I was getting tired of looking."

"I know what I've got and I love Hank to death," she said. "I guess the thing is, sometimes it just seems like such a *retro* position to be in. This is the only job I've ever been passionate about and I'm chucking it in to follow my husband to a city I don't even like. *No offense.*"

"None taken," I said.

"I'll bet your mother would read me the feminist riot act."

Funny how my mother keeps coming up as the standard of political correctness, but

I didn't want Flora to be too hard on herself.

"The truth is," I said, "my mother is in no position to talk. She's getting ready to take a job at Spelman and move right into the Rev's backyard, so what kind of example is she setting?"

"A great one." Flora laughed.

"Well, I wish them the best," I said, "but I'm glad I won't be around for the fireworks."

She looked at me and put down her cup. "Does that mean there's absolutely no way I could talk you into taking over the Grower's Association when I leave?"

The Von Trapp children, under clear skies, were now romping in the Alps, presumably singing their asses off.

"What are you talking about?"

"It's perfect," she said, and I realized the idea had not just occurred to her. "You could do this job with one hand tied behind your back."

"That's not the point. I'm not moving back here, I just —"

She interrupted me gently. "I know, but I'm just saying *if* you end up . . . staying for a while. This wouldn't even have to be full time. I know Precious Hargrove could use somebody with your expertise and you could spend some time with your parents, too."

She was on a roll, so I didn't point out that the parents thing wasn't her strongest selling point.

"These gardens are the heart and soul of West End," she said, "and you never have to raise a dime for operating expenses. We don't even have a board!" She stopped suddenly then grinned at me sheepishly. "No pressure or anything."

I smiled back. "Listen, Flora, I love West End as much as you do, and I know what an amazing job all of you have done rescuing this one small community, but that's not the only work that needs to be done. We have to rescue the whole country! And maybe it's crazy to love living out of a suitcase and flying all over the place talking to people I've never seen before and never will again, but I did love it, because I could see the difference it makes when people all come together to do something for themselves. I could see it, just like the Rev could see Atlanta as a city too busy to hate, and Dr. King could see that beloved community he used to talk about, and Blue Hamilton could see West End as a peaceful oasis."

"And our new president can see a new America?" she said gently.

"It's all changing," I said, wondering if she had a Kleenex I could borrow, since all of a sudden, I was feeling a little sentimental, too. "And I want to be part of that more than I ever wanted to be part of anything so that when I get old, I can look around and see the changes and say, *Yeah, I helped make that happen.*"

We just sat there for a minute. I think I was talking to myself as much as I was talking to Flora.

"Well," she said finally, "I think you can stop worrying about looking for that real good man."

"Why is that?"

"You just fell in love with your country, girlfriend, and nobody can compete with that."

# FORTY-THREE: TARGETING THE WARRIORS

Flora and I sat there for another two hours. We watched the rest of the movie and talked a little bit about the Grower's Association, but mostly we just sang along with the Von Trapp kids and watched Maria blush in the arms of the handsome, but emotionally wounded Captain Von Trapp, thereby melting his heart and ending forever her earlier ambitions to enter a convent. Neither of us could do much more than carry a tune, but we sang along at the top of our lungs anyway. I figure if you can't sing off-key when the Nazis are coming, when the hell can you?

I told her we'd make another appointment to talk business and as I headed down her front walk and turned back toward home, I was really happy she was coming to D.C.

Whatever direction work or love took us, I knew we would be friends. I had turned off my phone so Flora and I could do our interview uninterrupted and hadn't bothered to turn it back on, but I reached into my pocket now to see if the Rev had checked in from the road. He hadn't, and no word from anybody in D.C., but there were three messages from Miss Iona. I didn't even listen to them. I just punched in her number.

She picked up on the first ring. "What is the point of having a cell phone if you never turn it on?"

"What's wrong?"

"It's him."

"What's him?"

"Didn't you tell me that Wes Harper offered to set your father up with a tour sponsor?"

"He said his clients would love that kind of exposure."

"I'll bet they would," she snapped. "I'll just bet they would."

This was getting us nowhere. "Please slow down and tell me what's going on."

"My reporter at *The Sentinel* said that program he told me about where they're targeting the warriors?"

I loved that she called them *the warriors*. I loved that she thought of them that way.

"What about it?" I said.

"It's full steam ahead," she said, "and in

this first wave, they are rolling out the big guns to woo these guys. Book contracts, radio shows, and, are you listening? *Tour sponsorships!*"

My stomach did a little flip when she said that, just like it did when the Rev first told me Wes was interested in the list, just like it did last night when I was at Brandi's with Wes and he was talking about how he could *help* the Rev.

"I'm on my way."

# FORTY-FOUR: THE MATTER AT HAND

"This political shit is wreaking havoc with my sex life," Toni said when they pulled up in front of the Rev's neat Victorian. After he talked to Oscar last night, sex had been the last thing on Wes's mind and Toni didn't appreciate it. "I like it better when we're just figuring out how to sell more barbeque pork rinds."

"Doesn't pay as well," Wes said, looking around the front yard and the driveway like he'd never seen them before.

The Rev's house, complete with the elaborate gingerbread molding that gave the West End Victorians their distinct character, was set farther back from the street than its neighbors on either side. The Rev had never been one for West End's fanatical gardens, so he had picked the house for its rolling front lawn, not because it had space enough in the back to grow two rows of collards, two or three of tomatoes, and maybe some

339

sweet corn.

The narrow driveway meandered along the side of the house and deposited visitors at a brick walkway up to the big front door with the stained glass window. Another brick path from the street ensured that no one ever had to walk on the Rev's perfectly manicured front lawn, which, even in mid-February, was almost impossibly green and neatly clipped. Sometimes people actually stopped walking by and reached out to touch it to be sure it was real.

"Do you think he dyes it?" Toni said.

"His hair?"

"His grass."

"Who gives a fuck?" Wes said, wishing she would focus on the matter at hand.

Toni narrowed her eyes. "Politics isn't doing much for your disposition either."

"See what I was telling you last night?" he said. "If you drive the van right up there, nobody's even going to notice it."

"It won't matter if they do," Toni said, flipping open the mirror on the visor in front of her seat and checking to be sure there was no lipstick on her teeth. "Who's going to question a van from the New Orleans Children's Relief Fund?"

He turned to her. "What?"

Satisfied that she was as lovely as she

remembered herself to be, Toni smiled at Wes so he'd remember it, too.

"Two magnetic signs. One for each side of the van. They'll be ready tomorrow morning."

"New Orleans Children's Relief Fund?"

"Pretty good, huh?"

"You're going to hell, you know that?"

"I love you, too," she said. "Now let's go case this joint."

# FORTY-FIVE:
## INVISIBLE HORNS

Miss Iona and I were in the Rev's office getting her settled in at the computer when that awful sound that passes as the Rev's front doorbell blasted us both half out of our skins.

"Showtime," I said. "You ready?"

"Hardest thing for me is going to be not telling him all about his sorry self the minute he walks in that door."

"That's not the plan," I said quickly, hoping Miss Iona would stick with our hastily drawn scenario and not *go rogue* on me à la a certain Alaskan governor who shall remain nameless.

"All we're trying to do is buy some time until I can convince the Rev that we're on to something and get him away from Wes long enough to bust the folks at the top."

"I know, I know," she said, restacking the pile of cards we'd staged next to the Rev's rarely used computer. "Go on and let them in before they ring that awful bell again. My nerves can't stand it."

Mine couldn't either. We hadn't been able to get the Rev or Mr. Eddie on the phone, which meant we were left to our own devices as far as dealing with Wes, who I had only recently considered breaking my chastity vow for and now wanted to turn over to the Justice Department as fast as I could find their number. Except we didn't have enough proof yet. Miss Iona's guy was working on it, but these guys were pros. So far, no hard evidence had shown up and nobody would go on the record for fear of reprisals. What we needed now was to protect the Rev and his shiny new voters while we gave Wes enough rope to hang himself.

Wes and his assistant smiled and greeted me in unison when I opened the door. "Good afternoon."

They looked like a corporate diversity ad in *Black Enterprise* magazine — smart, stylish, *amoral*. I added the *amoral* part. Or they did.

"Good afternoon," I said. "Please come in."

She was younger than I expected and prettier than I hoped she'd be, even though it didn't matter anymore since no way I was sleeping with a man like Wes Harper. He was as attractive as he'd been last night, except now I could see the invisible horns growing out of his head.

"Ida Dunbar, Toni Cassidy."

"My pleasure," I said, extending a hand. "I'm sorry my father isn't here to greet you. He's in South Georgia until tomorrow."

"Moultrie, right?" she said, with a little condescending smile.

"South Georgia."

"Wes told me his father often travels with Reverend Dunbar."

"Two old road dogs," Wes said like it was an affectionate joke we shared. "The schedule they keep would kill most men twenty years younger."

Toni was looking at the pictures hanging in the hallway. The Rev and Dr. King sharing a laugh. The Rev and Nelson Mandela on an Atlanta stage with their fists raised in solidarity. The Rev and Mayor Jackson on the night of the first inauguration. The Rev and Julian Bond outside the Georgia Capitol when they refused to seat Julian because of his opposition to the Vietnam war. The Rev and Mr. Eddie as much younger men, on either side of Mrs. Fannie Lou Hamer.

"It must have been amazing to grow up like this," Toni said.

"It was."

She turned toward me, the *Black Enterprise* smile still in place. "I'm surprised there're no pictures of your mother."

"Do you know my mother?" I said, surprised at the question.

"We read her book in my Women's Studies class at Barnard," she said. "I think that's when I became a feminist."

"My parents are separated," I said. "She lives in San Francisco."

"Oh, I'm sorry." And she actually looked like she was for a minute. "But to tell you the truth, I never understood how she could have been married in the first place. Your mother was one angry woman."

Sensing dangerous conversational waters, Wes jumped in quickly. "Shall we get down to business and take a look at what we came to see?"

"Of course," I said, leading them down the hallway to the Rev's book-crammed office. "Follow me."

Miss Iona had closed the door to the office, already improvising, and when I opened it, she was sitting at the computer, peering over her glasses at an index card. She looked up and shook her head, annoyed. "Can you read this, Ida B? Is it *Corrina* or *Calinda?* I swear these people need to just go on and make an *X* like they used to and be done with it."

"I think it's *Calinda*," I said, handing the well-smudged card back and turning to our guests.

"Miss Iona Williams, meet Toni Cassidy. Wes Harper, I think you already know."

"Of course I know Wes Harper," Miss Iona said, looking at Wes with a tight smile. "Been knowing him since he was born practically."

"How you doin', Miss Iona?" He rounded his accent to reflect his southern roots like that would make her more comfortable.

"I'm doin' just fine, Wes. How about you?"

"Can't complain," he said.

Miss Iona turned to Toni. "Is that your job?"

"Ma'am?"

"The complaining?"

Toni smiled and shook her head. "No, ma'am. My job is to solve people's problems."

"Then you're right on time," Miss Iona said, handing the card to Toni. "Is it *Corrina* or *Calinda?*"

Toni squinted at the card just like I had, but had no more definitive answer. "Corrina?"

"Is that one of the cards?" Wes said, reaching for it, but Miss Iona snatched it back first. Startled, Wes drew back his hand.

"What else would it be?"

I shot her a look and jumped in. "One of many," I said, crossing to the Rev's closet and pulling open the door to reveal the neatly stacked boxes taking every inch of available space. The one box that Miss Iona was ostensibly working on had left the only opening when we slid it out carefully to complete our charade. The sight of all that very raw, and very valuable, data seemed to render Wes and Toni temporarily speechless.

Miss Iona was happy to fill the void. "The man's crazy. When he first showed me all these cards and started talking about me typing them up into some kind of master list, I said, are you crazy? And he said, Iona, you're the only one I trust to do it. And I said, I ain't studyin' you, Horace Dunbar. My days of typing up mailing lists for men who can't be bothered are over."

Toni and Wes walked slowly over to the closet. They still couldn't believe it, but there they were, all two hundred boxes, neatly labeled with the date they joined in the stack, waiting patiently for processing.

"He wanted you to type all these up?" Toni said.

"He didn't *want* me to; he *expected* me

to," Miss Iona said. "That's the way the Rev is."

"All by yourself?" Wes said, reaching out to run his hand over the stack closest to him.

"Of course all by myself. That's the whole point. The Rev won't hardly let anybody even look at these cards. I think you're the first ones other than me and Eddie. Ida B hadn't even laid eyes on them until yesterday."

"And not a moment too soon." Toni turned from the cards back to Miss Iona. "We'll get some guys in here to load up everything and I'll take it from there."

"The Rev didn't say anything to me about moving them," I said calmly. "It's my understanding that he wants the cards to stay here. For security reasons."

Toni looked at me. "So how do you propose we get it done?"

"Don't worry," Miss Iona said. "I've had a change of heart. Call it a Black History Month miracle, but I've decided to take on the task myself, as per the Rev's expectations."

"Miss Iona, if you'll forgive me . . ."

"Don't have much choice really," she said. "Ida B isn't much of a typist on her best day."

She was laying it on thick and they were getting more confused by the minute. Wes smiled at Miss Iona again, totally unaware that his charms had no effect on her at all. "Do you have any idea how long that will take you?"

She shrugged as if the question were beside the point. "I have no idea. As long as I'm done in time enough for Precious Hargrove to use it when she gets ready to run for governor, I'm good to go."

"That's two years from now!" Wes looked shocked.

Miss Iona actually patted his hand reassuringly. "It shouldn't take me any longer than that."

Toni looked at Wes and raised her eyebrows like *you've got to be kidding*. He turned to me.

"I thought we were on the same page about this," he said, chiding me gently.

"It's not my choice," I said. "What happens to these cards — where and when and how — is up to the Rev. I thought *you* understood that," I chided him right back.

"I'm going with the first initial only," Miss Iona said, squinting at the *Corrina/Calinda* card again as she typed it into the computer and reached for another.

Wes's smile was less sincere, but he offered it anyway. "You're right, of course. It's clearly something I should take up with the Rev."

Recognizing an exit line when she heard one, Toni tucked her purse under her arm.

"He'll be back tomorrow," I said, like I was being helpful. "But he's preaching at Rock of Faith on Sunday, so he probably won't be available until Monday."

That would give us time enough to make our case and get the Rev back on the good foot.

"You got that right." Miss Iona nodded in agreement. "Don't nobody disturb that man when he's getting ready for Founder's Day, even if they are *almost* family." She underlined that *almost* with her voice.

"Monday it is then," Wes said.

"I'll be here," Miss Iona said brightly, the sound of her tap-tapping receding behind us as I showed them to the door.

# FORTY-SIX:
# THE SMALLER THE
# CREW, THE SAFER
# THE SECRET

"See what I mean about people writing in pencil?" Toni said as they left West End and headed back to midtown. "You can go blind trying to read that shit."

"Nobody's asking you to read it," Wes said. "How many guys you think we'll need to get the damn things out of there?"

"Wouldn't it be easier to just call the man and try to talk him into letting us come and get them?"

"You heard them! He can't be disturbed until Monday. That's too late. I told you what Oscar said. We've got to do it Sunday when they're all in church."

"All right," she said. "Get me one guy. The smaller the crew, the safer the secret. You got anybody in mind?"

"Yeah, I do," he said, reaching for his cell phone and punching in a very recent number. "Estes? I need to talk to your son."

# Forty-Seven: Home From the Wars

I had convinced Miss Iona that it might be easier if I talked to the Rev alone and she reluctantly agreed. She made me promise to call her as soon as I could and helped me fix the Rev a dinner fit for a king. She was a firm believer that the way to a man's heart is through his stomach and even though I reminded her that we were aiming at the brain, she said it couldn't hurt.

After we got it all done, I set the kitchen table for two since he'd know something was up for sure if I tried to get him to eat in the dining room, and went to get the card I'd bought at the CVS that afternoon when I realized Saturday was Valentine's Day. It was a kid card, something an eight-year-old would sign and seal with a kiss, which was probably appropriate since I felt like an eight-year-old. The closer it came to the Rev's estimated time of arrival, the more nervous I got. The last and only time I'd tried to question my father's judgment was a disaster. He wasn't used to it, least of all when it came to how he handled his business. I was his child and even though I had carved out a niche where my opinions were sought and my skills were valued and people who knew about such things bandied around the idea that I might be invited to work at the White House one day, in the Rev's eyes, I was still his baby girl. It was outside the realm of his possibility that we could exchange ideas with something of value being offered from both sides. His role was to teach and lead and my role was to follow. But not this time. There was too much at stake, for him and for me.

My grandmother told me a story once about how she and her father were crossing the tracks in their old Model-T Ford and her father, who had lost an eye in a hunting accident years before, didn't see the train backing up in their direction. My grandmother, who was about six or seven years old at the time, saw it bearing down on them, but didn't want to embarrass her father by implying he hadn't seen it first and removed them from the danger, so she said nothing.

My grandmother would laugh when she told this story because the train was going so slowly it just pushed them gently a few hundred yards down the track. The car was slightly damaged, but they walked home just fine. My mother, of course, saw this as a story about how little girls are trained from birth to protect the male ego, even at the cost of their own lives.

The hard thing about this conversation wasn't going to be telling the Rev there was a nefarious plot heading his way from the twisted minds huddled in the heart of darkness. He already understood that kind of evil. He'd spent his life fighting it. The hard thing was that this time he didn't see the train coming. This time he wasn't the one providing the protection. He was the one who needed protecting. And maybe that was because he was getting older and wasn't quite as sharp as he used to be, or maybe it was because they sent his godson to bring the bait and as the Rev likes to say, *when the brother holds the door for the murderer, the deed is unstoppable.*

But maybe it was just that as much as we want to make the Rev and Martin and Malcolm and Mandela all perfect, godlike creatures, deigning to walk the earth in human form in order to lead us mere mortals to the mountaintop, they are only men, fully and completely as human and as flawed as any of the rest of us. The quality that makes them different is that they can look at us and where other folks only see a bunch of wild, scary, defeated, disheartened, disorganized people, they see what we might look like if we would stand up once and for all and take responsibility for being the free men and women all people are born to be. They see the best of us even when we can't and their words paint such a vivid picture that for just a moment, *we get it, we feel it, we see it,* and somewhere deep, deep down, we know that *we can be it.*

The saddest thing to me about the whole Jeremiah Wright episode was that he is one of those who has always been able to see how beautiful we are. He's spent his life holding up that mirror and one day, to even his surprise, one of his parishioners saw a president looking back, but now all we remember is the incendiary ten-second sound bites and the ignominy of his appearance at the Press Club. I wasn't going to let that happen to the Rev. My father needed for me to speak to him as a grown woman and make him listen. Otherwise, I might as well pull up a chair at the children's table and sit on down.

I signed the card "all my love," and then heard the front door open and the Rev's voice booming out a greeting.

"Where are you, daughter? I'm home from the wars!"

In the kitchen, nervous despite my self-pep talk, I tucked the card in my mother's apron pocket and reached in the refrigerator for a bottle of cold white wine, poured two glasses, and met him in the hallway as he shuffled through the mail I had left lying on the key table.

"Welcome back," I said. "Were we victorious?"

He kissed my cheek and accepted a glass of Chablis. "Close enough. Something smells awfully good in here."

"Dinner in fifteen minutes," I said.

"Well, isn't this an unexpected pleasure." He took a swallow of wine and grimaced slightly. "Why can't they make a wine that tastes like a bourbon? Somebody could make a fortune!"

"I'll work on it."

"It's a deal," he said, laying his phone down beside the mail and heading upstairs. "In the meantime, let me go wash up and we'll see what damage you've been doing in my kitchen."

"I think you'll be pleasantly surprised," I said, taking a sip of the wine that was just fine being exactly what it was. Then his phone rang.

"Get that for me, will you?" The Rev turned halfway up. "Wes has been trying to catch up with me all day. I don't want to miss him again."

I froze. Of course Wes had tried to call him. He wanted to ask about the cards. About the process. About the deal. About the crazy old lady who said she's going to type them all by herself. *As per your instructions, Rev.*

"I'll take a message," I said. I wasn't ready yet. I hadn't had a chance to fortify myself and follow Miss Iona's advice about the way to the Rev's heart yet.

He looked at me. "You haven't even looked at the caller ID. What if it's not him?"

The phone was still chirping in that annoyingly insistent, electronic way. "I'll take a message."

"Hand me the phone, daughter. It's easier to just answer it myself." He started back down.

I looked at the phone then and Wes's number was definitely the one showing: Harper, W. E., and a 212 area code.

"It's him," I said. What could I do? I answered it. "Hey," I said.

The Rev waited for me to greet Wes and hand him the phone. "It's Ida."

"Oh, hey," he said. "I've been trying to get hold of your dad all day. Is he . . ."

"Just walked in the door," I said. "Can he call you right back?"

"Sure," Wes said, as the Rev reached for the phone. "No problem. I'll see him at service on Sunday."

"I'll tell him you called." And I snapped the phone shut and dropped it into my mom's apron pocket right next to the pink envelope with the Valentine card in it.

The Rev looked at me like I had lost my mind and I swallowed hard. His frown was a thundercloud. "Didn't you hear what I said?"

"I'm sorry, Rev," I said. I hadn't intended to tell him standing in the hall like this, but it was too late now. "Before you talk to Wes, I have to tell you something."

"I'm listening, daughter."

"Can we sit down for a minute?"

"I'm fine right here."

"There's no easy way to tell you this," I said, putting down my glass. "Wes Harper is part of a scheme to target black leaders who have been critical of the president and encourage them to work against him."

His frown deepened. "Has Iona been filling your head with this mess?"

"It's true, Daddy," I said, surprised I

hadn't called him *Rev.* "You're one of the first ones they're reaching out to because . . ."

"Because of what?"

There was no turning back. If he was going to help, he had to know where he stood *right now.* Not as an icon, but as a man making decisions every day that he had to be judged on. "Because of the Jeremiah Wright stuff. Because of those things you said on YouTube about the enemy of your enemy. Because they think you're open to being used against him because your feelings are hurt. Because . . ."

"Enough!" The Rev's voice cut through my babbling. He walked into the living room and set his glass down on the coffee table. I followed him. He just stood there with his back to me for a minute, then he turned around and every word stood alone and accusatory. "Because they hurt my feelings?"

I wished I could take it back or figure out a way to say it better, but I couldn't. "Yes."

"Just exactly when, daughter, did you wake up and decide that you know more than I know?"

I didn't answer. How could I?

"Or should I say, when did you *and Iona* wake up and decide I needed the two of you to help me avoid the traps white folks set for *bad niggas* like me who never take low?"

"Daddy, I . . ."

He didn't even slow down. "When did you two start figuring you could spot a turncoat or a traitor faster than I can? When did you decide you could protect me from danger better than Ed Harper could after he's risked his life for me more times than I can count?"

"When we realized it was his son!" I blurted before I could stop the words coming out of my mouth.

The Rev looked at me like I had thrown my wine in his face, although I had left my glass in the hallway. "Have you told Wes any of this nonsense?"

"No," I said. "I wanted to talk to you first."

"Well, now you've talked to me," he said. "And I hope this will be the end of it."

And he headed for the stairs.

"It won't be," I said, desperate now to make him listen to me. "That's why they want your list!"

He stopped with his hand on the banister and looked at me. "This is unacceptable, daughter. My cards, and my people, are my responsibility, not yours. When I need your advice and counsel concerning any decision

I make, you may rest assured I will not hesitate to ask for it. But until I do, and as long as you are in this house, you will abide by my wishes."

His voice was low and terrible. I couldn't remember my father ever speaking to me that way. "Do you understand me?"

I had done the best I could. It was time for me to go. Back to D.C. Back to my own life. You can't save a person who doesn't want to be saved. It was like Mr. Eddie always told the new gardeners: *Everybody's got to kill their own snakes.*

"I understand," I said, hating the tremble I heard in my own voice.

As I watched him go on upstairs, I realized there was no way I could sit across from him at dinner and pretend everything was okay. The pictures, the plaques, the proclamations. The Rev's lives, past, present, and future were smothering me. For the first time, I knew how my mother must have felt, but this wasn't just some tired old man being conned out of his personal nest egg. *This was the Rev.* His weakness left us all vulnerable.

I slipped the apron over my head and reached for my jacket, but I felt the Rev's phone in my pocket right beside my little pink Valentine. I laid them both beside his plate, turned the oven down to warm, and left.

# FORTY-EIGHT:
# THERE ARE ALWAYS
# CONSEQUENCES

I don't think I consciously headed for Flora's house, but when I found myself standing in front of it, I wasn't surprised. My hands were still shaking and it didn't have anything to do with the cold. My attempt to protect my father from a clear and present danger had not only failed miserably, it had driven us even further apart than we were before I came down here. Even worse, without the Rev's help, the dirty tricksters were free to pursue all manner of voter suppression in those little Georgia towns where people were just beginning to exercise their full citizenship without fear of reprisals. Why couldn't the Rev see what I was talking about? There he was, a race man, a fearless warrior, reduced by his ego to being a part of the problem when he had been such an important part of the solution. There had to be a way to make him see that this was real.

I rang the bell, half hoping she wasn't home. I didn't know how much I could explain without bursting into tears. Flora was laughing when she opened the door and over her shoulder, I could see Lu, sitting on the couch in the crook of a man's arm who could only be her father and he was laughing, too. In her lap, Lu was holding the biggest, brightest, heart-shaped box of Valentine candy I'd ever seen.

"Ida! Come in and meet Hank!" Flora sounded delighted until she caught a glimpse of my face. "What's wrong?" she said, drawing me inside.

They all looked so happy, I felt like the bad fairy showing up at Sleeping Beauty's birthday party.

"Nothing's wrong," I said, still sounding shaky even to my own ears. "I was just out walking and . . ." There was no lie to cover it, so I didn't try. "I should have called. I'm sorry."

"Don't be silly," Flora said. "Come in and take off your coat."

The man stood up and held out his hand. "I'm Hank." I recognized him from the photograph Aretha had taken of him in the garden. His Afro was shorter, but he had the same small mustache and kind eyes.

"Ida Dunbar," I said.

"The Rev's daughter?" He squeezed my hand. "I am a lifelong admirer of your father's."

"That's a long time," I said, managing a smile as Flora took my coat to the front closet.

"Daddy just got in from D.C.," Lu said, beaming up at her father. "Better late than never!"

Hank winked at me and went back to sit beside his daughter, draping one long arm affectionately around her shoulders. "I got held up looking for some Valentine candy for my two best girls."

"You're not fooling anybody," Lu said. "This is just a bribe so you and Mom can abandon me and go off to Tybee *alone*."

Flora, perched on the arm of the sofa next to her husband, rubbed his back gently. "I'm still trying to figure out how you got it past security. No way that this could fit in the overhead bin."

She had a point there. The candy box was easily two feet across the top of the heart. "I told the flight attendant I hadn't been home in three weeks and if I didn't come correct, my wife was going to slam the door in my face while my daughter threw my clothes out the window and set fire to my BMW."

He was remembering the famous Angela

Bassett revenge scene in *Waiting to Exhale*. Home girl got a lot of people in trouble who didn't seem to understand that in real life, there are always consequences.

Lu laughed. "You don't have a BMW."

"Lucky for me," he said, kissing the top of her head.

A kettle in full boil sounded in the kitchen. Flora stood up and looked at me. "I'm making tea. Would you like some?"

"I'd love some," I said. "Can I help you?"

Of course, she said yes. We left Lu and Hank carefully unwrapping the granddaddy of all Valentine candy and headed for the kitchen. Flora turned off the tea kettle, the whistle dying off slowly like the end of a sigh.

"What's going on?" she said, pouring the hot water into a big red pot and dropping in a tea ball. Flora was the kind of woman who made her tea from scratch. She probably grew it in the backyard.

"Grab another cup out of the cabinet over there," she said. "And tell me what's up."

I handed her the cup, which she added to the three she'd already taken out, and tried to sum up what had just happened. "It's the Rev," I said, hating how helpless I felt.

"Is he okay?"

"No," I said, feeling tears forming, trying

to blink them back. I had been through so many hard days in the campaign, but I never cried. Even when you love the candidate more than you ever loved a candidate in your life, he's still not your daddy. "He's not okay."

# FORTY-NINE:
## THE CONFIDENCE OF
## A SLEEPWALKER

If I had come to Flora's looking for some assistance, I hit the jackpot. Standing there while the tea was steeping, I told her everything, then she pulled me into the living room and made me tell it all again. This, as Flora reminded me, was Hank's specialty, but he didn't say much. He asked me a couple of questions, but mostly he just listened. Lu sat beside him, listening intently, too. Occasionally, she'd reach into the giant candy box lying open on the table before us, take a piece without looking, and pop it in her mouth.

Even as I told them about Wes and Toni and Miss Iona's reporter, I knew I had never done that in my life. I make my assorted chocolate selections carefully, if possible consulting the key that sometimes appears on the lid. Then I nibble around the edges a little bit to confirm the wisdom of my decision before actually putting the whole thing in my mouth. I was in awe of Lu's fearless faith in her own decisions. I envied her that. And the obvious closeness of her family.

"When are they supposed to pick up the cards?" Hank said.

"They're going to talk to the Rev on Monday," I said. "So I guess that's when they'll schedule a time."

He nodded. "I think your reporter is clearly onto something . . ."

"He works for *The Sentinel*," I said, not comfortable claiming the guy since I'd never even met him.

"Great paper," Hank said. "I haven't heard about this one specifically, but we know they've got stuff going all over the country and this would be right up their alley. Why don't I make some calls tomorrow and see what I can find out?" He looked at Flora, who nodded her approval, even though I was horning in on her Valentine's getaway trip.

"We'll be back Sunday night in time for the Rev to change his mind before Wes makes his move. Would that help?"

I was so relieved, I almost hugged him. "Would you?"

"Consider it done," he said, smiling, reaching for a piece of candy without so much as a sideways glance, just like his daughter, and popping it in his mouth with the confidence of a sleepwalker.

# FIFTY:
## NO REGRETS

The next day, I went by Miss Iona's to tell her about our new best friend, Hank Lumumba. She was as relieved as I was, and as worried about the Rev.

"This is all your mother's fault," she said, as we sat in her kitchen talking about everything that had happened and trying to anticipate what would happen next. "If she hadn't broken his heart and driven him half crazy none of this would have happened."

I laughed. "Listen, after last night, I have new respect for the woman. She's a saint for even trying to stand up to the Rev."

"Don't get carried away." Miss Iona rolled her eyes. "Is she still headed this way?"

"She's got an interview next week," I said. "That's why I'm going back to D.C. on Monday."

"Aren't you going to wait and see what happens with the Rev?"

"I'll catch him on YouTube."

Miss Iona frowned. "That's not funny, Ida B."

She was right, but what's that saying about laughing to keep from crying? All I could do now was hope that by adding Hank to our team, we could make a stronger case to the Rev. Of course, it wasn't over once we convinced him of what was going on. Somebody would have to tell Mr. Eddie. I couldn't even imagine how that conversation would go.

As far as further conversation with the Rev, none seemed to be forthcoming. We didn't even have dinner together. He had been in his office all day working on his Founder's Day sermon while I holed up in my bedroom working on my résumé. I figured this Obama fantasy had a shelf life of about another two weeks. If I didn't get an offer by the end of February, I'd start Women's Herstory Month on March 1 with an email blast to any and everyone on my list who might have some leads on job possibilities. At that point, whether it was me not making the cut on my own, or being edged out because of the Rev, it wouldn't matter because sometimes I'll turn on the TV or the radio and some journalist is talking about *President Obama* this and *President Obama* that and I know whatever happens next, I was a part of that moment, and that movement, and I have no regrets.

It was after ten and I was curled up with Alice Walker's *The Temple of My Familiar,* which is so wonderful and wise that you can't possibly get it all the first time you read it. This is my third. I was so deep into its tale of love and rebirth and family and friendship that when my phone rang, I had to blink to remember where I was. I didn't recognize the number, but that didn't mean anything. My professional tribe is highly mobile.

"Hello?"

"Ida? This is Lu. I'm sorry to call so late, but my mom and dad are already down at Tybee and I need to tell you something."

"It's not too late," I said. "Are you okay?"

"I'm fine. Can we come over for a minute? Me and ShaRhonda are walking from the West End News."

I had no idea what Lu could need to tell me, but she sounded serious as hell. "My father's working," I said. "How about I meet you at your house?"

"Great," she said. "We're on our way."

They were coming down the street when I turned the corner and threw up a hand. Lu waved back and they waited for me at the end of their front walk. ShaRhonda, who had been so bubbly at WEGA the other morning, looked like she'd been crying.

"What's going on?" I said when we got inside. "Has somebody been bothering you?"

Lu looked at ShaRhonda. "Do you want me to tell her?"

ShaRhonda's response was barely audible. Lu squeezed her hand and took a deep breath.

"Okay, here's what happened. ShaRhonda and Cornell had a date tonight for Valentine's Day. They were supposed to go out to dinner and then meet us at a party some of our friends are having, but he called at the last minute and said he couldn't make it."

ShaRhonda stood up and started sort of pacing around behind the couch. She was really agitated, but I was no closer to the reason. Lu turned to her friend.

"Do you want to tell it?"

ShaRhonda looked at Lu helplessly. "I don't even know if I want *you* to tell it. He made me promise, Lu."

"I know that," Lu said, "but it's not just about him. I told you that, remember? It's bigger than him."

"He's only doing it because his dad told him he won't be able to stay in school if he doesn't and what's he supposed to do then?"

"Calm down, sweetie," I said. "Only doing what?"

"He made me swear on the phone before he'd even tell me, but I told him if he stood me up on Valentine's Day without a good reason, it was over." She was pacing again. "I thought he had killed somebody or something."

"But it's nothing like that," Lu said quickly.

"He wouldn't have to do this," ShaRhonda said, "but his father gambled away all his school money and didn't even tell him because Cornell would have gotten a job. He would have figured out something better than this!"

"Why don't you sit down," I said, "and tell me what he said."

ShaRhonda came back and sat down beside Lu, who moved closer and took her hand, either for support or to keep her from jumping up again, I couldn't tell.

"Tell her," Lu said.

ShaRhonda looked at me. "They're going to rob your father's house."

The hair stood up on the back of my neck. He was there now, alone. I tried to keep my voice calm.

"They're going to do what?"

"Tomorrow when you're all over at Rock

of Faith for Founder's Day, they're going to rob your house."

"Who are *they?*"

She shook her head miserably. "I don't know."

Lu took up the story. "But they told Cornell he had to move a bunch of boxes out of your father's house and they needed him to meet them tonight to go over the plans. I remembered what you were talking about with my dad, so when ShaRhonda told me that, I put two and two together."

"You did good," I said. "Did he say anything else you can remember?"

ShaRhonda wiped her nose on the back of her hand. "Just that if anything happened, he loved me."

"Nothing's going to happen to Cornell," I said, standing up and reaching for my coat. "I appreciate you telling me. Don't say anything to anybody else about this, okay?"

They nodded in unison, still holding hands. "We won't."

"Do you know who it is?" ShaRhonda said as they walked me to the door.

"Yes."

"Lu said they're trying to do some stuff against the president. Is that true?"

"Yes."

"I know Cornell wouldn't do anything like

376

that if he had a choice," ShaRhonda said. "He's not like that."

"Everybody has a choice," I said. "That's the whole thing about it. You *always* have a choice."

"Can you stop them?" Lu said.

There was only one answer and I gave it to her. *"Absolutely."*

# FIFTY-ONE:
# BURGLARS AND
# BETRAYALS

After I told Miss Iona what ShaRhonda's boyfriend had said, she picked up the phone and called Mr. Eddie without even asking me. Of course he was at home. The Rev was in his study and Wes was somewhere doing dirt. *Where else would he be?* Miss Iona, who seems to regard coffee as a universal cure-all, made a pot while we waited for him to walk the four blocks from his house to hers.

"This is going to kill him," she said, shaking her head, and then she quoted the bible. "How like a serpent's tooth is a thankless child."

But she was wrong. It didn't kill him. He sat right there, sipping his coffee, and listened while we spun our tale of lies and deceptions, burglars and betrayals. Miss Iona talked more than I did, but when I told him the part about Cornell breaking into the house tomorrow to steal the cards, he put his cup down and looked at me for a long time. I was waiting for him to offer some defense of his only son that we'd have to reluctantly refute, but he didn't say a word.

"You all right?" Miss Iona said finally, touching his arm gently.

Mr. Eddie nodded slowly. "I'm sorry, Ida B. There are no better words to say it, or none I can come up with. I'm just truly sorry and I do apologize for my son."

"You don't have to do that," I said. "You don't ever have to apologize to anybody for anything."

"Thank you for that," Mr. Eddie said.

"Should we call the police?" Miss Iona said.

"They haven't done anything yet," Mr. Eddie said. "Police don't care about you thinkin' something. You gotta do it."

"When are we going to tell the Rev?" I said. "Me and Miss Iona can't convince him, but he'll believe you."

Mr. Eddie picked up his now cold coffee and put it back down. "The Rev has to come to things in his own time," he said. "Let him bring the word tomorrow morning. Then we'll tell him what we know."

"Well, if you're not going to call the police, and we're not going to call the Rev, what are we going to do?" Miss Iona said.

Mr. Eddie looked at her.

"I'm just saying," she said. "We need a plan, don't we?"

"I've got one," he said. "When you all go over to Rock of Faith tomorrow morning, I'll tell Wes I'm not feeling good and stay at home."

"Are you sure Wes is going?"

"He promised the Rev. He'll have to go so it won't look suspicious if he doesn't."

"That's why they got that man's child all up in it," Miss Iona said. "Little Miss Thing can't do it all by herself and Wes has got to be over at the church cheesing at the Rev to make sure they got a cover story."

I hoped her description of Wes didn't hurt Mr. Eddie's feelings, but if it did, he didn't register it on his face. You would have thought we were talking about plans for any other Sunday morning.

"Go on," I said.

"Once Wes is out, I'll head over to the house and stand guard over those damn cards. Until we get it all sorted out, nobody's takin' them anywhere."

That made sense to me, but Miss Iona was still frowning. "You don't think they'll try to push past you and come on in anyway, do you?"

Mr. Eddie stood up. "Now you hurtin' my feelings."

"Oh, sit down," Miss Iona said. "I just wish my Charlie was here."

"What's he gonna do?" he said, sitting down as ordered and taking Miss Iona's hand. "Iona?"

"What?"

"Do you trust me to look out for the Rev?"

"Of course I do."

"How about you?" he said, turning to me.

"Always."

"Then both of you get up in the morning and go to church and let me do my job."

I'm sure my mother would have pointed out that there was more than a whiff of patriarchy in his assumption of the leadership role of our little group, but at that moment I trusted Mr. Eddie to do the right thing. I think this is what politics always comes down to anyway, a willingness on the part of the good guys to stop the bad guys from going too far. Even when they're family.

# FIFTY-TWO:
# BLOOD ON THOSE
# BALLOTS

When Wes came downstairs for breakfast on Sunday morning, he had already spoken to Toni twice. She assured him that everything was ready to go. She and Estes's son were parked in the van a few blocks away near West End Park, waiting for the appointed hour. Toni had even had a couple of T-shirts and baseball caps made over at the mall so that from a distance, they looked like two neatly dressed young deliverymen, out on a mission of mercy.

Of course there would be some immediate fallout about who took the cards and why, but Wes already had his rap on that. *Why do you think I wanted to get them moved someplace secure? I'm just sorry we got here too late,* he'd say, outraged. He'd suggest to the Rev that he keep the theft on the down low to avoid spooking potential tour sponsors who hated any kind of political infighting and then give him the number of a discreet private investigator. That should keep him busy long enough to copy the cards, pass the disk on to Estes, tell the PI where he could find them in the Dumpster behind the offices of the Georgia Democratic Party, and get the hell back to New York. Plus, even if the Rev suspected something, Wes knew he'd never tell. It would break his best friend's heart and at the Rev's age, good friends are hard to find.

He was surprised to find his father sitting at the kitchen table, still wearing his bathrobe and a pair of black leather house shoes Wes had given him last Christmas.

"We better get a move on," he said, not wanting to be late. They had to pass the Rev's house on the way to Rock of Faith and he wasn't going to take a chance on his father spotting the van in the driveway and stopping to investigate. "You know they're holding seats for us down front, but after ten thirty, I wouldn't count on it."

"I'm not going," Mr. Eddie said. "You go ahead."

*Oh, shit,* Wes thought. *Now what?*

He sat down across from his father. "Are you sick?"

"No, son, I'm just tired."

"Too tired to be with the Rev on his big day?" Wes said, smiling encouragingly at his father like you would to cajole a reluctant toddler into potty training.

"It's not the first time I let him do one on his own." Mr. Eddie smiled back and crossed his legs. "I might stop over there later just to share some fellowship."

*Damn,* Wes thought, *what the hell does that mean?* What kind of window of time was his father talking about? An hour? Two hours? Time for Toni and the kid to get in and get out with no complications? Why was everything so hard when he had to deal with these old muthafuckas, his father included. They change their minds on a whim but once they dig in their heels, that's it. First, the Rev thinks one old lady can do a job that requires twenty or thirty young ones. Then his father flakes out on one of West End's major Black History happenings and decides not to go see his best friend do his thing, which leaves him wandering around the neighborhood, poking his nose in where it doesn't belong.

"Come on, Pop," Wes said. "I'll drive."

Mr. Eddie was looking at him strangely. "Do you know who Fannie Lou Hamer was, son?"

"What?" Wes wondered if his father was having a stroke.

"Mrs. Hamer. From Mississippi."

"Mississippi Freedom Democratic Party, right?"

His father nodded, then stood up and took his cup over to the sink slowly. He didn't look so good. Wes wondered if his railroad pension would pay for long-term care if Mr. Eddie needed it. "She almost got beat to death just trying to register to vote."

What was he supposed to say to that? "I remember you talking about her when I was a kid, but what's she got to do with getting ready for church, Pop?"

There was that funny look again. "It hasn't been that long ago, son, that we can take it for granted. There's still blood on those ballots."

*Jesus!* There wasn't time for all this. If he didn't call Toni, she was going to head over to the Rev's, thinking he was handling things on his end, but here he was getting a private black history tutorial. Maybe she was right. Maybe they ought to stick to bar-beque pork rinds and leave the politics alone.

"I understand, Pop, but we're going to be late if we don't get going."

"You go, son," Mr. Eddie said again. "I'm going to lie down for a while and rest my eyes. They're taking the Rev for brunch at Paschal's after service. I'll catch up with you over there."

"You sure?" The Paschal's gathering wasn't even scheduled to start until two. There would be plenty of time to get everything done before his father ventured out.

Mr. Eddie nodded. "Go on, now. The Rev will understand me not coming, but you'll have some explaining to do."

"I'll have my cell on vibrate, so call me if you need me, okay?" Wes picked up his keys.

"Son?"

"Yes?"

"Is there anything you want to tell me?"

Something in his father's voice made Wes wonder where the hell that question was coming from. "Not that I can think of."

His father's expression never changed. "I love you, son."

"I love you, too, Pop."

After Wes left, Mr. Eddie went upstairs, took a shower, shaved, and picked out his suit. Then he stood in front of the mirror to tie his tie and wondered how he ever got so old.

# FIFTY-THREE:
# FEET OF JESUS

"I thought Ed would take it harder," Miss Iona said as we sat in a front pew at Rock of Faith and watched the sanctuary fill up with the Rev's *other* family. The usher who said his name was Julius promised to come back and get me when it was time for me to play my part so I could enjoy the rest of the service out front. The Rev was in the tiny pastor's holding room where he always prayed alone before services.

"Well, the Rev's taking it hard enough for both of them," I said. "He hardly said two words to me this morning. I kept waiting for him to tell me he'd asked somebody else to introduce him."

She shook her head. "He'd never do that. Your name is in the bulletin."

That was as good a reason as any, I guess. The truth was, I was half hoping he would give me a way out. I didn't relish the idea of standing in front of the Rev and singing his praises when we were hardly speaking to each other. Plus, I was worried about Mr. Eddie. He had called me right after Wes left, heading this way, and said he would give them fifteen minutes and head over to the house to catch them in the act. I kept imagining Toni and Cornell showing up, armed and dangerous, even though we had no reason to think they would be. I would never forgive myself if anything happened to Mr. Eddie.

"Did you write something special?" Miss Iona said.

"No," I said. "I'm just going to read what's on the back of the bulletin."

She looked surprised. "And waste this opportunity to tell him how you really feel?"

Of all people, I thought Miss Iona would understand. "What do you think I've been trying to do ever since I got here?" And it was deeper than that. "What do you think I've been trying to do my whole life?"

"Well, now's your chance," she said. "Take it!"

"This is hardly the time or the place for true confessions," I said.

Miss Iona pointed at the altar, which was dominated by a huge painting of a beautifully brown Messiah. "You're at the feet of Jesus, girl. This is where you are supposed to confess so you can be forgiven."

"I haven't done anything to be forgiven for," I said, but she wasn't going for it.

"We all are in need of forgiveness, Ida B, but the point is, your father is a man who is always at his best in front of a crowd. Especially a crowd that loves him. If you want to tell him how you feel before you leave here with all this mess between you, this is the place to do it!"

Before I could argue the point, she leaned over and pinched my arm. "Don't say anything! Here he comes!"

I turned around to see Wes Harper striding up the aisle. He stopped right in front of me. He was shameless, with that big, fake smile, but at least his presence here meant everything was going according to plan. So far, so good.

"Got room for one more?" he said.

"Of course," Miss Iona said. "Sit right here, Wes. We've got to leave Ida B on the aisle since she's introducing the Rev."

Wes stepped over me carefully and sat down between us.

"Do we need to save a place for Mr. Eddie?" I said, looking around like I didn't know he wasn't coming. Miss Iona did, too.

"He's not coming to service," Wes said, looking concerned. "He said he was going to lie down for a while and come over to Paschal's later."

I feigned concern. "Is he okay?"

"He's fine," Wes said. "I've got my phone on vibrate in case he needs to get me."

Miss Iona clucked her tongue in fake exasperation. "I told these old fools they need to quit ripping and running around the way they used to."

"That's what I've been telling him, too," Wes said. "But so far, I haven't had much success effecting a slowdown."

"Don't worry," Miss Iona said. "Your father is as strong as an ox. Don't let his lean lines fool you."

Wes smiled. "I never do, Miss Iona."

Then somebody tapped her on the shoulder and when she turned around to say hello, Wes turned his smile on me. "I want to apologize about the other night," he said. "That wasn't quite the way I'd envisioned winding up our evening."

Is there another word for shameless?

"We'll have to do it again sometime," I said. *Maybe right after Hank Lumumba helps us blow your cover and stop this shit once and for all.* I tried to calm down. I knew I hadn't said it out loud, but I'm sure God doesn't appreciate that kind of language in his house even if it is all in your head.

"I'd like that," he said, but then the organist hit the opening chords of the processional hymn and the choir came marching down the center aisle in their best Founder's Day robes, so I stood up with everybody else and sang along the best I could. The Rev was sitting in one of those big chairs on the pulpit next to Rev. Patterson, and if there were any hard feelings between them, you couldn't tell it. Looking over at me staring up at him, the Rev gave me a nod and I nodded back. Was it ever going to be right between us again?

The service proceeded according to the bulletin, but my mind wasn't on it. Just before the offering, the Rev left the pulpit quietly and disappeared, something I had never seen him do. Before I could figure out why, the usher came to tap me on the shoulder as the choir started singing the offertory hymn. I just hoped I could get through my introduction without bursting into tears. As I stood up, the usher leaned over and whispered to Wes that he should come, too. There was a phone call for him.

Wes looked surprised, then concerned, but we followed the usher through a door at the side of the altar that led to the small pastor's room. He opened the door and there stood the Rev and Mr. Eddie. I had no idea what was going on. In the sanctuary, Rev. Patterson was encouraging people to give generously, but when the usher closed the door, it was suddenly silent. Wes looked even more confused than I felt.

"What's going on?" he said, sounding annoyed.

"Why don't you tell us?" the Rev said, cold as ice.

Wes looked at his father. "What's up, Pop? I thought you weren't coming?"

"Let me ask you something, son," Mr. Eddie said, and I was relieved to see he looked just fine. "How stupid do you think we are?"

Wes took an involuntary step backward. Mr. Eddie's tone was hard as a diamond drill bit.

"I . . . I don't know what you're talking about," Wes stuttered a little.

Still in his robe, the Rev looked even bigger in this small room. "We know it's you, Wes. We know what you've done and we know what you were trying to do."

"I haven't done anything."

"That's not what your assistant told me and Hank Lumumba."

"Hank Lumumba?"

I was surprised at Wes's reaction to his name. I was surprised, too. I thought Hank was down at Tybee celebrating Valentine's Day.

Mr. Eddie nodded. "He's over there at the Rev's talking to Miss Cassidy right now. Had some conversation with young Estes, too. Both of them seemed to have a lot to say to Hank once he told them what we already knew."

Wes's face was an angry mask. "And what do you think you know?"

"Let's give Hank a call and you can ask him," Mr. Eddie said, turning to the Rev. "You don't mind if me and Wes miss part of your sermon, do you, Rev? Me and my son got some talkin' to do."

"I understand," the Rev said, taking my arm gently. I was standing there staring at him and Mr. Eddie with my mouth open. Had they known all along? Why hadn't they told us?

When we came out of that room, the big usher was waiting outside. The Rev nodded and he took up a position at the door. Mr. Eddie could talk to his son as long as he needed to. Wes wasn't going anywhere until Mr. Eddie said so. We could hear the choir singing.

"Pass me not, oh gentle savior,
Hear my humble cry."

"You knew?" I said.

He nodded. "Hank told me the way they were going to come at me would give him the best chance to cut them off at the pass here and in a lot of other places, too. That's why I did that fool interview. To make them think I was ripe for the picking."

"You did that whole tacos and sangria thing *on purpose?*"

He nodded again. "Sometimes you have to show them what they want to see in order to get them to show you who they really are."

My mind was whirling. "You always knew Wes was working for them?"

"We found out just after you got here. I had to tell Ed, but Hank said it was too dangerous to let you in on it. In case things went awry, they didn't want the Obama people anywhere near this."

I smiled at my father. "I was a Dunbar person before I was an Obama person, remember?"

He smiled back because he knew exactly what I meant. Before I knew anything about politics, I knew the smell of my father's aftershave lotion, the gentle touch of my father's hands and the strength of his arms, the sound of his warm private laugh and of his voice singing to my mother in the quiet of our late night house. Before I knew the words to "We Shall Overcome," I loved the gentle way he'd lean around the front seat to tease me about my latest crush as Mr. Eddie guided the car down the road to wherever black folks needed somebody to stand up and be counted.

In the sanctuary, the ushers were bringing the offertory trays forward for Reverend Patterson's blessing. It was almost time.

"Lying to you was the hardest thing I've ever had to do," the Rev said as the congregation sang the last verse of the offertory hymn.

"Do me a favor," I said. "Never do it again."

"You've got a deal, daughter."

Then I heard Rev. Patterson introducing me and it was my turn to introduce the Rev. Miss Iona's words were ringing in my ears: *Now's your chance. Take it!*

So I stood on my tiptoes and I put my arms around my father's neck and I hugged him as hard as he was hugging me back, and there we were, *family strong and freedom high.*

"Ready, daughter?" the Rev said.

"Absolutely," I said, and when we walked out together, the congregation burst into applause like they were seeing us for the first time and Miss Iona clapping as loud as anybody.

"Brothers and sisters," I said, "my father is a man who needs no introduction, especially here at Rock of Faith Community Church."

"Amen," said a room full of people who had known me all my life. "Amen."

"I grew up in this church, in these pews, in this pulpit, pretending to preach while my dad was upstairs talking to somebody or downstairs taping that old furnace together so folks would be warm when they came to church on Sunday morning."

A collective chuckle. They all knew even the fieriest sermon didn't make up for cold feet. I took a deep breath and tried to figure out what I really wanted to say about my father. When I looked over at him, he nodded as if to say, *Go ahead, daughter. You've got the floor!*

"A few days ago," I said, figuring if I just started talking, something would come to me, "I was thinking about what I could say about my father this Founder's Day morning that you don't already know — or that I won't get into trouble for telling!"

Another little laugh from the congregation. They were with me wherever I wanted to go and I felt myself relax a little bit.

"While I was trying to figure it out, Mr. Eddie said something that stayed in my head. Mr. Eddie said that sometimes when we have true greatness in our midst for a long time, we get used to it. Sometimes we start to take it for granted and forget to even acknowledge the people we should be thanking each and every day of our lives."

People were murmuring *amen* and nodding their heads at me.

"Because they are the ones who brought us here; the ones who stood up with us and for us. The ones who made us brave because they had more than enough courage to go around. The ones who never doubted for one minute that we could get this country to live up to the promises it had made."

"Teach, Lil' Rev!" somebody called from the back. I was on a roll!

"The ones who believed in us even when we faltered. The ones who brought us here, to this amazing moment, and said, 'Here. This is your country now. Make something out of it!' "

"My Lord!" said old Mrs. Bailey, sitting with the Ladies Usher Board in her best white uniform. "It's our country!"

"And while you're at it, make something out of *yourself!*" I said, feeling the Rev behind me, but afraid to look at him again since I felt myself getting a little emotional. "That is my father's gift to us. The chance to live as free citizens of our own country, and for that, on behalf of all of us here, and all of us whose names we don't even know, I thank him and I honor him here this morning!"

The congregation applauded enthusiastically and then almost in a wave, they all stood up and kept clapping. Miss Iona stood up, too, and I could see tears on her cheeks even from up here where I was standing.

"Amen!"

The Rev finally had to wave at them to sit back down and when they did, I watched Miss Iona dabbing at her eyes and I decided she was right. Confession is good for the soul.

"But I was raised to believe that truth is the light," I said. "So let me admit that it's not always easy to be a great man's daughter."

"Amen!"

"It's not always easy to get a word in when so many people have so many urgent messages to convey, sometimes messages of life and death, when all you're trying to do is show off a perfect history exam or model a new dress or introduce a thoroughly intimidated prom date."

That earned another chuckle. My father was notorious for terrorizing the brave boys who dated me in high school.

"It's not easy when the meetings run so long that I'd fall asleep downstairs, trying to wait up for my dad, and not realize he'd arrived and carried me to bed until I woke up in the morning and heard him laughing with my mother in the kitchen while he whipped up some of his famous French toast."

When I said that, suddenly I could see the whole scene: me in my little girl bathrobe, my mother with her hair pulled up in a ponytail, my father in his shirtsleeves and a great big apron my mother had tied around his waist. Just the three of us for one private moment and it was so precious that of course I wanted more. We all did. But that's not who my father was, and I had never understood it more clearly, or respected it more deeply, than I did standing there that morning, thanking him for giving up more than anyone would ever know because he had the work of history to do, and it couldn't wait.

"It was in this church that I learned my father never belonged just to me. He belonged to all of us."

"Amen! Teach!"

"He didn't change my diapers because he was too busy changing the world."

"Amen!"

"He didn't come to my dance recitals because he was somewhere refusing to dance to any tune but his own."

"Yes he was!"

"He didn't make it to my high school graduation to hear me give the valedictorian speech . . ."

A collective groan of sympathy, but I didn't need it.

"Because a kid in Savannah whom he'd never met had been arrested and his mother called the Rev for help."

"Yes, Lord! Who did she call?"

I could see my father nodding and smiling. "Teach, daughter!"

"But none of those disappointments matter, because he's here today and so am I, and so are all of you. Brothers and sisters, neighbors and friends, it is the honor of my life to present a great teacher, a great leader, and the best father anyone could ever have, my daddy, the Reverend Doctor Horace A. Dunbar."

Then everybody jumped to their feet again and the Rev hugged me and stepped forward to bring his Founder's Day message, but in the front row, Miss Iona caught my eye and gave me a discreet thumbs-up in her green leather Michelle Obama gloves. *Well done, Ida B. Well done!*

# FIFTY-FOUR:
## ON THE RIGHT SIDE
### AGAIN

"You sure you can't hang around a little longer?" the Rev said as I got ready to go to the airport the next afternoon. "Black History Month is almost over and we could really spend some time together."

"Every month is black history month now, remember?" I said, glad I'd been able to convince him not to come to the airport with me. Airport good-byes are crazy now with all the security restrictions and the lighting is horrible. Besides, we'd had our moment and, once we got home, we also had that marathon talk I'd been waiting for all my life. Everything was right between us.

Miss Iona called to say good-bye and let us know that Hank had told Wes he'd get him a fair shake with the Justice Department if he would tell what he knew about the efforts to illegally purge voter lists all over the country and Wes was singing like a bird. For Mr. Eddie's sake, I hoped he wouldn't get jail time, but it was out of my hands. Flora called to say we could do our WEGA transition interview when she's in D.C. next month to look at houses and I've already got a few in mind to show her. Until then, I sure had other things to think about. Like finding a job. I had some prospects and Hank had even given me a couple of good leads, so things were definitely looking up.

"Don't give up on the White House," the Rev said. "Now that I'm on the right side again, who knows what might happen?"

"I guess you're right about that," I said, and a part of me still hoped it was true. After all, it wasn't March 1 yet. I had another week or so to picture myself walking to work in the West Wing before my self-imposed deadline ran out.

"Have you had a chance to talk to your mother about all this?" the Rev said, reaching for his coat to walk out to my car.

"Maybe you can do that for me," I said. "She's headed this way."

"What do you mean headed this way?"

"She's going to be the director of the Women's Center at Spelman."

At first he just looked at me and then he threw back his head and laughed so loud the dishes rattled in the kitchen. You could have knocked me over with a feather. If I live to be a hundred, I will never understand my parents.

"Aren't you worried about her coming back?" I said.

"Worried?" He laughed again, not quite as loudly, then took out his big white handkerchief and dabbed his eyes gently. "You know why she took that job, don't you?"

"It's too good an opportunity to turn down?"

He shook his head slowly, grinning from ear to ear. "She can't live without me."

So there it was. I knew suddenly without a shadow of a doubt that he was right. I wonder if my mother knew it, too. "Then I guess the only question left to answer," I said, grinning back at him, "is can you live without her?"

"Daughter, I wouldn't even try!" he said, and hugged me so hard I had to catch my breath, which was fine with me. I can breathe anytime. *Soul mates indeed.*

"Ready, daughter?"

"Ready," I said, and then realized I had left my briefcase upstairs. That was a sign, as if I needed one, that it really was time to head back to D.C. I was getting careless. In my world, forgetting a briefcase is like a cowboy forgetting his horse: unforgivable. "Oh, shoot, Rev! Hang on a second!"

I heard my phone ringing in my purse as I dashed up to my room. "Get that, will you, Rev?" I called back over my shoulder.

But the phone kept on ringing as I grabbed my briefcase and looked around to be sure I hadn't forgotten anything else. Maybe he couldn't figure out how to answer it, I thought. No one knew better than I did that technology wasn't the Rev's strong point.

"Just push the button in the middle," I said, heading back downstairs, but the Rev was just standing there staring at the caller ID.

"What's wrong?" I said.

"You'll want to get this one yourself," he said, handing me the phone. "I think a friend of mine wants to talk to you."

"Hello?" I said, wondering why he was being so mysterious, and then the voice on the other end said the most beautiful words in the English language.

"Miss Dunbar? Will you please hold for the president?"

# ACKNOWLEDGMENTS

Thank you and love to my husband and constant collaborator, Zaron W. Burnett Jr.; to my daughter, Deignan; my son-in-law, Will; and my grandchildren, Michael, Chloe, and Bailey. Special thanks to Kris and Jim Williams, their children and grandchildren, Jilo, Abeo, Osaze, Hasina, Ife, Sydney, Sean, Ayanna, Tulani, Tatayana, James, Kylett, and Cabral; and to my West Coast family, Zaron W. Burnett III; Meghan, Skylar, and Griffin Underwood. Thanks also to Miz Johnsie Broadway Burnett, who wanted to know what happened to Brandi; to Lynette Lapeyrolerie, Glenda Hatchett, Walt Huntley, Cecelia Hunter, Ingrid Saunders Jones, and Jimmy Lee Tarver for their friendship and support; and to Dr. Beverly Guy Sheftall, Founding Director of the Spelman College Women's Research & Resource Center for her vision. Thanks also to Ron Gwiazda for taking care of business; and to Bill Bagwell, because a deal's a deal.

# ABOUT THE AUTHOR

**Pearl Cleage** is the author *of What Looks Like Crazy on an Ordinary Day . . .* , an Oprah's Book Club selection; *Some Things I Never Thought I'd Do,* a *Good Morning America* Read This! book club pick; *Babylon Sisters,* for which she was named the 2006 Go On Girl! Book Club Author of the Year; *Baby Brother's Blues,* winner of the 2006 NAACP Image Award and the African American Literary Award for fiction; and *Seen It All and Done the Rest.* The first author selected for the *Essence* Book Club, she collaborated with her husband, writer Zaron W. Burnett Jr. on the poem *We Speak Your Names.* She is also an accomplished dramatist whose plays include *Flyin' West, Blues for an Alabama Sky,* and *A Song for Coretta.* Cleage and her husband live in Atlanta.